The Designated Drivers' Club

Shelley K. Wall, author of
Numbers Never Lie and *Bring It On*

CRIMSON
ROMANCE
F+W Media, Inc.

Published by
Crimson Romance
an imprint of F+W Media, Inc.
10151 Carver Road, Suite 200
Blue Ash, Ohio 45242

www.crimsonromance.com

Chapter 1

The wind shoved Jenny Madison through the bar door into the mass of noise and people. A paper sign taped to the window fluttered next to her, an advertisement for the play *Home is Love*. A clever patron had crossed out the word "Home" and penned *DRINKING* over it.

Jenny concentrated on the prior word and squelched a desire to go there.

"Yeah, and you'll be locked out of it if you don't get busy," she muttered. Her boss' words rang heavily, scratch that, ex-boss'. He had fired her because her attitude didn't fit their work environment. A stack of bills pended disaster if she didn't forge ahead.

Jenny walked with faked confidence into the crowded club. She carried business cards, monogrammed notepads, and refrigerator magnets with her new business name. This was her fourth stop of the evening. She adjusted her denim skirt down over her legs and tugged the lapels of her black jacket forward. Admittedly, it wasn't as professional as she wanted but it sufficed. She had not worn heels in a month and now that she donned a pair, her feet complained.

"The Designated Driver's Club." A petite brunette with studs in her eyebrow read from the business card. "What does that mean?"

"It's a membership thing. You pay either annually or monthly. We pick you up anywhere you want and take you home, then back to your car the next day—or we deliver it if preferred. Our drivers are safe, alcohol-free, have good driving records, and we guarantee you won't get a DUI." Jenny mustered up her best cheerful smile. "And all for a price that's less than the cost of a ticket."

"You'll pick up anywhere in the city?" The girl's stud lifted along with the brow attached to it.

"Yes. Anywhere."

"Wow. Great idea."

"Thanks. You can sign up on the website listed on the card, or call that number there." Jenny ran her finger along the print. "We take all major credit cards. Oh, and we don't lecture anyone or give them a hard time. Our drivers are courteous and confidential. We recognize everyone needs to have a good time once in a while—we just want it to end well, too."

She flashed a final smile at the table, ran her tongue over her teeth and moved on. Her cheeks ached and her lips cracked from forced cheerfulness. A few more tables and she would step back outside and teeter her heeled feet to the car.

"Hey!" A tall twenty-something guy with shaggy dark hair called after her. "How many drivers do you have?"

"Enough," she answered with fake assurance. Okay, a little white lie—but she doubted it would matter. If, by chance, she had more calls than she could handle, she could recruit a few friends to help. Or—even better—hire someone. Her own staff. That sounded impressive.

Jenny whipped around to get the final tables just in time to meet a cocktail waitress head-on. The waitress was quick and evaded the collision. Jenny wasn't as speedy. Her hand full of cards and goodies fluttered to the floor, spreading out in a small carpet of paper. Footsteps threatened to trample her stash. She let out a curse, bent, gathered them quickly and rose with a huff.

"Nice." A male voice admired from behind her. She turned, catching blue twinkling eyes focused on her backside. Her face reddened as she remembered her denim skirt had "bite me" emblazoned on the pocket. She had a black jacket over it and thought it would cover everything enough to look professional but casual. Ignoring his chuckle, she plopped a few business cards and notepads on the table. The men with him picked up the cards and read.

"Check this out, Buzz." A man with highlighted brown hair and a torn handkerchief around his neck flipped a card in front of the blue eyes.

"Hmmm." He lifted the card with long, slender fingers. "So…bite me girl, what's this about?"

Jenny launched into her monologue, consciously aware of the blue eyes boring into hers as she spoke. When she finished, he lazily glanced down to her hands, then back up.

Mr. Highlights and handkerchief leaned over, both elbows on the table, and grinned. "Do you have a quota on how many times a person can call?" he asked. The other two guys with them laughed. "See, Buzz here, has a tendency to overdo it—a lot. You know, brokenhearted, luckless guy…drowning his sorrows. If it weren't for me, he'd use a service like this almost every night."

Buzz Blue Eyes shot him a murderous glare. "John, you know you'd be lonely if I didn't call you. You can't stand to stay home every night anyway." He tapped the business card up and down on the table. "I'm David."

"Not Buzz?"

"Nickname. Thanks to these idiots." He jerked a thumb at the group flanking him and introduced them one by one. "John, Kevin, and Grady."

"I'm Jenny…and a membership allows you two pickups a month. Anything more has a minimal charge attached." She forced the smile and held out her hand. She made it up on the fly, but they wouldn't know that.

"Yeah." David lifted the card. "Jenny Madison. The girl with two first names." Observant guy.

"And bite me on her bum," Grady chirped in a British accent.

Jenny glanced at the Paul McCartney wannabe and said, "You're British?"

"No, Grady's from Kansas City. He just does that to attract chicks," David clarified.

"What do you expect?" John laughed, "Look at him—if you look like that you better have a gimmick."

Okay, they're somewhat funny, in a brother-trying-to-be-bad-boy way, she thought. "Well, nice talking to you gentlemen." She tossed a wave at them, dropped some cards at the next table and headed for the door. Cory, the bartender, nodded once in acknowledgement.

Jenny glanced back over a shoulder briefly before shoving out the heavy wooden door. Buzz Blue Eyes waved before turning to the redhead that had slipped into the booth next to him.

*

Jenny patted the hood of her black Mercedes. "Maybe I'll get to keep you after all. Let's cross our fingers and hope." The car had been a splurge last year. She had driven an almost-antique Toyota until that point. When the heat went out on it, the cost to repair was more than the Blue Book value. A trail of repair costs had haunted her so long; she finally gave into her friends' urging for a replacement when she got the pittance of trust money from her dad. Had she predicted the current outcome, perhaps she'd have chosen a small, used Chevy at the time.

*

Three weeks later, Jenny happily set up an automatic pay schedule for her car payment and rent. A monumental step from the scrimping and saving she was used to. Steady income was not to be overrated. She decided to celebrate and meet the girls at Foxy's, their normal bar. She would not drink this time—just in case a call came in.

Presently, there were forty clients signed up for her service and a steady stream of calls for pickup. Her work schedule had completely flip-flopped from the old office job. Now she usually started around six p.m. and received calls as late as three or four in the morning. Sleep came during the day, rather than night. Her new forced wake-up time was noon. Mainly because she had to get out and enjoy the daylight or she would go crazy. The nocturnal vampire lifestyle was interesting but wearing.

The stuttered tone of her new hands-free phone interrupted her thoughts. She looked at the display—a work call. "Great," she muttered. She had just pulled into the lot at Foxy's.

A customer pickup at the cliffs was a novelty—one that piqued her interest and drew fear at the same time. Jenny hadn't been there since high school. Still, her service guaranteed a pickup anywhere. The absence of streetlights would have been creepy but for the full moon lighting the way. Regardless, when a rabbit jumped into the road and bounded for the trees she freaked and let out a squeal, then giggled nervously at her skittishness. A subtle noise motivated her to roll down the window despite her fear. She heard…singing. A lilting, strong, male voice belted it out somewhere ahead. Her headlights shone on the frame of a man sitting on the ground at the edge of the cliffs, his head back, and his mouth open. Singing.

Jenny got out of the car. Saying anything at all might send the person over the edge, so she eased up next to him and sat too. A comfortable distance initiated between them. No way was she going to dangle her legs like that. It was too far to fall; she just let her feet hang slightly over.

"Scared of heights, Jenny Madison?" the man asked. She peered into the shadows caused by the headlights on his back.

"David, right?"

"Yeah. Thanks for coming. I didn't know you also did the driving."

"Uh, we're a little short-handed tonight." *And every other night too.*

"Isn't this place great? I love the natural acoustics."

Over his shoulder, fireflies blinked a scattered dance in the dark sky. He leaned back in the dirt and put his hands behind his bushy hair.

"You okay?" she asked.

"Good enough. We had a bad night tonight. The fans were flat." Fans? She knew he couldn't see her look at him, but she lifted an eyebrow anyway.

"What constitutes a bad night?"

"I'm in a band. We play small gigs around the city." He said it nonchalantly, as if she should have known.

"That's cool. What's the name of your band?"

"Blind Optimism."

"Hmmm. I don't think I know it." Funny name.

He laughed. "We played at the Jazz House tonight. We sucked."

"Is that why you're here?" She leaned back and laced her hands behind her head too, staring up at the stars and fireflies.

"I guess. I like to come up here and try a tune out occasionally—without all the back—up music. It gives me a chance to listen to the voice and the words on their own."

"Makes sense. It sounded good when I walked up. Was that one of your songs?"

He chuckled. "The one they hated."

"Oh, well—it sounded good to me. Maybe the backup was the problem and not the song. So, the guys with you last month were your band?"

"Mmm hmmm," he acknowledged, his eyes starting to close.

"Well, David—the rock star—Buzz. Let's get you home."

She lifted up and pulled on his arm to move him away from the cliff and get him to his feet. Jenny noticed the pile of bottles on the ground behind him when they walked into the headlights' glare.

She punched in the destination on her GPS and turned the car around. A few minutes later, his head was laid back against the headrest, eyes closed. The open mouth and soft huffing told her he was asleep. His head rolled to the side when they pulled into a clean but aging subdivision. From the rearview mirror, she thought his eyes registered their location.

David adjusted his lanky frame to a sitting position. "Are you from here, Jenny Madison?"

"No, Texas." She met his eyes briefly.

"Me, too. Where in Texas?"

"Wayward. You know it?" She glanced again.

"I've been through it once or twice. Near Austin, isn't it?" She nodded. He laughed. Not a loud boisterous laugh—just a lyrical expression of humor.

"What?"

"I just wondered what the parents of the small town girl with two first names…and bite me on her ass, felt about her being this far from home."

"They always told me that Wayward fit me great but I didn't necessarily fit it."

"That sounds like a riddle. What the hell is it supposed to mean?"

She laughed this time. It startled her to hear it. "I think that's a very polite way of calling me a misfit." She turned off the engine in front of the house. "Do you need help in the door?"

"Is that part of the service?" His eyes widened as he spoke.

"Don't start getting ideas, Band Boy. We just make sure you get inside, we don't go in."

"I didn't mean… No, I'm good. Thanks!" He got out. With

hands in his pockets, he strolled slowly up the drive and into the house. Jenny went home and looked up Blind Optimism on the Internet. She downloaded and listened to the videos. Not bad. A little too cheerful for her, but they had talent. Or at least he did.

*

Two months later her business had grown to seventy members. Out of boredom Katy agreed to help part-time. David was now officially a regular. He called every two weeks, mostly from the cliffs. Once, she was summoned from the bar where she met him. Each time, he was alone when she arrived. He never really seemed like he needed a ride home.

She wondered if it would be rude to start giving clients sobriety tests. It would kill her to admit it but she looked forward to his calls. He was nice to talk to. At the cliffs, she had listened to him for hours. She had even bared her soul a little too.

Now that Katy was helping, she decided to take her first night off in three months. It was Sunday and Katy had mocked her. They rarely got more than one call on a Sunday anyway so it almost didn't count as a day off.

The doorbell to her apartment chimed. She peeked through the small hole. A delivery. Why would anyone deliver on Sunday?

"Ms. Madison?"

"That's me."

"I have your tickets here. Can you please sign right on that line there?" The man pointed to a dotted line.

"I didn't order tickets."

"There's a note." He handed her an envelope. "Have a good time," he said as he turned to leave. She opened the envelope. One ticket to Rock Fest in the Canyon. The note read:

Jenny,
You were never meant to fit in.
In Wayward or anywhere else.
You were born to stand out.
David Keith

A man with two first names sent her concert tickets? No. She looked at the lone paper addressed to her business, which was also her home address. Correction. Concert ticket. Singular. The list of bands on the ticket included his. The time was—today. He wanted her there.

*

It took her two hours to talk herself into going. She hated going solo to public places. It was so awkward to be alone in a crowd of people. She voiced her concerns outwardly, as she shoved her way through the crowd to her seat. Blind Optimism was the opening act. Jenny practiced a response should his earlier evaluation of their talent be accurate. Listening to him berate his group was one thing, but if he gave her the ticket in order to see a supportive face in the crowd—well, she hoped she didn't have to lie. She prayed her own evaluation was more accurate than his.

He waved when he walked on stage. He looked right at her when he sang…and the other ten thousand people in the park, of course. With all the lights, she doubted he received more than a glimpse of her. Yet, she imagined otherwise. The idea that he harmonized only for her breezed cheerfully through her head along with the tune they performed. She was rewarded between songs. He sent her drinks with a note. *I am the designated driver today.* Charming. She raised a glass to him in thanks. The drinks waited on the floor as she rose with the rest of the crowd and danced to the music. His voice could charm the chrome off a car. The glare of the lights enhanced the sparkling color in his blue eyes as he serenaded her and the thousands of people around her. She thrilled at his success and could see he mirrored the feeling.

"What do you think of them?" the man sitting next to her asked. She turned to a middle-aged, friendly faced black man with a bit too much fashion sense.

"I like them! They were pretty upbeat, don't you think?"

"I guess," he answered.

"You didn't like them?"

"The bigger question is…would you buy their music?" Strange question from a random stranger. Jenny looked past him to see a man with dark waves talking to someone on his other side.

"Of course I would! The guy's got a great voice, a happy smile, the kind that makes you want to…"

"Yes! That's the answer I wanted." The guy gave her a quick smile. He patted Jenny's arm and turned back to his company. "Let's go." The man and the two sitting with him rose and left, without even seeing the headliner.

Fifteen minutes after David's band cleared the stage, a man plopped into the empty seat next to Jenny. Apparently, this guy only cared about the main act. She mused that he missed a pretty good show by arriving late. She watched the band warming up onstage. The man's leg rubbed hers. Jenny edged away and frowned. The nerve! His fingers tickled her side. Now, that was too much.

"Hey buster!" she spat, knotting her fingers into a fist. Then she turned. Her mouth dropped. It seemed laughter and blue eyes were a very sexy mix.

"Hi, Jenny Madison." David's voice was melodic, even when saying her name. "What did you think?"

He had changed shirts and wore a hat to cover his hair. He smelled good. Spicy. He had showered. She stared for a second, and then cleared her throat. "Your drummer gets too loud, and your backup singer was off key on the second song for a short while."

He laughed and touched his lips lightly with hers. She didn't hit him but thought about it.

"And I see you're happy to be here," he responded.

"Some guy has been plying me with alcohol," she quipped. "Here, have one. I have three." She waved a hand over three glasses, one empty, and two full.

"What a creep." A slow grin crossed his face. "I'll pass."

"Since when?"

"Since two months ago."

"But I've driven you home four times."

"Yeah. I wanted to make sure I got my money's worth, even if I didn't need it anymore. Besides, how else was I going to see you?" His lips turned up again. "Devious, aren't I?"

"Absolutely sinful." She tried to keep her mouth straight but couldn't. The corners lifted and she let her teeth show.

"Did that hurt?"

"What?"

"The smile. I haven't seen it much since you dropped your business card on our table." He laced his fingers into hers. "It looks good on you."

"Well, don't get used to it."

"I'd like to." He turned to face her. "Isn't this fantastic?" Excitement in those blue eyes was even sexier. He continued, "I mean—look at us—I'm opening for a major band. Your business is soaring." He fell back into his seat. The look of pure pleasure on his face was refreshing.

"Yeah, I guess it is fantastic." She would have never believed it herself four months earlier.

"Jenny Madison from Wayward?"

"Hmmm?"

"I think you're my good luck charm, can I be your designated driver tonight?"

She thought for a minute. "Okay, but only because the service I use is short-staffed." She giggled.

"This is going to sound cliché but…I like you, Jenny. You make me laugh, and it really jazzes me when you laugh."

"Well, don't get used to that, either."

"What? Liking you?"

"No. Me laughing," she stated. "I don't do it much."

"We'll have to work on that."

*

Grant Tucker had noticed the girl in the seat next to Hodge when she sat down. Brown waves, big chocolate-colored eyes, long legs, and a smile that filled her face. She was entranced by the music and alone. A groupie for this little unknown band? Surely not. They're not that good. Why else would she come alone though? He watched her for a while and found it interesting the way she tried to contain the smile that hinted at dimples. As if she enjoyed the music but wanted not to. Or maybe she just had trouble enjoying herself period?

When Hodge asked her opinion of the band, a thing he always did when checking out new talents, Grant found himself listening to her rather than the band's current agent sitting next to him. The voice almost didn't match. It was low, husky, and almost gruff. Incredibly sexy.

Upon Hodge's signal to leave, he escorted his boss and one of their clients from the concert. They weren't interested in the main show. Since the band was already a client, they'd seen this performance more times than could be counted. As they slipped behind the curtain and headed for the back gate, he glanced back to see if she was still there. She was, but the seat next to her was no longer empty. He shrugged. No matter. He had no desire to strike up a conversation with a fame-seeking fan anyway. Been there. Done that. Had the bruised wallet and empty apartment to prove it.

Chapter 2

Stupid Rain. Jenny peered from under her umbrella in search of Lauren, her current client. Hopeless. All that could be seen was a colorful mix of vertical paintbrush strokes—an abstract that started out as a city view blurred by the drizzle around her. The downpour had completely obliterated visibility. It was cold as well, penetrating her jacket and jeans even with the umbrella's protection.

The possibility of identifying anyone exiting the club was gone, washed down the street with the rain. She had to get closer or they'd miss each other. Deftly dodging puddles in her new boots, she worked her way across the lot to the overhang above the entry. A cold ache in her shoulders threatened to work into a case of shivers. She needed hot soup, hot chocolate, hot coffee—hot anything. The achiness was always a predecessor to a fully-fledged cold. She didn't have time for that now. Her schedule was full. She had clients back-to-back tonight. People waiting on her to arrive. Even Katy was booked solid. She expected more calls later when the spooks had done their ghoulish good and needed to head home. It was Halloween night. One of the few big party nights of the year.

So far this evening, she had picked up a barrage of interesting guests adorned in costumes that included Martha Stewart, Pippi Longstocking (who did that anymore?), the Fruit of the Loom underwear guys, Bonnie and Clyde, and now she was waiting on Lady Gaga, a.k.a. Lauren Follis. Lauren was a new client. She had only picked her up once before and it was her kid that called, not her. That had been a first for Jenny, and sad, too. The child called and asked her to go to a bar on Fifth Street and look for a woman who needed a ride home. The child described Lauren in loving detail, and then said, "She may not think she needs to come home 'cause she's talking or something, but we need her here." There were many firsts in this business, she mused.

"Hey! Sheath the sword, lady," a masculine voice snapped in front of her. Through the fabric of the umbrella, she saw the darkness of a form. The form pressed against the cloth, sending rivulets of water showering down her hands and arms. The shadow of another arm pushed back.

"Oh. Sorry," Jenny mumbled. *Isn't there anywhere else to stand besides right in my way?* "Maybe you could move over just a little." She pulled the latch and collapsed the umbrella, making sure to stay under the protection of the overhang.

"Thanks. I thought you were going to stab me with that oversized tank of a tent." A tall, dark, and very wet person glared at her.

"It's a golf umbrella." She had purchased it for just this type of occasion.

"For two?"

"No smarty pants. For a person and their clubs."

"So, where's the clubs? Inside having a drink?" He smirked. The guy thinks he's a comedian.

"I just use it for work." She peered up through wet, sticky hair at the dark face. "I'm picking someone up."

His mouth clenched. When his eyes wandered down her clothes, she realized the misconception. "No. I'm not *hooking*, you idiot. I'm giving them a ride home so they don't have to drive. Get your mind out of the gutter."

"Thanks for the clarification. Glad you set me straight on that. You didn't really look the part anyway." He shrugged and shifted toward the door, dismissing her. Obviously, he didn't think her attractive enough to pick up anyone at the moment in her rain-soaked hair and clothes. She wished she could say the same for him. "Except maybe the boots. I'm waiting on someone too," he said.

"Why don't you go wait inside, Mr. Happy Pants?" As soon as the words came out, she clamped her hand over her mouth. Man, she really needed to work on her self-control. She'd done pretty well with the clients. Her friends were used to the crankiness and tolerated it. David had done a good job of curbing it to a degree. Now, she just needed to stop allowing random strangers to ruin her good mood. She lifted the edges of her mouth briefly, "Oops. I guess that was a little harsh. Sorry. It's the rain. I think I'm catching a cold and I need to be anywhere but standing out here waiting."

"I hear you. I've got a million other things to do myself." He glanced up and put his hand over her head to catch the steady drip that hit her shoulder. "Still, a friend's a friend, right? Maybe you should move in just a bit." He backed up more to give her space and she pressed toward him. The warmth of his breath reached her. It felt like steam rising off a nice cup of coffee and she quelled the urge to cup her hands toward it. Not to mention he smelled delicious—spicy.

There were several people sheltered under the overhang besides them. Very likely, they were waiting for someone, too—or waiting to get in. Some of them were in full costume. She grinned at the white powder puff on the behind of a very hairy-legged Playboy Bunny. The heels must have been a size fourteen. In profile, the bunny also sported a very thick beard and mustache, along with bright red lipstick. Good thing it was Halloween. A person could get shot dressed like that in this part of town.

"Ah, there's my passenger," she said. "Have a good night." Jenny flicked a casual wave at the man and worked her way forward through the crowd.

Lady Gaga, in full pink hair and overly exposed cleavage tripped out the door. Yes, it was a little odd that the woman was black but then, a lot of people wondered that about the up and coming star when she first debuted anyway. Besides, when a person had Lauren's body, they could pull off almost any costume. A shiny red, four-inch platform heel clattered on the wet pavement as she walked right out of it. Jenny moved to her, grabbed the shoe, and pulled the chute on the umbrella. "Hey, Lauren. Did you have a good time?" She licked her teeth and forced the business charm smile. Out of the corner of her eye, she caught the unfriendly, dark, umbrella-hater staring at her.

"Oh, hello there. Are you giving me a ride again? Yes, it was great. Really great. You want to check it out?" she slurred.

"No, that's okay. Time to go home, girl. Your daughter's getting worried. Here, get under this with me and I'll get you to the car. It's across the way." Lauren shot her a puzzled stare.

Jenny held her hand and shoe as they maneuvered through the puddles. Forty minutes later, she had successfully deposited Lauren at her door. There was still another pickup waiting before she could make her way home to her apartment. Lauren's delay had left her no recourse other than to ask Katy to pick up a couple of extras. Jenny ran her fingers through her hair, flicking it away from her face. After a drenching downpour, clothes tend to stick to the skin, hair mats and tangles, and makeup runs. Jenny knew she had hit all three—a home run as far as wet days go. A quick glance in the rearview mirror confirmed her fear. She was a complete mess. Some girls could run through a day like this and look glowing. She wasn't one of those girls.

Tires. She reminded herself. She needed to get new tires. The tread was practically gone. On a normal day, it wouldn't matter. In pouring down rain, it could prove dangerous or worse—cause an accident. She grabbed the pencil from the cup holder and added *tires* to the ever-growing list she kept lodged on the dashboard. Jenny had acquired affection for making lists. It was almost obsessive the way she made sure to write down new tasks, and then crossed them off when complete. Crossing the tasks off certainly brought a measure of self-satisfaction. With so few accomplishments to measure her progress, the lists were her only measuring stick. A quick glance proved that more tasks had lines through them than were added. "Good." She grinned. If she actually chose to buy into the positive psychology thing, her cup was half-full today.

Jenny slipped and slid along the deserted road to the cliffs. She was late and she hoped he wasn't completely drenched. As the car reached the end of the path, she looked through the glow of the headlights for his silhouette. The rain had subsided to a slight drizzle but it still hindered her view. She couldn't see him. With the aid of the umbrella, she picked her way to the edge and called out for David. He wasn't there. She panicked and took a quick glance over the edge, then chastised herself for doing so. He wasn't drinking much lately—he wouldn't fall, and he was anything but suicidal. He was an up and coming music talent with loads of fans and great reviews. He had either stood her up or grown tired of waiting. She tried his cell to no avail.

She slopped back to the car and drove home to her apartment on the off chance that he went home instead. David had taken to crashing at her place a couple of nights a week. Sometimes he called for a pickup, others he just arrived at the door with that happy smile. As she pulled into the parking lot, she glanced at her dark windows. A disappointed, uneasy feeling settled upon her. Her cell summoned her as she stepped out of the car and she glanced to see if it might be a customer. It was Katy.

"Hey, there. Where are you?" Katy said with barely masked impatience.

"Home, why?"

"I have David. He waited for you and you never showed, so he called back and got me." Katy's phone went muffled as if she'd covered the mouthpiece for a few seconds, and then she let out a giggle. *Holy Cow, is she flirting with my boyfriend?* Jenny didn't care if the woman was committed, a surge of jealousy slammed through her. *Is he really a boyfriend?*

"No problem, I'll come get him. Where are you?" She tried not to sound annoyed.

"Don't worry about it. I can bring him to you." She sounded sickeningly sweet. David's voice sang in the background as he often did when he tried to work through a problem with a new song.

"Are you sure?" Jenny's voice clipped. "He hasn't been drinking, right?"

"No. No." Another muffled conversation as Katy whispered behind a clamped mouthpiece, "Here, why don't you talk to him?" There was a short set of whispers, and then David was on the phone.

"Hey there, Jen. Where've you been?" He giggled. "Oh, my God, that rhymes, doesn't it?" His voice was lilting and soft.

"Are you okay?"

"Fantastic, babe. We had a great night. It was awesome. The crowd loved us. We couldn't get out of the place in one piece. This girl tore my shirt. You have to see it. She nearly ripped the sleeve right off!" He laughed. "I can't believe it. Hey, Katy, babe, can you stop here for a second?" *He called Katy 'babe'?* Jenny felt alarm bells go off in her head. She thought that was a word he'd reserved for her.

There was a commotion and a loud noise, and then Katy's voice came on. "Sorry, Jen. David went in this store here. Look, we should be there in twenty minutes or so. Okay?"

"Thanks." Jen hung up and tromped into her apartment, where she changed out of the wet clothes and combed her stringy hair before he arrived.

Chapter 3

Another gift, this time a charm bracelet with a tiny guitar, graced Jenny's arm as she headed out the door to pick up her first customer of the day. It was 4:30 p.m.—an early start, especially for a Wednesday night. According to Katy, David had arrived late the other night because he spent an hour searching for just the right gift. He was lucky to find anything open at that time of night.

The sunlight caught on the chain and cast a small rainbow across her wrist. She smiled, remembering how sweet he'd been when he gave it to her. He was so excited about the concert and he wanted to celebrate. She very quickly forgot that she'd heard him call Katy "babe" at least twice on the phone. The entire situation with David was confusing to say the least.

The sun was bright for a November night, but its rapid departure behind the trees signaled the pending time change. Her call was at least forty-five minutes away on the far side of the city. Jenny punched the gas, hoping they wouldn't mind the wait. Traffic was horrendous—she'd forgotten how bad rush hour could be when everyone else was heading out of town. She fumed and pounded the steering wheel as everyone slowed to a crawl in front of her. If it weren't for her waiting client, she'd enjoy the twinkling lights of downtown against the dusk. She didn't have the time now. She sighed briefly. All she could see in front of her was four lanes of stacked cars. There must be an accident. As she crept forward, she strained to see what was causing the delay. No sirens or lights. That was a good sign.

"Great," she muttered. "Now, I've seen everything." A guy chased a black and white great dane amongst the traffic. All four lanes of cars were at a standstill waiting on him.

"The entire freeway is shut down for a dog lover. Get the stupid thing on a leash, guy."

The dog bolted right, and then left, as the man lunged after it. Apparently, the canine had no sense of urgency due to the surrounding cars—he just wanted playtime. His front paws went down low as he wagged his tail in an almost rotating gesture while waiting for the man to come close. Some of the car riders had stepped out and were trying to assist with herding the small horse toward the man.

After several chases and lunges, the man finally latched onto the dog's collar, snapped the leash in place, and yanked him toward a waiting BMW on the side lane. The man shoved the dog into the back seat of the car, slammed the door, and walked to the back.

Traffic began flowing again. The man pulled his spare tire and jack from the trunk of the car. Not only did the goofus let his dog block traffic, now he intended to change a tire during rush hour on the side of the freeway?

There was a familiarity about the man's stance as he contemplated the flat. The closer she moved, the more she thought she knew him. Still, she couldn't place the car, the dog, or the profile. Then he turned and looked straight at her. A flash of recognition crossed his face. His brows jutted down before he turned his head, moved around the car, and bent down to his tire. Mr. Happy Pants from the bar on Halloween night. On a whim and a glance at the sky, Jenny careened her car in behind his and stopped. She crawled to the passenger side and stepped out on the asphalt shoulder. "Need help?" she asked. He slid his eyes sideways briefly.

"I'm good," he answered. Jenny debated that statement. She peeked around him at the tire iron sprawled on the ground and the spare that looked worse than the one that had spread itself like cheese on the road.

"Good at dog catching or changing a tire?" Her thoughts spewed involuntarily out of her mouth.

"You just can't hold back, can you? The sarcasm just pops out of you like hiccups." He frowned up at her, squinting his dark, smoke-colored eyes into the sun that was diminishing behind her in a bright orange burst. "Not playing golf in the rain today?"

"Look, Mr. Happy Pants, I thought you might want some help," she spurted. "I guess I thought wrong."

"Yes, you did. Don't you think it's a little ironic calling *me* 'Mr. Happy Pants'? That's kind of like Scrooge calling the Grinch grumpy," he snapped, pressing down on the edge of his spare. She wasn't sure, but she thought he'd just insulted the both of them. Did he realize that? "How exactly did you intend to help with this? Have you ever even *changed* a tire?"

Okay, that was it. An uncanny urge flowed through her to yank the tire iron away and wrap it around his head. Or maybe just fling it across his shin a couple times. She checked the urge and scowled at him. He's on his own. She whirled around and stomped toward her car without answering. What a jerk. What an ass. What a…

"Wait." She heard a clatter as he dropped the tire iron on the concrete. "I'm sorry. That was out of line." He rose and walked toward her, stopping as the dog plunged its head out the window into his gut. He let out an exasperated grunt then shoved the head back into the car before taking a few more steps toward her.

"Nice dog." Jenny smirked. "You have a way with him. If I were a dog whisperer, I'd probably say that he doesn't care too much for you."

He glanced back at the drool hanging off the dog's lower jowl and shrugged. "Then the feeling's mutual. I swear that thing is like a 200-pound toddler. Always drooling and eating, thinks everything's a game, and has no control of any body function whatsoever. He's not mine. He belongs to my boss."

"Your boss? Why do you have him in your car?"

"Because I'm too accommodating for my own good." The dog barked at him and Jenny could swear the man growled back. Immediately the big pointed ears fell back and the dog ducked his head into the car.

"I doubt that," Jenny snipped, and then once again slammed her hand over her mouth. She stifled a giggle.

"Yeah, you should keep it there for a while. Listen, I didn't mean to growl at you. It's just been a rough day." The man then grinned and Jenny was startled. He actually looked nice when he did that. All those harsh, angry lines just melted away. It gave an aura of—she hated to admit it—niceness. Dark curls framed his face which had the angular, solemn, sexy look of a—what? She wasn't sure. "Look," he started, "the spare's flat too, and I need to pick up my boss at the airport in thirty minutes. Would you mind giving me a ride to my apartment and I'll grab my car?"

Jenny dropped her hand. "The car isn't yours, either?"

"No, it's his. He's…odd. Wants to be picked up in his own car with his 'family' in tow. Hence, the dog."

"His family is that thing?" She pointed to the dog. The beast shook his head sending swirls of drool showering around him. Fortunately, he had his head back out the window. The slobber foam landed neatly in a line across his nose. Jenny screwed her mouth up at the sight.

"Now it is," he admitted. "He's been divorced twice. The dog seems to be the only relationship he's good at. Or at least that he cares about."

Jenny looked at her car, then back. "Sounds like a great guy. I can give you a ride, but I'm not so sure about him." She pointed at the dog again.

He stared at her. "He has to go too. I can't leave him here—he'll eat the inside of the car. Have you ever seen a dog act out when it's left alone? It's not a pretty sight, especially when the dog's that big. He's already chewed up the back seat when Hodge left him in it once before. The man would probably fire me if I did it. Besides, it's not safe."

Jenny nervously looked at her Mercedes. The boss's name was apparently Hodge. She wondered if her car looked like a doggy snack to that small horse of a mutt.

"Don't worry. I won't let him eat yours."

"Okay, but you're gonna pay for any damage. Understand?" She sent him her most scorching stare. It was lost on the man—he had already opened the car door and yanked the dog out. Ironically, the dog sensed his annoyance and showed impeccable manners as it strutted alongside. It looked at Jenny and she had the distinct feeling that if he'd been a person, the dog would have had a smug grin on its face. Jenny eased them gingerly into traffic. The spacious car seemed a lot more cramped with a 200-pound dog in the back seat, along with Mr. Tall, Dark, and Grumpy sitting shotgun.

"What's your name?" she asked. "I want to know who to send the cleaning bill to." She motioned to the back seat where another six-inch piece of slobber hung from the dog's mouth.

"Grant." He held out a hand. "Tucker." He whisked the towel in his other hand back to catch the pending goo from the dog's lip.

"I'm Jenny." A brief shake of his hand, then she returned hers to the steering wheel. She glanced at her watch and sighed. The constant juggling of schedules in order to meet her business objectives was frustrating. Between Katy and herself, they had to call each other numerous times throughout the day and switch customers just to keep up. The surge in customers was great—the toll it took on the cars and drivers was worrisome.

"It's right there." Grant pointed to the apartments at the next exit as if he felt her impatience. Five minutes later, Jenny had pulled up behind his bright red, sporty convertible Audi.

She took one cautious glance at the car and raised her eyebrows at him. "You're kidding, right?"

He gave her a startled glance. "No, why?"

"You're going to pick up your boss in that car, with this horse in the back?" Surely, he saw the futility in it. "Which one is going in the trunk?"

The guy glared at her for a minute, then relaxed and laughed. "You know, if you weren't a little pretty, your mouth would be downright annoying. What the hell else am I supposed to do? That's the only car I have." He looked out the window, she assumed he was willing the car to change into a Jeep or a Cadillac as the dog licked the back of his head. He slapped at the beast. "Knock it off, Bugsy."

Jenny registered the backhanded compliment, or insult. She wasn't sure which it was. "You're not going to get there on time if you don't hurry. I recommend you leave the dog in your apartment."

"Can't. My boss is pretty picky about that." He opened the door and reached for the back latch to let Bugsy out. "Besides, I don't want the stupid thing eating my furniture while I'm gone. It's leather and brand new. He'd probably think it was a rawhide chew."

Jenny quickly dodged the wagging tail that was facing her, and sighed. She lowered her forehead onto the steering wheel for a second and let out a small groan. "Get in. I'll take you."

"Take me?" He sounded hopeful.

"To the airport. It's impossible to get the three of you in that sardine can." It took the man all of two seconds to jump back in the car with relief written all over him.

"You know, behind the abrasiveness there's a nice streak in you," Grant said with a smile. Damn that smile.

"If the dog ruins my car, you'll think differently. And you'll find out what else I use that golf umbrella for," Jenny responded.

"A nice streak that you keep hidden deep. Real deep."

Jenny cast him a glare, then hit the speed dial on her hands-free. "I need to make a quick call."

When Katy answered, she explained that she wasn't going to make her next stop and asked if Katy could help out.

"Jenny, you know I have something going on tonight?" Katy pleaded. "You really need to think about hiring another driver." They had talked about hiring several times lately. Jenny was increasingly dependent on Katy's help. It would be pointless to try to run the business without her.

Grant looked out the window as she spoke. The slobbery towel rested in his lap, clasped between both hands. He pretended to ignore the conversation, entranced by the city zooming past.

"I know. I'm sorry," Jenny said. "If you could take care of this one, I'll start looking tomorrow. I promise." She had no clue when she'd find the time, but she would do it.

Katy let a few seconds pass before responding with an exaggerated sigh. "I'll be late then. You know this business of yours is killing my love life. Speaking of love life—what's that panting noise?"

Katy glanced sideways, startled to see the dog standing over her shoulder with his tongue hanging out. No one could say the beast didn't have a good set of lungs.

"What panting noise? I don't hear anything," Jenny answered innocently. Grant snickered at her coy response, adding a very masculine tone to the panting dog's background noise.

"Jenny Madison, you're with someone! Is that David?" Jenny couldn't help but giggle too.

"No. It's not David and I'm not *with someone*. It's just a dog." She didn't look but knew Grant was shooting daggers at her. *Okay, and a hot as hell guy but who's checking.*

"Yeah, right."

Jenny couldn't blame her skepticism. If she'd heard it, she probably would have thought the same thing.

The dog licked Jenny on the ear and she whispered, "Stop" at the beast and shoved him away. Grant laughed softly in the passenger seat, barely attempting to conceal his voice. His body started racking with silent laughter when the dog sighed heavily, made some smacking, licking noises, and panted stronger. Jenny glared at the man, who obviously did not intend to contain his dog.

"Katy, I have to go. Thanks for your help. I'll call you tomorrow." Jenny clicked the "end" button on the phone before the dog could make some other disgusting sound.

"You're a lot of help," she snapped.

Grant let out a loud howl of laughter and clutched his stomach. "Oh God, that was funny." He stomped his foot on the floorboard as if to get a grip on himself. "Your friend obviously thinks you're making out hot and heavy with someone— apparently someone named David—and it's just a 200-pound slobbering dog!" He had tears in his eyes, the jerk.

"I'm glad you're enjoying the fact that my best friend and business partner now thinks I'm cheating." Jenny frowned. That rumor would make the rounds by morning, knowing her friends. "Cheating?" He stopped laughing and stared at her hands. "You're married?"

"No. Not married. Just…involved. Sort of. I think." *Was she?*

"I gather a guy named David is the 'sort of, I think' guy?"

"Yeah, and he's out of town, which Katy is definitely aware of."

Grant straightened in his seat before responding. "Well, it's still funny. You want me to call her and explain?" He reached back and scuffed Bugsy's ears. He was practically commending the dog's performance.

"Hmmm. Let me think about that." Jenny tapped a finger to her chin for a second. "Sure, why don't I have a random guy that I hardly know call up my friend and tell her that it was his dog panting on the phone in the car? Especially while that same guy is the reason that I am missing work and is in the car with me at the moment. That probably will go over even better than the dog story. Sure, that's believable."

"You have a point," he muttered. "Maybe I could go talk to her?"

She took one look at Grant and said. "Not a good idea." If Katy saw Mr. Tall, Dark, and Grumpy, she would certainly never believe Jenny was just giving him a ride. He was the type that women drool over—even with the bad attitude.

He looked at her skeptically. "You don't think I can behave myself, do you? I could take Bugsy with me and she'd see right away."

Sure." Speaking of drool, could you wipe the dog's mouth again?" Jenny felt the dampness on her shoulder.

He looked at her funny then passed the towel under Bugsy's head. "We weren't talking about drool," he responded.

No, I was just thinking about it. Oops.

"The airport!" Jenny announced their arrival. "Where should I wait?"

Chapter 4

There's nothing like circling the airport continuously with a giant black and white slobber machine breathing in your ear. Jenny was certain she looked like someone that just stepped out of a sauna and needed a shower. She opened the back window so the beast could deposit some of his overflowing moisture outside the car and went around for the fourth time. When a person talks of hot breath on their neck, this is definitely *not* what they mean. Still, for all the wetness, she had to admit the dog was cute, in a huge, oversized, happy-go-lucky way.

She eased the car slowly down the pick-up line and darted her eyes from person to person, seeking out Grant and his boss. She passed a family of four, a woman in a business dress, two men in suits, and three young men in jeans. No Grant.

One of the two men in suits flashed a waving hand at the cars and lunged in front of her, jolting her to a stop. She let out a loud squeal just as she recognized the face. She nearly ran over him and she had to admit it might have felt good for a second or two. At what point did Grant don a suit jacket and comb his hair to look like he stepped out of a men's fashion magazine? Her mouth fell open and she stared as he thumped the hood of the car and glared briefly at her. She was still dazed with the change when he pounded on the trunk.

Jenny jumped out of the car and pressed the trunk button to flip it open. "I'm sorry, I didn't see you." She forced her customer friendly smile and helped him drop the newly acquired bags into the hatch. She ignored the raised eyebrow that Grant flashed her way and extended a hand to the middle-aged man with him.

"I'm Jenny." She grinned. "How was your flight? "The man smiled and clasped her hand in his vice-like grip and introduced himself. Hodge. A well-dressed black man that spoke to his dog like it was an infant. He looked familiar but she couldn't place him. Within minutes, Hodge was strapped into the back seat with his adoring hound and Grant planted himself next to her once again.

Hodge looked at the dog standing over his lap and frowned. "Bugsy, *SIT.*"

Amazingly, the energetic, car-eating horse dropped his behind into the seat and watched his master. Hodge leaned over and pulled the seatbelt around the dog, strapping him safely in. Wow. Jenny looked at Grant with a "why didn't you do that?" look.

Grant scrunched up his nose and gave her a snarl, and then amazingly he broke into a very charming grin. "Pretty smart dog, huh?"

Wow. She couldn't help but stare at the clothes, the combed hair, the suit, flashing dark eyes, and the seriously pleasant smile. Even though she realized he had let the dog drench her purposely, she warmed. He looked like a different person. She was certain the show was for his boss and she didn't have the heart to ruin it for him. So, she played along—smiling pleasantly, talking with Hodge, and teasing with Grant. She poured on the flirtatious charm. At least she thought she did.

*

"So, how do you know my boy Grant?" Hodge peered at her through the rear view mirror.

"We met outside a bar on Halloween. He thought I was a hooker and hit on me."

"I did not." He hadn't said that, she jumped to conclusions.

He had never meant to imply—anything. It was just the boots, they didn't fit. And he hadn't hit on her.

She laughed, "It was raining like crazy and I had this big umbrella—"

Grant finally eased up and lifted an arm over the seat back toward Hodge. "She had on these stiletto heeled boots and black suit. With a red umbrella that was bigger than this car."

Hodge leaned forward. "Cat woman! Awesome."

Jenny shot a glance at Grant, "How'd you know what I was wearing? I was soaked."

"I noticed. It was black and the rain made it—cling in all the right places." *Not to mention the white top had been almost translucent when wet.*

Jenny turned to the traffic and slammed on her brakes when a car swerved into her lane. She bumped the horn twice; the dog punctuated it with a soft bark.

Hodge reached up and stroked the hound. "Ooh, I have these visions of Halle Berry in all that black shiny shit with zippers everywhere."

Cool it, Hodge.

"It wasn't like that."

Grant tensed when Hodge stuck his hand into Jenny's hair from behind and squeezed. "You should come over some time, Jenny Cat, and bring the black shiny thing. I've always wondered how hard it was to get out of all those zippers."

Okay, this was going way too far. Grant wanted to yank the hand down. Jenny smiled and pulled at Hodge's wrist instead.

"Back off there, Batman, or I may have to have Robin here use a couple of Judo moves on you."

Hodge leaned back in the seat, his voice a bit softer. "Cat woman does judo moves too, you know. As I remember, she used those stiletto-heeled boots pretty damn well in the movie. It'd be more fun with you than him."

Grant couldn't believe his uncle was actually making a move on Jenny. Seriously? She could be his daughter. "You might need to take a dose of Cialis first, old man." Yeah, he shouldn't have said that but it felt good.

Hodge glared for a second. "Harsh, man, harsh. Just because you hate women doesn't mean I have to." Thankfully, he decided to change the subject. "You like music, Jenny Cat?"

"Sure, love it. I have a friend that—"

"We're in the business. Grant didn't tell you?"

"Nah, we haven't really talked much about work."

Hodge obviously thought that meant something else and patted his shoulder. "He wouldn't. Too modest and serious if you ask me. Especially since he's about the best damn manager on the west coast. Probably the east coast too."

Grant turned and looked out the window, keenly aware she was staring at him. Why did he say that crap?

"Hodge's real name is Benjamin Hodges Larson," Grant explained. He was relieved when the name didn't register. "He's fairly well known as an agent in the entertainment business."

"I wouldn't go that far." Hodge interrupted. "We're very small, only a few clients. Mainly because we choose our clients selectively. I don't touch anyone that's not of sound mine, clean body, and has a good work ethic. I don't have time to risk my career on bad seeds."

Jenny turned back to the traffic. "Smart move, since most of those bad seeds are spoiled, addictive personalities with a whole host of problems following them around."

"No shit."

Grant adjusted the volume of Jenny's Sirius radio when a long lull in conversation occurred. He hoped it would silence the banter between the two of them. Surely, she's not falling for his spiel? A quick glance in the rearview mirror showed the man admiring the back of Jenny's head just before his eyes drifted closed. Jet lag had finally set in. Thank God. If he had to listen to any more of her flirting and laughing with his aged, gray-headed, overweight boss, he was going to be sick. Yeah, she was beautiful doing it but that wasn't the point. And Hodge. What the hell was he thinking? Grant thought to say something but bit it back. Must be professional. Clearly, he himself didn't really know what the point was.

"He's asleep," Grant whispered. "Jet lag. That flight from London is a killer. It'll take him a couple of days to recover."

"I can't believe how different the dog is. The crazy thing is barely moving. Does Bugsy always do that when he's around?"

"Actually, Bugsy's like that most of the time. I don't know what got into him today. Maybe he smelled another dog—or the traffic bothered him. Who knows?"

Jenny's GPS instructed them in a musical female voice to turn left at the next intersection and go 1.2 miles to their destination. They silently followed suit. A few minutes later, Grant stepped out, leaned over his boss and unlatched both seatbelts before shaking the man awake and leading the dog out to the fence. He jogged back and helped Hodge get the bags from the trunk, then leaned in the passenger door and looked Jenny in the eye.

"Give me five minutes to get him settled and I'll be right back," Grant asked as he flashed an appreciative smile. Her eyes popped up to meet his.

"You want me to wait?" Apparently, she thought she was just going to dump him here. Then he'd have to call a cab and a tow truck. He glanced at his watch. He supposed he could do so, but admittedly he'd rather not.

"Please. I need to swing by Hodge's car and get it towed. If you can't take me, I'll call a cab." He watched her hesitantly. She looked at the clock on the dash and furrowed her brows.

"My day is shot anyway but I need to hurry; I have to pick

someone up in an hour." He looked at her confused before sliding the door softly closed.

*

Jenny whizzed them back to the car where the tow truck he'd called was already lifting Hodge's beamer and preparing it to move. Grant silently prayed that the tow wouldn't dent or scratch the precious automobile. Once the tow driver was ready to go, Grant jogged back to Jenny's car and jumped into the passenger seat one last time.

"You saved my life tonight, Jen. I owe you. What can I do to make it up?" His eyes searched hers. *STAY.* The word bolted into his brain and echoed with the thought. Much as he hated to admit it, he was reluctant to leave. He realized she was in a rush, but the idea of her driving away and possibly disappearing was hugely disappointing. He started to say, "What about lunch?" then stopped. No.

"Don't worry about it. Just consider it my good deed for the day." She waved a hand, dismissing him. He doubted good deeds fit into her lifestyle very often. Grant didn't know why he decided to lean in; it was a stupid thing to do. He didn't even know the woman and she'd already mentioned that she was "involved, sort of." Still, he was overwhelmed after listening to her wit all night. Her grating grouchiness had ironically grown on him.

Without thought, he leaned over to place a kiss on her cheek. She was small; reaching her was a stretch that required him to place an arm across the console. His fingers brushed the warm flesh of her forearm and she flinched. Damn it if she didn't turn right into him, accidentally of course. His mouth was abruptly on her lips instead of her cheek and he panicked. Soft, pouting lips that felt incredibly warm against his. He sank back and waited for an angry quip of some sort to slip from her. Nothing came; she just stared at him.

"I guess no good deed goes unpunished," he whispered and reached for the door handle. Her fingers clamped over his forearm and he looked down to see her slip something into his palm. A business card?

"You're a strange guy, Grant," she stated. "I don't really understand what you're doing with that dog and Hodge, but this was—interesting. Definitely entertaining. If you ever get stranded again, feel free to give me a call. Driving is what I do for a living." She smiled briefly then sobered up. "Don't bring the tiny horse, though. I'm gonna have to vacuum all the hair out tomorrow, and I believe I'll have to shower all the slime off my neck. Just curious—why didn't you strap him into the seatbelt to begin with?"

He stared at her. She'd completely flipped from the angry, crabby girl he'd first met, but he sensed it was all pretense. Glancing at the business card, he realized what had happened. She was making a sales pitch. This was her sweet and charming business personality. "Because I liked watching him aggravate you. So, how much do I owe you?" he blurted.

Her eyes widened. "What?"

"You said you do this for a living. Based on the calls earlier, I'm guessing I made you lose some business. How much?"

She blinked a couple of times then stuttered an answer. "I said don't worry about it and I meant it."

He slipped the card in his suit pocket and shoved the door open. Clarity hit Grant like a baseball to the brain. She had pulled over to him hoping to make a new client—not out of interest or any Good Samaritan tendencies. "You're a little strange yourself, Jen, but I have to admit I don't like the faked sweet you. The sarcasm fits better. Being genuine is always a plus with me."

She looked at him as if he had slapped her, "Ouch. Being a genuine ass, you mean? You know, I could have just left you on the side of the freeway."

He started to speak, to apologize, then closed his mouth. He stepped out of the car, pushed the door shut and strode toward the flashing lights of the waiting tow truck. He *was* an ass and he had no idea what bothered him about her motives.

Why did it disappoint him that the entire experience was just a business thing for her? After all, that wasn't uncommon. He did it all the time. In fact, his entire career was based on strategic relationships. Working for a man that would help him get into the business. Meeting people that might someday be clients. Building relationships that could prove financially successful. Funny that even his personal life had an agenda—one that supported his career. He thought about Emma Howell—gorgeous, bleached blonde, incredibly perfect Emma. What a bitch. Had she ruined him permanently? Admittedly, he had better lose the bitterness at some point. Not yet.

Grant watched Jenny's car veer around the truck, the red taillights were quickly engulfed in the traffic ahead. Within minutes, he couldn't determine which were hers. How ironic that surface personalities often hid a much thicker, more sincere, or perhaps more menacing basement of complexity in people. Both Emma and Jenny obviously wore their outer selves like a winter coat, hugging it against them to hide the real person. The inner self was not even close to the exterior. He wasn't really sure what Jenny's inner personality held, but he knew for sure it had to be better than what he'd found in Emma. That woman was an empty, calculating, selfish—okay, he needed to stop thinking about it. Jenny was the opposite, burly on the outside, but he sensed her real self was much more genuine and likeable.

Grant shook his head and struck up a conversation with the driver as they headed to the tire shop. He hoped he would get home in time to get at least five or six hours of sleep before Hodge's first phone call.

Chapter 5

Jenny plunked a beer down in front of Katy and slid into the seat across from her at her tiny kitchen table. She dispatched the thought of asking about the night Katy had driven David home. It was ridiculous to superimpose a flirtation onto something that, in all likelihood, was just joviality. After all, David was a lighthearted guy—he couldn't help it. She studied her friend's face, contemplating the possibility that Katy would cheat on Bruce, the professed love of her life. No, she wouldn't. Katy reviewed the resumes for drivers that Jenny had already inspected. Jenny wasn't sure it mattered. Her feelings for David seemed a little platonic after meeting Grant. "I did background checks on all these guys," Katy announced. "And I rated them by my thoughts." Thick, red ink numbers at the top of the pages communicated her preferences. She shoved the papers back at Jenny and waited. Jenny flipped through. Only two had a number above seven. One was a clear nine (her best score), with a plus mark.

"Why a nine plus?"

"His driving record is impeccable. He's the only one that hasn't had so much as a speeding ticket in ten years," Katy clarified.

"Then why not a ten?" Jenny questioned.

"He's…old. I know. I know. Don't give me that look." Katy held up a hand. Jenny's wrinkled forehead must have given away her thoughts. "It's not just that. He was almost too eager. Maybe too cheerful. I don't know; it just didn't feel right."

Katy referred to their phone interview with him earlier in the week and she was right. Something about him communicated a feeling of carefully executed optimism. Almost as if he didn't really mean it—just blindly said what they wanted to hear.

The thought made Jenny smile as it conjured up images of the CD cover David had shown her the night before. His band now had a contract with an agent and scheduled tour dates for the next six months, with rumors of a possible contract with a larger firm that could take them worldwide. Blind Optimism was stampeding into fame and his time with Jenny had dwindled to a few hours a week as opposed to almost every other night just weeks ago.

She supposed that was why Katy's perceived flirting motivated a jealous twinge. The phrase "absence makes the heart grow fonder" was total fiction. Still, he had showed up last night with the CD jacket, and a new charm to add to her bracelet. He'd kissed her and teased with her as he chased her around the living room, singing. She didn't even mind when he fell asleep on her lap without even so much as an attempt at more than the few kisses. She understood the demands of the music industry had worn down on him. She shouldn't let herself jump to irrational conclusions just because both he and she were working hard and trying to get their businesses going.

Jenny shook off the reservations on mister nine-plus and gave him a call. He quickly accepted her offer and she had her first bona fide employee.

"Cheers to our first staff member." She dinged her beer against Katy's in a mock celebration and they chugged down the cans.

"Hey, what am I, chopped liver? Don't I count as your real first staff member?" Katy admonished.

"No, actually, your official title is partner." Jenny grinned. She'd drawn up the agreement the prior week. It was only fair that Katy shared in the profits since she was instrumental in the startup. Jenny had solicited the help of an attorney for the first time in her life. The Designated Driver's Club was now a

Limited Liability Corporation. Actually, it would be as soon as the state approved the documents.

Katy's mouth dropped. "You're kidding, right?"

"Ha. Don't you think it's about time you made more than just a pittance off all that hard work and late hours? Besides Bruce needs to know that you really are working and not just running around on him at night."

Katy's face turned pink. She looked out the window with wet eyes. "I don't know what to say." Jenny thought the reaction a little odd except for the tears. There was nothing embarrassing about working hard.

"I want you to say you'll do it. If not, I have to hire employee number two also. There's no way I can keep going at this pace. I don't know about you but I miss the days I could come home at night and take a bubble bath, then curl up and watch television. I haven't seen one single reality show since this gig started." She giggled, "I don't even know what reality is doing these days because I'm too busy living it. So, what do you say partner? Are we doing this or not?"

Jenny rose and pulled a bottle of water from the fridge. She held one up for Katy, who politely declined.

"We are—on one condition." Katy asserted her controlling tendency and added, "No, make that two. I want to train all incoming staff. Otherwise, they'll all end up scaring off our customers with your surliness and negativity. Plus we both get at least one full day off a week, scheduled in advance of course. A day where we don't take any calls, no matter what." Katy gave her best admonishing glare. "Not even in an emergency. If we do well, we up it to two days."

Jenny wiped the condensation from her hand and held it out for a handshake that sealed the deal. "Done."

"What are you doing for Thanksgiving?" Katy quickly moved on to new business.

"Have you and David made a plan?"

"Not yet, he's supposed to be in Dallas for a concert the night before so I doubt he'll be around."

"That's a shame. This would have been a good time for him to meet the fam. That is, unless you're not ready for that. Come to think of it, I've never really asked—is this a serious thing? Or just, you know, casual?"

"Since when have I ever been casual about anything?" Jenny asked.

"Good point. You're the definition of serious. Or at least you pretend to be, but we all know it's just a front to cover up your 'softer soul'." Katy's voice became sugary on the last two words. "We're just waiting for you to realize that and expose it to us."

Jenny laughed and held up her drink. "Here's to the wait. I hope it's worth the while. Speaking of waiting, when are you and Bruce gonna start bringing little midgets into the world? Are you planning to jump right into it—pun intended—or wait a while?"

Katy exhaled a slow curse. "Off limits, partner. I get that enough from my parents. You don't need to go there too."

"Yikes. Sorry. I didn't realize that was a touchy subject. Thinking back though, I guess you did have a lot of relatives dropping hints at the wedding." Jenny clunked the bottle on the table and stood up to act it out. Rubbing a hand on Katy's arm, she dissolved into a coughing fit as she pretended to be Katy's aging aunt, who suffered from a chronic cold.

"Oh, Katy." She pinched her friend's cheek. "Hurry up and get us another baby to torment. You're reaching the top of your prime you know."

"Thanks partner. I appreciate that you can find humor in my torture and frustration." Katy shot her a smile. "Well, I'd better get home and busy myself 'jumping' my husband. I'd hate to disappoint everyone."

Jenny laughed.

"I was kidding. At least about disappointing everyone, not the jumping—we're not on the fast track to baby land right now. We just got married. We need to learn how to tick each other off first."

Jenny watched as her friend plodded out the door of her apartment to her waiting husband.

Chapter 6

Jenny smoothed her hand over the leather upholstery of the first automobile to be inventoried into their business. She examined the dashboard with satisfaction. Her first fixed asset was a beauty and upheld her confidence in the success of the business. The copy of signed documents was neatly folded in the glove compartment as she fiddled around inside, figuring out all the buttons, getting the seats and mirrors adjusted, and programming the radio for her favorites. Her first employee needed a vehicle, and she decided he would get her old one. This new one was hers, at least for now. After all, being the owner had a few perks, right? She needed to break in the new vehicle and tonight served that purpose perfectly.

Dusk bloomed, and then faded as the clouds developed a mesmerizing pink and gray haze to them when the sun dipped its final bow behind the cityscape. With the Thanksgiving holiday just two days away, Jenny expected a slow night. Her common sense reminded her it would be short-lived. As soon as Thursday was gone, a steady slur of holiday parties promised to keep all three drivers in constant movement.

The car purred out of the dealership, gliding freely toward her first pickup of the day. A new customer was the perfect way to celebrate the new car. She rehashed her phone conversation with David last night, frowning. His concert went well. The fans loved him, of course. He was ecstatic, chattering rapidly about the music, the band, and the crowd—but he was 600 miles away. He sounded distant in more ways than just physical miles. She couldn't really place it, but something had changed. His rushed call between the show and his trip to his hotel disappointed.

The constant news releases about him over the past weeks just made his phone call substantiate her concerns.

She lectured herself that perhaps their affection was based more on the excitement of "beginning" than on each other. Maybe it had simply been a strange support system that bolstered them through the first rough seams of building businesses and careers. They were polar opposites. Together they didn't make sense. Maybe there wasn't any relationship at all.

Jenny pulled the car to a halt in front of a convenience store, and tapped some buttons on the display to browse through the GPS. She needed directions to the new customer's location. The GPS was her lifeline during work hours. She pondered if a similar device existed for personal lives and relationships.

Were there steps that forecasted success in developing stronger ties? A guide map, so to speak? Her prior track record symbolized a serious lack of ability in the love realm. In all relationships, if she evaluated herself honestly. Abrasiveness sometimes had a downfall. She shrugged. Big deal. It also conveniently disguised the vulnerabilities one preferred unshared.

Jenny sped along the feeder road of the freeway on cue, ready to make the right turn encouraged by her best friend, GPS. The apartments ahead caught her eye. Actually a movement in front of them alarmed her.

A little girl with dark curls and a determined face bounced a ball next to the street. She focused on slapping against the ball to push it down against the pavement then back up to her. Jenny squinted into the sun, looking at the apartments for an adult to attach the child to. Nothing. Didn't anyone notice this child standing next to a busy intersection? It was the oldest cliché in the book. Unattended child, bouncing a ball—the next thing to happen was a given.

Jenny slowed. The back of her neck cooled. The girl laughed at fumbling attempts to control the ball, yet her eyes remained solidly focused on her efforts. Her voice jingled and Jenny had no idea why or how she heard it. Then her eyes rose and rounded. Her mouth opened in panic.

"Walky, stop!" she screamed.

A figure darted in front of Jenny's car and she slammed on the brakes. Her heart flung to her throat and pounded against her esophagus, cutting off her breathing. "No!" she blurted as she yanked the wheel and slammed the car to the curb. The car jumped the curb with a thud and glided forward. She couldn't stop. It hurtled straight toward those dark curls. The little girl's open mouth no longer screamed; she just stared. It was the last thing Jenny saw before she slammed into the corner light post and wrapped the hood of her new car around it.

Chapter 7

As Jenny fluttered her eyes open, an immense dread filled her. She stared up at clouds and blue sky. "I'm *so sorry,*" she uttered. "He just ran out in front of me. I didn't even know he was there." Pain throbbed in her forehead. She raised a hand to feel the knot forming above her left eye.

"Who ran in front, ma'am?" the paramedic asked as he shone a light into her eyes and danced it from left to right. He ran his hands down her left arm, then right, proceeding to her legs with mild pressure.

"I'm fine," Jenny affirmed. "No need to do that." She pushed against the hard, cold cement underneath her and rose to sit.

"Stay down. You've had a pretty bad blow to the head." He pressed her shoulder back to the cloth on the pavement. "Can you tell me your name ma'am?"

She gave her name, then he asked for her address and if she had any significant health issues he needed to be aware of.

"Can you tell me what happened?" he asked, as he checked her blood pressure.

"Where's the little girl? She was in front of me on the roadside here. She tried to warn him. Wally, Walty, or maybe it was Walky—I think. He ran in front of me. She screamed. I jerked the wheel to miss him but I think I was too late. Is he okay?" Jenny tried to look around, the hand still pressed against her. She processed the police redirecting traffic, the cars backed up, and the ambulance beside them. That was all. What happened to the little girl and her friend—or was it a dog?

"There wasn't anyone else around, ma'am." His matter of fact voice punctuated the strange look on his face. He didn't believe her. "The car behind you called it in. See the lady over there? She said you jumped the curb and hit the post with no warning. Were you on your phone maybe? Or texting? Distracted in any way?"

"No, of course not. I was—I'm not sure. I can't remember." Jenny hesitated to say more. She blinked her eyes.

"Hmmm. Well, nothing's broken and you don't seem to have any internal injuries other than that nasty bump on your forehead. Still, we need to take you in and check you over to be safe. You might have a bit of a concussion. Fortunately, as head injuries go, that's the best place to get one. The old saying 'hardheaded' isn't a myth. The bone on your forehead is there to protect the brain, and it does so quite well."

"That's good to know." She peered up at the sky, strumming her fingers over her head. A bulge of skin shaped under them. She glanced at the paramedic.

"It will probably swell a little more and bruise up, but don't worry." He motioned to his partner. "Now, we're going to pick you up and take you to the hospital. Just lay still okay?" She shut her eyes.

*

The ride to the hospital proved brutal. The paramedic wouldn't shut up. She just wanted to close her eyes and rest, but he kept yakking away asking all sorts of questions. At the hospital, the nurse did the same. She couldn't wait to get home where it was quiet. Jenny persuaded them to release her after almost three hours of observation. They forced her to call someone to pick her up—no going it alone. She tried David with no luck, and then opted for Katy.

"I'm sorry," Jenny said. "I'm really sorry."

"It's okay. Don't worry about it. I'm just glad you're not hurt." Katy eyed her as they drove away from the hospital.

"Keep that ice on your head or you're going to look like a unicorn."

"Can you take me by the intersection where it happened? I just want to see it."

"Not tonight, girlie. You're going home and we're icing that bad boy down for the rest of the evening. Bruce is meeting us at your apartment and we're staying. Got it?"

"Got it partner." Jenny looked out the window with her frozen hand gingerly snuggling the icepack. Katy reached across the car and patted her knee like a mother would a child. Jenny analyzed the sympathetic nature of the action. Had she been told what Jenny said to the paramedic?

The following day, Jenny sprawled on the couch with an ice pack on her head. Many miserable hours had elapsed since the accident. She craved sleep but the sleep-Nazi couple refused to allow it. The fourth time Katy jolted her out of an anticipated nap Jenny snapped and flung a shoe at her. Katy confessed they were instructed to keep her awake as much as possible. Apparently with a concussion, the patient should remain awake in order to prevent further damage or—worst case—a coma. Jenny promptly offered to concuss the both of them if they woke her one more time.

"Don't talk to me. Don't shake me. Don't prod me. And definitely, don't even *think* about turning on that damn light," Jenny cursed as she pointed toward the bedroom. She tossed the ice pack from her forehead into the kitchen sink, and then went to bed, closing the door decisively behind her. She eased herself under the sweet comfort of the waiting sheets, closed her eyes and promptly drifted into a blissful slumber. Jenny briefly considered locking the door but chose not to get up. The sheets felt amazing; closing her eyes was heaven.

Chapter 8

"Hey, Babe." David's voice interrupted the fog blanketing her brain. Jenny flicked her eyes open, stared at the blue eyes and bright smile and groaned. "Oh, God. You've come to throw me over the cliffs." She pulled a pillow over her head to block out the overhead light.

"No, I just brought you a Tylenol." He laughed. The pillow was yanked away. The bed lurched as he leaned to pull a water glass from the table beside them.

"Oh, in that case, you're an angel."

"Ha. Hardly." He grinned.

"Where's Katy?"

"She and Bruce had to go to work. They answered your phone when I called."

"I'm sorry they bothered you with this."

"It's fine. I'm only here for a little while, though. I have a flight to Miami this evening. We snagged a gig there for a few days." He patted her arm gently. "So, it appears you finally lost a fight, babe. Maybe you should think about that saying, 'make love, not war' and try not to attack things that are hard and don't move when you push them. You know, like light poles?"

The bed shifted as he rose and moved to the door. "David?" she murmured. When he turned she said, "Thanks for being here."

"No problem, babe. Get some rest." The door clicked behind him. Her eyes fell shut.

*

Jenny lifted a hand to brush it across the bump. She dropped the hand back to the steering wheel and looked out the windshield. Fog surrounded her. It laced in and out, lightly teasing to cloak her in blindness. Ahead, on the side of the road, she noticed the intersection where the accident occurred. The fog whirled back to reveal the little girl. She waited for Jenny to creep up alongside. Jenny slowed to a halt and bent her head down to peer out the window. The fog behind her twisted itself into all sorts of animal and human shapes, then unfurled into trees and houses. *She's okay*. Thank God.

The girl entered the car on her own and turned to smile at Jenny. "They were right," she said in her sweet, small voice.

"Right?"

"They told me if I waited, you would show up."

"I wanted to make sure you were okay. I was worried. I thought I'd—"

"I'm okay," the girl confirmed. "And you're gonna help me."

"Sure. Of course. What can I do?" Jenny turned toward the little girl, before asking.

"Do you need a ride home?"

"Yeah. I'm Shilo. Don't ask me why my mama named me that 'cause I don't know. Everybody asks. It's a stupid name, 'specially for a girl, but I'm stuck with it." The girl nervously scratched her leg. A dark spot of dirt smeared over her left eye.

"It's a good name, Shilo. I like it. It's different and different is good."

"No. It's dumb. What's your name?" She flicked a curl back from her grimy face.

"Jenny Madison. Nice to meet you. Can you tell me where to go?"

"It's up there." Her little finger, covered in dirt, pointed to a street they approached.

"Just turn and go to the second house."

"No problem. Tell me, Shilo, where's your mom? Does she know you're out here? This is a pretty busy place for a person your size to play."

"She's resting."

Jenny pulled the car to a stop in front of a modest, Mediterranean-style home of yellow stucco with red clay tile roofing. Shilo opened the car door, stepped out, and leaned toward Jenny. "Thank you, Miss Madison." She smiled.

"Just call me Jenny."

"My mama says that's not polite. Good girls always say things right and use Miss or Missus. Like Miss Madison. It's 'spectful. But if you want, I can call you Miss Jenny. She's okay with that. Says it's 'spectful too as long as you say it's okay."

"Sure, Shilo, it's okay."

"Good. See you around, Miss Jenny." The little girl waved.

Jenny felt a shove against her back. She turned and looked out the window to see a tanned hand moving toward her, toward the window. She lunged backward in alarm. It shook her. She checked it again in confusion, and then woke up. She blinked twice as David's grinning face came into focus.

"You have to stop doing that," she mumbled.

"Stop doing what?"

"Smiling like that—it's spooky." She fisted up her right hand and rubbed the remnants of sleep from her eye. "What time is it?"

"Almost three in the afternoon. Look, I have to jet—and you've had way too much rest. Get up. Let's grab something to eat before I leave for the airport." He patted her leg impatiently. For the first time, she saw the smile slip.

"Everything okay?" She threw the blanket off, stood, and opened her closet to pull out clothes.

"Fine." His lips noticeably tensed. "I really need to go, babe. Let's book." He clapped his hands twice to punctuate his message. She jumped at the sound and grabbed her jeans from the shelf. Jenny looped a shirt off its hanger with one hand and turned. He was reading the display on his phone. His expression indicated there was trouble in band paradise.

Jenny rushed to be ready in fifteen minutes with combed hair, brushed teeth, clothes on. She stepped out of her room to a David she'd never seen before. A dark, angry scowl twisted the charm from his features.

"What took so long?" he spat.

"Long? I was only in there fifteen minutes from the time you woke me."

"Jenny, you've been in there all day. You haven't moved. You're killing me. I have things to do. People waiting on me." His cell chirped out a tune, his tune, and he glanced at it.

"Just go on then. You don't need to hang around here. I don't need that."

"Quit being so bitchy. Katy said not to leave you."

"I'm fine." She watched him consider her proposal for a second, and then he shook his head.

"No, come on." He grabbed her hand and yanked her out the door. "I'll feed you then I'm out of here. You look like you need to eat."

*

They spoke little until they arrived at the restaurant, a quaint but speedy sandwich shop minutes away from her apartment. They ate in silence while David pecked away at texting someone on his phone. Jenny pulled her hair down over the forehead bump with her fingers. She scanned the restaurant while waiting for their food. Pictures of various city locations, taken in black and white, graced the walls. Where no pictures hung, the walls were covered in rustic brick with a brown lumber support beam threaded in periodically. The lights hanging over each table glowed through the thick glass of wine bottles that had the bottoms cropped off and a light bulb inserted. An open brick oven graced a corner behind the counter where a man in a white chef's coat rolled and kneaded mounds of dough into rounds. A task he'd obviously mastered over time. He then slid them into the oven on long handled boards. The scent of yeast and flour baking into bread made Jenny's mouth water. She inhaled deeply and closed her eyes. Heaven.

A blast of cool air hit her face when the door opened. She glanced toward it to see a crowd of people enter the restaurant, cheerily talking and laughing. As the group moved in to accommodate the ones behind, Grant emerged from the back along with Hodge, who shepherded another person through with them. He was an early twenties, blonde youth with long bangs that hung into his eyes like sticks. Grant held her gaze briefly before Hodge recognized Jenny and called out.

"Oh my God! Look who's here!" Hodge said. He clapped as if to applaud her arrival and strode to their table. Jutting out a hand to clasp hers, he smiled broadly.

"I just asked Grant about you this morning and what do you know—here you are." He pulled Jenny into a short hug, crushing her face into his shoulder. While her cheek smashed against him, she looked warily into David's eyes.

"Yes, here I am. How are you, gentlemen? Car fixed, dog still drooling, and life is good?"

Hodge laughed and nodded. "Yes. Yes. All is great."

David interrupted his texting to take in the men that approached. His mouth dropped briefly then he composed himself and flashed a bright smile. "Hello. I'm David Keith." He held out a hand to Hodge, who was so busy talking to Jenny that he didn't notice. Grant took the hand and introduced himself.

Jenny turned, "I'm sorry. Hodge, Grant—this is David." She swept a hand toward him. "I don't believe you've met but you might just have a lot in common."

David stood, scraping his chair loudly over the wood floor. "Yes, I—"

Grant interrupted. "David Keith, local musician and lead singer of Blind Optimism. Yes, we've seen a lot about you lately. Sounds like your band's doing pretty well." He darted a glance from David to Jenny then cleared his throat. "Our party's leaving us so we'd better let you get back to your lunch."

Hodge registered the trail of people headed toward a booth in the back and squeezed Jenny's hand. "So great to see you, Jenny. You look terrific, as always."

He started away then turned. He swished a finger in the air as if he'd had an epiphany. "Hey, I have this thing on Friday night at my house—sort of a social for our new client. Oh my God, I forgot. Jenny, this is Clyde Hill, he's going to light up the charts—an amazing young talent." Hodge grabbed the young man's arm and pulled him forward. Close up, she realized he was younger than she first thought. A teen still battling the effects of acne and shyness around adults. The young man nodded with his hands fisted in his pockets.

Jenny smiled and waved. "Hi."

"Anyway," Hodge continued, "we have this party on Friday and I'd love for you to come if you're free. It's sort of a pre-holiday get-together and of course, a celebration of our new talent here." He patted Clyde on the back. "I know Grant would love for you to be there. Wouldn't you, Grant?"

All eyes turned to the dark-haired man in the gray pinstripe suit that shadowed Hodge.

"Yeah, that would be terrific," he answered.

Jenny was sure she detected less than enthusiasm in his response as he met her gaze. Behind her, David placed an arm on her shoulder and responded, "Of course we'll come. We'd love to."

They quickly moved away through the tables to join the group in the back. Grant glanced back for a second and shrugged, then mouthed the word "sorry" at her.

"How do you know *them*?" David blurted. "Holy cow, I can't believe it." His cell buzzed and skated on the table trying to get his attention, but he ignored it and leaned toward her. "You never told me you had contacts like that, babe. Geez, you could have said something. That man's like, one of the best entertainment guys around. I'd kill to get signed with him."

Jenny stood there amazed that twice in one day she'd observed sides to David she didn't even know existed—sides that punctuated how little she really knew him.

A wonderful waft of warm bread greeted their table as their food arrived. David was ecstatic. He pumped Jenny for information about Hodge. What was he like, what kind of hobbies did he have, what did he talk about? She thought it odd that he didn't ask how she met him or any details about Grant either. Jenny frowned and glanced at the pictures on the wall, realizing David had accepted the invitation for her and intended to go even though she was certain it had been directed at her initially.

"I thought you were out of town this weekend."

Chapter 9

Grant reclined in the booth and draped an arm over the back to position himself so he could see the room. The conversation boomed around him and he smiled occasionally but remained detached. *So that was David.* He hadn't expected Jenny to be involved with a vocalist. He watched her nervously surveying the room, picking at her food, casually listening to David talk. Something wasn't right. He couldn't put a finger on it, yet. The man talked animatedly and she just sat. Her fingers played with her hair, twisting it around them as she waited on him to eat. She reached up and brushed the bangs back from her forehead and he saw a bump. It startled him, a nasty swollen protrusion with a slightly yellowed tone. She pulled the hair back down over it, said something, and then rose to go to the ladies room.

"Excuse me folks. I think I'll wash my hands," Grant said to the group, and then waited for them to move so he could get out of the booth. Grant observed that as soon as Jenny left the table, David picked up his phone and began texting someone.

The bathrooms at the restaurant resided down a short hall lined with the same red brick that covered the other walls. The noise of the people had drowned the background music in the open dining area. In this isolated hall, he absorbed the rich tones of opera vocalists belting out an Italian rendering of "Silent Night." He twitched his lips. Christmas music before Thanksgiving, even in Italian, signaled a flurry of parties coming. He hated parties.

Grant rested his hands in his pockets and leaned back against the brick a few feet from the door. When the door opened, he pretended to step toward the men's room positioned further along the corridor.

Jenny lunged straight into his chest, a heavy thud that charged against him. "Oh! I'm sorry. I wasn't watching. Are you okay?"

"Sure." He lightly grasped her forearms to steady her. "The question is are you?"

Her hair was strategically hiding the bruise. She fingered it, and then tilted her chin.

"Good. Peachy."

"Liar." He lifted a finger and pushed the bangs back to reveal the damage. "How'd you get the knot on your head?" Up close, there were grayish blue smudges of bruising surrounding the area that protruded. He frowned as he surveyed it.

"Car accident."

He raised a brow and ran a finger over it. That better not be human-induced.

"I ran my brand new car into a telephone pole."

"Seriously?"

"Yeah. I thought something was in the road. I swerved so I wouldn't hit it."

He frowned a moment then lifted his lips into a grin. "It looks like you did. You hit it pretty hard by my guess. Did someone get in your way, or piss you off, Jen?"

She shoved against his chest and stepped back. "Very funny. I'm glad you find my little concussion humorous."

"Not funny. When I first saw it, I thought he'd hit you. I guess I overreacted. It would have explained things better though."

"What things?"

He was wrong. Her anger came from somewhere else. Why is it that every time a man sees a bruised woman, he immediately thinks she's battered? Is that a protective instinct? Admittedly, he would have liked to deck David. He wasn't sure why, but the thought appealed to him. Something about the guy just pissed him off. She averted her eyes to the doors at the end of the hall.

Two circled windows fitted into swinging doors. Behind them, the kitchen crew bustled around preparing orders.

"Why you go from docile to pending explosion in seconds. Why you protect your personal space like a knight guards a castle? And it practically kills you to flash a smile, unless of course, there's business involved. Then you can't stop and it's strange because I can't tell which one is the real person, and which one is the fence."

"I'm not like that." She paused. "What do you mean by 'the fence'?"

"You know—the wall that you put up on the outside, not the inside. So people can't tell what's going on inside there." He tapped a finger to her forehead forgetting about the bump behind her bangs. She winced. "Oops, sorry. There's something interesting about it though—especially because under all that crap, you're obviously a decent person."

The kitchen doors crashed open, a dish cart followed by a young woman shoved into the hall. The girl moved between them, offering muffled excuses. They flattened themselves against the wall to make room.

"Glad to know you think so highly of me. I need to get back, Grant. It was good talking to you." She watched the cart rattle away from them. There was something else going on. She nearly leaped out of her shoes when the doors opened. Something told him there was more to the bump on her head than a fender bender. He grasped her wrist.

"You sure you're okay?"

"Fine." She hesitated. "But, thanks for asking. I guess I'll see you at Hodge's party." She pinched her face into a grimace. Ah, she doesn't like parties either.

"It's a semi-formal thing. Do you own a dress?"

"You think I don't?"

"I didn't say that, just…I haven't seen you wear one."

She eyed him with distaste. He apparently had just insulted her. He seemed to do that easily, without intention.

"You've seen me what—twice? Every girl owns a dress or two. Even ones like me. Grant, this whole entertainment agent business doesn't really fit you. If someone asked me what you do for a living, I'd never have said this. An accountant maybe or a computer guy, sure, but not an entertainment agent. Or is that not what you do?"

"Technically, people call it an 'entertainment executive,' but yes, that's what it is. I guess you thought me more boring?"

"Not boring, but not superficial either. Hodge and all those guys, they all seem obsessed with themselves. It's all about being seen, isn't it? Making sure your name is always in front of people so they don't forget it."

"Not *my name*…theirs." He nodded toward the dining area. "And Hodge isn't really like that. This is a calling for him. My name is irrelevant, though. I'm irrelevant." He was hidden behind Hodge's fame in the business, silently guiding the ship. He preferred it that way. It was easier to get things done without a cast of people trailing you all the time. Still, his name was beginning to carry weight. Not much recognition, just weight.

"You're definitely not that." She peered at him, a puzzled glance cast across her face.

"How's the beast?"

"Bugsy? He's good—goofy as always." A shadow filled the hallway. He turned to see David approaching them. Grant realized his hand was still on her wrist and dropped it as the young rock star, on the brink of discovery, approached them.

"Hey, babe." David kissed Jenny on the cheek. "I was getting worried. Everything okay here?" He smiled. Grant thought the man's over-whitened smile a little cheesy. He kissed her on the cheek, not the lips? Hmmm. Interesting. Normally, a man doesn't kiss his woman on the cheek when another guy is touching her. He goes straight for the lips, staking his claim. Unless the intruder's no threat—married or gay. Grant narrowed his eyes and measured David. Or maybe he just doesn't see a threat. Yes, interesting. He liked the idea of David's underestimation.

Grant glanced toward the dining room, recognizing the table probably missed him by now. He backed away from the two. "I need to get back to my group. You guys have a nice lunch." He saluted them both and walked out of the hallway. Even with a bump on her head and all that surliness, something about Jenny attracted him.

Chapter 10

Jenny sat at a streetlight, took a sip of her morning coffee, which now was really an afternoon coffee, and thunked the travel mug back in the cup holder. Back in the old Mercedes, she adjusted the Sirius radio to the modern country station and the sweet sound of Lady Antebellum singing "We Own the Night" filled the car. She smiled. She tapped her fingers to the steering wheel in rhythm with the clippity-clip of the drums in the song.

There were parts of her that she would never let go, and probably never expose either. This was one of them. She was a small-town girl from Texas. Country music had been a staple of her life growing up. Some of her high school friends had been into rock, rap, or pop, but a few, like her, still loved the upbeat storytelling of the country tunes.

College had changed that—a big school, a big lifestyle, big music. There, she learned and became attached to most of the rock music, and a little pop too. She liked the edgy hardness of bands like Nickelback. They were rough, sang things that most parents wouldn't want their kids to listen to, but that was their motivation she thought. Still, country was her favorite, and what she preferred. She always flipped the station to other music based on the client, but when alone, this was her mainstay. It had a way of wiping the dirt away from the work, so to speak, and reminding her of more important things.

A hard rap on the window knocked her out of her car dancing. She jerked a look at the side window. A young black man peered in at her, a teen with neat dark hair, a serious expression, and a green backpack thrown lazily over his shoulder. He looked harmless, but you never know. He smiled and waved, then signaled for her to roll down the glass.

Jenny pressed the button, held it for a second, and then watched the glass inch open slightly. She peered nervously at the teen. "Can I help you?"

"You're with the Designated Driver Company, aren't you?" he asked.

"Yes, that's right."

"You give my mom rides. Her name is Lauren Follis."

"Oh, yes! She's your mother?" Jenny recognized the resemblance right away. He had the same eyes, the same angular facial features, but his slight stature didn't come from Lauren. She was rounder, a woman whose curves were noticeable a mile away. No one would call Lauren heavy, but she was definitely not a waif. Her Halloween costume actually was an apt semblance of her true personality. She was the type of woman that turned heads. This young man was solid as a rock, even for a teen, and not an extra ounce of flesh to be seen.

"Yes, unfortunately. I was wondering. Since you give rides, and you don't have anyone in your car right now, do you think you could drop me off at the corner of the Bagley medical complex? I have a lab starting in 45 minutes and I missed the bus."

"You're a student?" She had obviously misjudged his age.

"Yeah, trying to be. I'm a senior, trying to get into med school. I probably won't make it. I can barely pass my organic chemistry class right now. I'm sorry to ask, but Mom's passed out—and she lost her license anyway. She totaled the car a few months back, and I don't have one." An angry scowl passed across his features. He quickly wiped it away and met her with a steady gaze. "So, what do you say?" he asked.

Jenny glanced at the dash, decided she had plenty of time to spare, and nodded. "Sure, hop in. You have a name, young man?"

"Josh." He slid into the seat behind her. She handed him a business card from her console then adjusted the rearview so that she could see his face. He noticed, averted his eyes out the window and shoved his hands into his pockets. She guided the car onto the freeway and pressed the gas, it would be a rush to get him on campus for his class, but she could do it.

"You might be a few minutes late," she admitted. "I'll see what I can do. So, med school, huh? That's pretty impressive, what made you choose that?"

"I used to think it would be cool to save people's lives. When I was a kid, I sat in an emergency room and watched a bunch of doctors trying to save this little girl, and I thought—wow, I want to do that. It would have been better to be part of the group than one of the people watching them."

"The little girl was sick?"

"No, car accident." He shook his head and darted a scowl into the mirror. "I need to study for this lab." He pulled out a notebook from the backpack on his shoulder, flipped the pages open, and effectively squelched any further questions she considered asking.

Jenny adjusted the radio to the rock station. He looked to be the rock type, maybe. The raspy, sexy voice of the lead singer of Whitesnake filled the car. She drove the rest of the way in silence. She envied him when they pulled up to the bustling campus with students milling around enjoying the sunshine between classes. College life was one of the most exciting times, every day proposed new opportunities and a bright future within reach. She shrugged. Then you graduate and reality smacks you harshly across the cheek.

Josh opened the door and stepped out before Jenny could put the car in park.

"Don't get out." He held up a hand to stop her from rushing to get the door. "I'm fine. Thanks. By the way, I appreciate what you're doing for Mom, and I'm really glad she called you. She's pretty screwed up right now. She hasn't been able to pull it together." Jenny shifted down so she could peer up at him through the window. "Your mom didn't call me, Josh. Your sister did."

A car horn behind her blared. Jenny pressed the gas and thrust the car back into traffic.

She surveyed the sidewalk in the mirror. Josh, mouth open, stared after her until she turned the corner and peeled back onto the freeway.

Nice kid, she thought. Too bad his mom was an alcoholic. She wondered if Lauren even knew what classes he took. Something about Josh communicated familiarity, as if she knew him. An uncomfortable sense of déjà vu passed.

*

Jenny felt the sense pass over her again two nights later when she entered the doorway of Hodge's sprawling Mediterranean-style home for his party. Something about it stimulated familiarity—not the comfortable kind—the kind that reminds you of a scary movie. She glanced at the expanse of white marble, crystal chandelier, and cream-colored walls that rose thirty feet to a faux painted ceiling. She shivered. "You cold, Jenny?" David raised a brow as he pushed her forward into the crowd. He patted her shoulder briefly and glanced around the room. She felt the excitement in his veins. His breathing hitched as he admired the food laid out on a massive, cloth-covered table at the opposite side. It was anchored by a fancy glass sculpture on one end that spewed some sort of gold-colored liquid, and an attendant dressed in a white shirt, black pants, and a bow tie on the other end. "Nice," David muttered.

They were a little late and the room was humming. David originally disapproved of the dress she chose, politely asking her to wear something more "feminine." She'd never worn a dress with him before and was miffed that the black sleeveless sheath she loved didn't appeal to him. It had a cleavage-baring, rounded neckline that she graced with a set of crystal beads Katy had gifted her last Christmas. The hem was short and swirled like chiffon around her legs. "Too boring and staid," David had scoffed. "Don't you have something a little more interesting?"

She quickly analyzed David's description of interesting as more overtly sexy. After showing him three other dresses, his approval trained on a red strapless stretch-silk number she'd forgotten. It resided in the back of her closet, a spur-of-the-moment purchase that Katy convinced her to buy. She'd never had the guts or desire to wear it. She considered it for New Year's last year but found she was constantly adjusting her boobs to make sure they were amply covered. If she wasn't pulling up the bodice, she was yanking down the form-fitting skirt that barely covered her bottom. Jenny hated clothes that made her self-conscious or drew attention. This one screamed something that she felt completely stimulated a persona she didn't have.

Yet David liked it. Insisted on it.

Jenny nervously looked around the room at the flashy figures and accepted that David probably chose well. She tugged the hemline down over her thighs, drew up on the bodice, and followed him into the throng of people.

Chapter 11

Jenny barely managed to keep her mouth from dropping at every ornate detail around her. So this was how the other half lived. The smell of exotic flowers permeated the air, draping her further in the dreamy richness of the room. A gilded chandelier twinkled above them. The stair rail draped with flowered cascades surrounded a second story open balcony. Bodies adorned in layers of sparkle floated everywhere.

David threaded his way through the throng of people with determination, pulling her along by the hand. A group burst into laughter as they passed. One of them backed into Jenny, breaking her grip on David's fingers and she lost him, just like that. The sway of bodies lunged back and forth like ocean waves, pulling her with them. Eventually, she popped out against the wall, much like a shell rolling up on the beach. A small amount of panic welled into her throat as she peered over heads in search of David. She thought she saw his mousse-spiked hair for a second, and then it disappeared behind a sparkling tiara in a girl's long, bleached blonde locks. A tiara? What the hell?

Jenny shook her head in amazement. She'd never seen so much sparkle and glitter in her life. Okay maybe when she'd attended her grade school theater performance it was similar, but those were children. This was just a grown-up version of the same type of display.

"Ah, so you do have legs," Grant rumbled in her ear, a loud almost yelling voice required to be heard over the roar of conversations and music. She frowned at him.

He looked perfect in that suit. Who would have thought *that*? Every time, other than at the airport, he wore the casual denim or khaki pants with a jacket or rolled-up sleeves. Tonight, he dressed to the nines, and wore it just as easily as crumpled jeans. He leaned to her ear and she felt the warmth of him hovering against the side of her face. "And nice ones too," he teased.

"Shut up. I'm dressed no different than the rest of these… fashionistas. What is this—a competition to see how many people one can pack into a tight space? I don't need to worry about pulling my dress up in this crowd. There are so many people here; it doesn't have room to fall off."

Grant studied her face, his eyes slightly alarmed. "So, it has a tendency to fall off?"

"No. I don't know—I've never worn this. It sat in my closet for months waiting for the right occasion. I probably wouldn't have worn it tonight, but David insisted. I feel ridiculous," she snarled.

"You look great. Not ridiculous at all. Although, it's not really what I expected when I wondered what you'd look like tonight. By the way, where is David?"

A man with two glasses of champagne lunged toward them, the golden liquid from the fountain sloshing dangerously toward the rims of glass. His eyes widened with fear, he fought to control his balance despite the flow of people around him. Jenny held her breath waiting for it to splash down her front. Miraculously, Grant reached an arm and shoulder out and took the full force of the impact with his sleeve.

"Yikes, sorry about that," the guy offered before continuing on to the group with two half-empty glasses.

"Thanks. I nearly ended up soaked in champagne without even enjoying the soaking process."

"No problem. So, you want to? Enjoy the process? Have a drink, that is. I can get a glass of it for you or wine if you'd rather. Unless you're on call for work, then I assume it's strictly water, right?" He raised his hand to signal a person near the food. She vaguely saw the top of a young man's head nod back.

"Tonight's my night off, first one in eight months, actually. And yes, I'd like champagne. I may even take that wine, too. After all, an eight-month dry spell requires some catching up, don't you think?"

His eyes darted down her neck, sending a brief feeling of discomfort along her shoulders when they rested on her left collarbone. He looked up as the young man he'd signaled earlier reached his elbow. He spoke into the man's ear, an interchange she couldn't make out with all the noise, then nodded as the man departed.

"One champagne on the way, and the wine will arrive when you empty that." He moved closer, shielding her from the ocean of people that surged behind him. She could see David over his left shoulder on the other side of the room, talking with tiara-girl. The crowd swelled again and Grant lifted his hand to hold his drink away while his chest crushed against hers. The curve of his neck hit squarely across her face, and a jolt of cologne went up her nose along with, she thought, his Adam's apple. An intense roll tickled her stomach.

"Now we know what it's like to be a sardine. Sorry to smash you into the wall."

Jenny stared at him, uncomfortable with the contact, suddenly motivated to open her mouth slightly and touch him there on the pulse point of his wonderful smelling neck. *What the hell kind of thought is that!* After all, she had a boyfriend, one that was here—somewhere. She looked at the spot she'd seen David last. The glare of the tiara disappeared into a doorway she thought, but David was unseen. Jenny swallowed hard and smiled up at Grant just as the crowd surged again, pressing him into her once more. *Crap. Lip locked. Grant's mouth is smashed into mine. Not voluntarily either but by the mass of people pushing against them.*

Jenny stared into his face. Dark pupils looked back. No surprise? No shock? No. Something else instead. He didn't move away, and she was helpless to do so, being jammed against the wall. Finally he shifted. His fingers tickled a path down her neck. Without reservation, Jenny's lids fluttered closed. Her mouth complied, submitting to the pressure. The fingers of Grant's left hand trailed down her shoulder; the right hand held the glass high.

"If I didn't know better, Jenny, I'd think someone kept forcing us into this position," he whispered against her lips. "Two accidental kisses from one pretty brunette. What a terrible position to be in."

With no available path for escape, she focused on the eyes, dark and shadowed, focused nowhere but on her. It was crazy. Still, the kisses, even if by accident, were hot. *Focus somewhere else, girl. Look at the crowd. Look at the people, the beautiful room, and the food—anywhere but at him.*

When the next crowd surge pressed them together, control fell away. She slid a hand into his hair and took the kiss full on. Lips searching, open, moving against each other, bodies firmly anchored together. Weak-kneed from the length of him pressed close and strong fingers clutched into her side, Jenny melted. His cologne seeped sweetly into her mind, causing a ripple of want to feed in behind it.

How confusing. David was the one she came with, the one she thought she would leave with. Still, David never kissed like this. His kisses tendered sweet, playful fun—sure. Not this. Why did this immediately make her feel want, and wanted?

"Holy Crap, Jenny," Grant whispered. She shook her eyes open and saw that the crowd had moved and the only pressure holding him against her now seemed to be her fingers strung through the hair at the nape of his head, along with the other ones clutching his back. His hand splayed across her spine, lightly circling and his breath labored. He rubbed his cheek to hers.

"I'll never say I hate crowds again." Grant grinned. "In fact, I think I'm in love with crowded rooms filled with drunken, staggering people." He turned to survey the mob around them, briefly settling on a point across the room. His shoulders raised and lowered in an exaggerated sigh. He extricated himself from her fingers just as the young man arrived with her champagne. "My boss is signaling. Gotta go."

He disappeared into the crowd, briefly glancing over his shoulder before it engulfed him as it had done David. Jenny gulped the champagne then looked again for the man that brought her. No success. Should she regret the kisses? No. Grant's sudden departure left her exposed and confused, yet desired. David left her feeling just the opposite.

She abhorred the throng of people swarming to get a glimpse of the latest celebrity, of which there were many. *I don't belong here.* She didn't have a clue what this industry was about. When people looked at her, tried to place her face, then shrugged her off as unimportant—it amused her, so completely that, when the champagne took effect, she giggled at each demeaning glare.

*

The young man Grant sent with champagne returned with a glass of white wine, something sweet yet sinful. She traded her empty glass for the new elixir, thanking him in the process. Holding it to her lips, she inched her way along the wall to the staircase, hoping to find a comfortable spot along the balcony. A spot where she could freely people watch without the threat of getting pancaked into the wallpaper.

Jenny heaved a sigh of relief fifteen minutes later when she secured her goal. Wine in hand, she stood at a rail and watched

Grant listen as Hodge shouted into his ear. He nodded twice before disappearing through a door behind the food counter. He returned a few minutes later with a small box and handed it to Hodge, who tapped him on the arm and sent him away.

She didn't care what he pretended; he liked this, admit it or not. People stopped him as he weaved through the crowd, hands on his arm covered in flashy clothes or jewelry. His sternness broke suddenly when an elderly man with silver-streaked hair animatedly spoke. His face opened up in laughter—big shoulder-heaving laughter. It caught her by surprise. Mr. Grumpy Pants had a sense of humor hidden behind all that surliness. Who would guess?

Admittedly, he had a lot more than that hidden behind the scowl. Jenny sipped the wine. Out of the corner of her eye, something flashed toward the far end of the room. The tiara had resurfaced from the back. The girl's tousled hair stuck partially in the tongs of the sparkling crown as she tiptoed into the room from the door that Grant had passed through earlier followed a few seconds later by a man. Jenny's man. David. She spit the wine back into her glass.

"I'm such an idiot," Jenny mumbled.

"No, you're not," a child-like voice responded from her left. It stood out in the ocean of adult voices. Jenny glanced down to see a little girl with dark brown curls smiling. The same girl she'd seen just before she wrecked her car. "You're not that at all," the girl added. The girl shook her head and frowned.

"Hello. What are you doing here? You live here?"

"Yes! Isn't it bootifull? Me and my brother's rooms are down here. Wanna see?" The brown curls bounced in circles as she whirled and ran toward a hallway off the balcony. A little hand lifted up, motioning come hither for Jenny to follow.

"We haven't been here long. I miss my old room but Daddy said this was the best place to be. The best place for us. Momma thought it was silly. She said it's too big, but she still did it." The girl walked backward as she spoke. She stopped at a door with a purple moon face painted on the outside.

"This is it! Go ahead, open it. You're gonna wish you had one like it, though," she warned. The brown curls bobbed in anticipation. Something about the face brought back the odd feeling that had crept over Jenny when she first arrived. Her face, round and cheerful, held nothing threatening, other than a smug grin that obviously hoped to make Jenny jealous of the room on the other side of the door. Her brown eyes were curious, one completely chocolate velvet. The other held a large gold speck in the pupil that made one stare at it, as if it would wipe away.

"So, whose room is this?" Jenny placed her hand on the knob.

"Mine, you silly! I told you that. Come on, open the door!"

Jenny turned the knob and slowly pressed the door open part way, then slammed it shut again. "Nice. Yeah, real nice. Thanks," she teased.

"Oh my gosh," Shilo blurted. "Come on! I want to show you something. Quit playing around." Her frown masked the giggles that threatened to erupt.

Jenny flung the door open again. A cool blast flew past her and before Jenny was aware that Shilo had passed, she was twirling around inside the room, dancing from one side to another.

"See! See! Isn't it great?" Shilo jumped on the bed and patted her hand on the purple, yellow, and lime striped spread. "That's where Mom likes to sit when she reads to me. She hasn't done it in a while but she used to. A lot. She doesn't come around much now." Shilo raised a small finger and pointed to the rocking chair nestled in the dark corner.

Jenny closed the door to shut out the noise of the party, and then reached for the light switch.

"No! I like it dark. Look." Chubby fingers pointed to the ceiling. Little star and planet shapes twinkled above them—shapes that a loving parent had placed to give the illusion of a night sky.

"You were right. It's beautiful." In the dim light, it appeared the windows were adorned with purple curtains lined with lace ruffles. Wood blinds shut out the exterior lights. The bed Shilo bounced on was a four-poster twin size with graceful curves and carvings, all painted bright white. A matching desk butted up against the window so a child could look out while coloring or painting. Jenny stepped closer to observe the many colors that had slipped generously off paper onto the desk surface. Judging by its rainbow, Shilo loved to paint.

"Paint me something, Shilo," Jenny urged. "I can see you're an artist in the making. Would you paint something for me?"

"Oh, no. Not tonight. Daddy doesn't want anyone messing up the house on party nights." While Shilo talked, Jenny ran a finger over the desk surface, leaving a dust trail.

"Besides, I quit painting a long time ago. That's for little kids."

"And you're definitely not a little kid anymore, are you?" Jenny smiled.

Why is it children want so desperately to grow up? Even as teens, they can't wait to cross the threshold into adulthood. The little lifetime markers are so important—leaving grade school, leaving junior high, driver's license tests, leaving high school. Then there's becoming a voter, and becoming a legal drinker. Ironic that once those thresholds are passed, most people want desperately to go back, to be a child again with their entire future ahead.

"No. Not anymore. Hey, sit down. I want to show you my dance. We had a school play. I was in it. I'll show you." Shilo ran to the rocking chair and patted the striped pad that matched the bedspread. She rested her hand on the arm of the chair and waited until Jenny sat.

The rest of the room had significant light coming from under the door but the corner where the chair sat was dark, too dark to see her dance.

"Shilo, I can't see you well—it's too dark."

"It's a night dance with stars and stuff. That's how we did it at school. Watch. You'll see."

Jenny sat quietly. Shilo twirled vicariously around the room. The noise from downstairs served as muffled background music to her steps, cajoling her along as she gyrated and bounced with arms extended. When pleased with her performance, she sank into an elaborate curtsey.

As if on cue, the door flung open revealing the silhouette of a dark young man. He paused on the threshold, then entered and sat on the bed. Shilo jumped behind the bed and hid, then held her hand over her lips to shush Jenny. She smiled as if they were playing.

Foreboding penetrated Jenny's senses. Something oddly familiar about the silhouette washed through her.

Shilo giggled. "He can't see me," she whispered.

"Well, I think he knows you're here now," Jenny responded to the less than quiet voice.

The young man twirled his head, peered over his shoulder, and searched the shadows. "Who's there?" He paced to the door and flicked on the light. He narrowed his eyes to adjust to the brightness.

Jenny smiled and waved. "Sorry to alarm you. We were just playing." She recognized the young man she'd driven to campus.

"What are *you* doing here?" he asked.

"I was invited—I'm a guest. I guess I'd better get back downstairs." She pressed her hands into the chair arms and pushed to her feet.

"Yeah, you better. You're not supposed to be in here. This is my sister's room," he snapped.

"Yes, I know. Sorry about that."

"Leave her alone, Walky. We're just playing." Shilo tugged lightly at Jenny's fingers. She looked up indignant. "He doesn't listen to me anymore. I talk and talk and he just *ignores me*."

"Maybe that's the problem—you talk and talk." Jenny winked at her.

"Excuse me?" Josh asked.

"Walky? What's the name Walky supposed to mean?" Jenny asked. His eyes widened in shock.

"Shilo used to call me that when she was a baby and it kind of stuck. She's my sister."

"Why that name?"

"My name is Walker Joshua. Walker was hard for her to say; she shortened it up. After…when I was twelve, I decided to go by Josh instead. I never liked Walker anyway. Where did you hear that?"

"I like them both." He fidgeted with an object in his hand, a small chain with an attached charm. He shrugged and sat back on the bed, then turned toward her.

"What are you doing in here? You don't like the party?" Josh asked.

Shilo squeezed her cold little fingers around Jenny's and frowned. She pulled her other hand up to her lips and made the zipper sign.

"The party's great. In fact, I'd better get back out there before my boyfriend wonders what happened to me. Nice to see you, Josh. You and Shilo are so lucky to have a home like this."

"This isn't our home. This is our dad's place. I just come here on the weekends. Actually every other weekend. The rest of the time, I'm with Mom."

"And you have rooms like this? Wow. He must really care for you."

"We used to live here before they divorced. Before… before…all the bad stuff."

"Well, the bad stuff just makes you appreciate the good even more." She wanted to slap herself for saying that. It was so cliché. The kind of crap her mother used to say. She hated it then—sounded stupid. She knew firsthand no one wanted to hear that when they're in a rough spot.

"Yeah. Right." He rolled his eyes. "You'd better get back to your boyfriend."

Jenny shrugged. Once again, the door flung open and another shadow figure appeared. This one she recognized immediately. Her stomach flipped. Grant.

"What's going on in here?" he asked.

"Not much. Just chit-chatting," Jenny responded. "How's the party going?"

He ran his fingers through the dark hair, which for the first time looked tame—until he touched it. "It's a party. In fact, you should probably get back to it. Hodge doesn't really care for people wandering around, especially in here."

"Understood. Although, it might help to section it off or something if you're really concerned." Jenny moved from the darkness and stepped toward the door. She smiled toward Josh. "Have a Happy Thanksgiving and a Merry Christmas if I don't see you again."

Josh waved, ignoring the questioning look Grant cast his way. She knew Josh wanted to talk more. She sensed it in the heavy eyes, but Grant's presence stifled his questions.

As Jenny nudged through the doorway, brushing briefly against Grant, she pondered the family drama that ran through these walls when no party festivities filled the foyer and hallway. A lot of pain walked around here, silently blanketing interchanges between the people. She didn't have a grasp on it, yet if she thought it through, most families have some sort of drama. So, it wasn't all that unusual.

*

Jenny moved to the rail and searched the crowd for David. She wondered if tiara-girl was one of many and if that explained his scheduling problems with visiting—more so than the work itself. He had entered the show-biz world with enthusiasm. To Jenny it was a glitz and glamour world that masked the real underlying personalities of the people. It was like cellophane wrapped over their lives to keep them fresh and interesting. It mimicked an attempt to be somebody more important or more fabulous than the real self. She tugged up on the bodice of her dress once and felt a tap on her shoulder.

"Your wine, ma'am." The young steward passed her a glass and a brief smile then left. Grant eased into the gap he'd vacated.

"He's not there, Jen."

"Who?"

"Your friend, David. He left a few minutes ago. That's why I came up to find you. He said he had a call and had to leave. Wanted me to let you know." He turned toward her, leaned an elbow on the rail, and wrapped fingers lightly around a drink glass. She wondered what it was. Clear liquid, bubbles, and no fruit. Vodka, perhaps? "He left without even talking to me? David wouldn't do that. He's not like that." Admittedly, a week ago, she thought he wasn't—now she wasn't so sure.

"He isn't? It's none of my business, but how well do you know this guy, Jen?"

"We've dated a few months." Seven months and ten days, to be exact. It was easy to keep up with because it correlated within four days of the start of her business. "We met when I had first started my business. He was one of my first clients. Kind of cute, really. He signed up so he could see me, so he said."

"That didn't really answer my question, but okay. Looks like you both got off to a good start at the same time, business-wise, I mean. Do you like what you do?"

"Sure, it's interesting. I meet new people all the time."

"Most of them intoxicated."

"Not necessarily…and they're still people. I get to see them at their best or worst, depending on what's going on. There's something wildly raw and real about that. No faked pretenses out of politeness like you'd see, say here, when someone has their party face on and wants to make a good impression. You know what they say, we always show our true selves when we're drunk. Most people have a little baggage and sometimes they dump it on me in the car, most times they just want to get home."

"You don't seem like someone who really cares, or wants to hear other people's baggage."

She faced him, swiveled her eyes to meet his. "That's a little harsh. I'm not completely cold-blooded you know."

"I didn't say that."

"Yes, you did."

His eyes flickered to her mouth and she hitched in a breath. "I might have said that before, but now I'd say your blood definitely runs hot. A little too hot, really."

"Knock it off, Grant." She slithered a hand along her hip and tugged on the stretch material of the skirt. It felt as if it had hitched up to the curve of her rear and it was driving her nuts. Of course, a tug on one side instigated a move on the other side and the top of the dress once again dipped lower on her breasts. She grimaced and tossed her hair back.

*

Grant watched Jenny's clumsiness, grinned, and averted his gaze. He raised his glass and sipped, checking the crowd.

Hodge seemed to have a homing device for finding Grant in the room; it was sort of like some married couples, instinctively knowing where the other is, without really searching. Hodge looked to the railing where they stood and raised a hand. When he recognized Jenny, his mouth dropped open then his lips raised in a huge smile. He gestured twice in a come-here manner.

"We've been summoned," Grant spoke into her ear. He slipped a hand behind her back and turned her to the staircase. "Don't tell him you were in Shilo's room, he'd get pissed about that."

Chapter 12

The crowd had grown and now rolled up the steps toward them, like the tide rising. A rail-thin Steve Tyler look-alike with long streaked hair and skinny black dress jeans seized the opportunity and launched himself over the throng of people to crowd-surf. Grant watched, rolling his shoulders.

"Damn it! Not again," he said. Stevie boy clapped his hands and yelled out to the music as hands and fists pushed him up and away. Nickelback's "Burn It To the Ground" blared through the Bose speakers mounted above them.

"He does this a lot?" she shouted into his hair as the noise grew.

"Yeah, he's the back-up vocalist for Cloudy Day, one of our bands. He plays a hell of a bass guitar and this is one of his gimmicks. When they're on stage and the fans are hot, he throws himself into the people and they pass him around. It was a big hit at first, but a nightmare for us. If he gets hurt, we're out one of the key members of the band."

"Has he ever been hurt? Not the stubbed toe or sprained ankle hurt. I mean really hurt. The kind that requires a hospital or doctor?" she asked.

"Not yet, busted his head onc time though. A girl got pissed about him tipping a drink on her. The chick's dress was ruined. She pushed his supports right out from under him just to pay him back. He hit the floor headfirst. Ended up with a gash right here." Grant trailed a finger along the top of his ear. "We tried to convince him his gimmick wasn't too well received and it was time to stop. That didn't go over well, of course."

"I don't see any harm in it, really. He's just having fun, trying to get people involved."

"Involved in what, exactly?"

"The fun, I guess. I don't know." The uplifted arms in the crowd shoved the man around the room. Some waited with eager anticipation for their turn, others scowled at the inconvenience.

"Help me get him down, will you?" Grant tried to work his way through the carpet of people covering the stairs. "I just need to get down there. Never mind, he's coming to us." A black leather zip-up boot had been removed from the man's foot and passed in another direction, then tossed across the room. His body still bounced up, down, and up again over the group—working its way up the first few steps.

"Grantmewishes!" the crowd surfer called out when he made eye contact with Grant.

Grant scowled. *God, he hated the stupid nicknames this guy made up for people.* "Dude. You need to get down before someone tosses you. We can't afford to have you in the hospital when you have a show next week." Grant calmly tried to grab an arm. The people below them apparently heard the interchange and shifted the man's body vicariously toward the stair rail. "Shit." Grant lunged for his legs.

Jenny grabbed a sleeve and dug in with her fingernails. "I have him." She reached with the other arm for something besides fabric to hold onto. The fabric ripped and Stevie-boy's head, arms, and torso tipped over the rail. Luckily, Grant had wrapped his arms around the man's legs. He anchored against the inside of the rail and strained to hold him upside down.

"Whoa! Did you see that? Grantmewishes, your girl there just ripped my shirt off."

Grant's patience wore thin. *No shit. Don't you care that you're hanging upside down fifteen feet in the air?*

Helpless to do anything but hold the bony legs, Grant braced himself against the rail. Jenny threw the torn shirt over her shoulder. She leaned over the rail and grasped at him. She glanced back seeking guidance.

"Yank him up by the belt, or get his arms, would you?" he asked.

Now shirtless and hanging in the air above a crowded room, the man apparently recognized the danger. He struggled for Jenny's hands, peering solidly into the opening of a not-so-form-fitting neckline that Jenny was completely fed up with.

Stevie-boy's eyes widened. "Hey, I see your—"

"Give me your hand, idiot." Jenny interrupted.

She couldn't very well fix the stupid dress when she was trying to keep the man out of the hospital, could she? No, Grant chuckled. Let him have the freebie. For a very brief moment, he felt a twinge of envy. He'd appreciate it later when he realized it kept him from a mass of broken bones.

Stevie-boy scraped his fingers across her hand wildly a couple of times, before she was able to get a good grip. With one hand in hers, she scooped her other hand under his belt and heaved backward. The skinny little fart came over the rail, tumbling on top of her and knocking the three of them down four stairs before they settled in a pile halfway down. His sweat-covered, smelly, hairless chest smashed into Jenny's face. Grant's palm had wedged between them and planted firmly in the bodice of her dress. *Go figure.* He flexed his fingers to try to wiggle them out from between them. She'll never believe *that* was an accident.

She sat up to see whom the hand belonged to, adjusting the bodice to its appropriate place. Grant jerked away, his face completely hot, and held both hands up in a convenient shit-eating grin.

"Oops," was all he had to say.

"Yeah, right. For a guy with an attitude, you sure have a lot of conveniently *accidental* moves."

"Seriously. I didn't intend that to happen. Jenny, this is Daniel Ray." Grant motioned to the bare-chested bandie.

She acknowledged the man as she pulled down on the skirt and moved backward to the safety of the stair rail.

"Thanks for the save there, girlie." Daniel smiled. "Never thought they'd launch me over like that. Nice dress. Nice eyes. Nice you, too." He gave her the once over. "How do you know Grant?"

"I don't really. We just keep running into each other."

"So, you're not in the biz?"

"Nope. I'm just a chauffeur," Jenny answered.

"Cool. Maybe you could run into me sometime then? Not as a chauffeur or in a car of course."

Jenny eyed him suspiciously.

"Not likely," Grant said. "She's already involved. Right, Jen?"

"Uh, well I thought I was when I showed up. Not so sure now. You know David Keith?"

"Guitarist for Blind Optimism. I think he's been talking to Hodge about signing up with these guys." Daniel gestured toward Grant. "Yeah, I saw him down in the den a couple of hours ago with Quonna Lynnaid. She was—"

Grant elbowed Daniel. "Who cares? Jen, let's go get a drink, then I want to show you something." Grant slid an arm around her and pulled her with him down the stairs. "I'd recommend you be careful around some of these guys. Daniel's pretty harmless but not exactly smart. We have a hell of a time keeping him in one piece."

"Really? How so?"

"Thrill seeker. Which, if you ask me, isn't all that bad compared to some of the things these other people do for recreation. Daniel likes to rock climb, hang glide, sky dive, bungee jump, and just about anything else that will get the adrenaline pumping. He's working on a pilot's license right now and that scares the hell out of me."

"What's wrong with being a pilot? I think that'd be great for an entertainer. Make it easier to get them to their next performance."

"He won't settle for that. More than likely we'll see his name in the paper someday because he tried to do some stupid trick in the damn thing and crashed it."

*

At the bottom of the stairs, Grant retrieved a key from his pocket. He opened a door, and then slipped through and pulled Jenny by the hand. The room was pitch black. He pressed a switch and blue lights came on around the perimeter of the room. A floor to ceiling fish tank with clear blue water was set into the wall. The tank rounded the corner of the room and came back toward them, two full walls of large and small aquatic creatures of all shapes and sizes. It was a screening room with leather plush chairs lined up facing another wall where, opposite the aquarium, there was a white screen for viewing films. A tap at the door caught her attention.

Grant opened the door a slit and reached out. He turned holding two wine glasses and leaned to close out the noise on the other side. He strode to her and handed her one of the glasses. Sinking into one of the leather chairs, he pointed at some of the fish and named their species.

"It's beautiful. Why does he keep the place locked up?"

"This was Lauren's favorite room. She loved to have parties and then show their latest find on the screen. Made a big deal of it. After they divorced, he did one party in here but some idiot threw a bunch of trash at the tank. He was so pissed he made it off limits to visitors."

"You like this room, don't you? Not that I can blame you; it's gorgeous. Who wouldn't?"

"It's soothing. I could sit and watch the fish for hours. Kind of puts me in a trance."

"Thanks for showing me." She glanced at her watch. "I'd better get going." She yanked up on the dress again before starting for the door.

God, he was in love with that dress.

"Jen, David took the car. You're probably going to need a ride."

"My car? He took my car?"

"Yeah, you left it with the valet, didn't you?"

"That doesn't make sense. He doesn't even drive. Or at least he doesn't like to. He normally has someone else take him everywhere."

"Like who?"

"One of his band guys. Or me. Especially if he drinks, which he hasn't done in over a year."

"Well, he's driving now. Has your car. And, you probably don't want to know this, but he *was* drinking. Come on, I'll take you home."

"No, thanks. I can get a cab." She slid her thumb along her iPhone and dialed. When it rang, she looked up at Grant.

He had watched her turn her back to him and fumble under her dress for the phone she'd slipped into the elastic of a garter that lined her upper thigh. Rather crude, but wow, it totally kicked him in the ass. What more can he say about the frickin' dress?

Grant narrowed his eyes and turned toward the fish tank. Get a grip, asshole. She's grouchy as hell. Completely complicated. Yeah, but look at her. She's completely gorgeous too.

He stood and pulled the phone from her fingers. "Jen, I'll take you. You don't need a cab. It's the least I can do after you drove me all over the city a while back." He smiled.

"Guess I figured out what that bump in your dress was that I felt earlier when you kissed me. What else are you storing down there?"

"Nothing. Where else was I going to put it? This dress has no pockets and I didn't bring a bag."

"Did you bring a coat?"

"Yeah, a short jacket that goes with the dress. Someone took it at the door."

He made a call, the jacket was delivered to them, and they exited out a side door to the fish room, walked down a short hallway, then turned to a concrete drive where his little red car was parked. Grant focused on the phone with hopes that he'd see it returned to its hiding spot. No such luck.

Chapter 13

Grant opened the little red convertible's roof and eased the car out of the drive, careful to avoid the crowd that spilled into the yard of Hodge's home. Millions of stars twinkled above them. The air was crisp and Jenny leaned her head back into the seat to feel the wind on her face.

"Cold?" he asked.

"Not really."

"I've turned up the heat and seat warmers so it ought to be pretty toasty even with it open."

"Thanks. Just curious—why do you drive something like this? It looks too small for someone your size. Aren't you cramped?"

His knees rested just under the steering wheel. "There's more room than you think. I guess I drive it out of spite and lack of choice. I dated a girl for a long time, in fact was engaged to her for a while. I bought her this car as a gift when we moved in together. She loved it. Women love convertibles, I guess."

"You bought your girlfriend a car? Wow. That's a pretty serious gesture. I think I'd settle for flowers or maybe a new coffeepot, even a gift certificate to Starbucks. You buy a car."

"Yeah, I hadn't intended to but she was a little demanding. She dumped me for someone more interesting. One of our actors. Then she had a fleet of vehicles. I kept the car when she left just to piss her off. Not that she really cared. She was a woman with a plan."

"Sounds like a pretty big one too."

"I guess. Funny thing is, her actor traded her in a year later on a younger model. She called me up and was all apologetic, said she'd realized her mistake and wanted to come home."

"Really? What did you do?"

"We represent the guy so we knew he'd sent her packing. That's the bad part of the entertainment business. An agent has to know all the sordid details of their client's life in order to control their image. We know who does drugs and how much, which ones are alcoholics, the violent sides, their sexual preferences or twists, all that stuff. We make money from their image just as much as their talent so what you don't know can hurt—not just you but the business."

"That's sort of callous. And creepy."

Grant shrugged. "It is what it is."

"So, you took her back?"

He shook his head. "Hell, no. I told her it'd be a cold day in hell before she set foot in my apartment, or this car, again. It gives me great satisfaction to drive this little thing. I never would have bought it myself, but it's actually a lot of fun. Want to try it?"

"No, thanks."

"Just try it please? It's pretty fun. Let me pull over." When she gave in, he eased the car off the freeway at the next intersection, and then whipped into a parking lot. She had second thoughts when they rolled to a stop.

"Really. I'd rather not. I've had two glasses of wine and one champagne. I shouldn't."

"You drank it over a four-hour period. You're as sober as a judge. Although I know a couple of judges that are serious alcoholics so I never quite understood that phrase." He strode around the car and opened her door. "Slide over."

"No."

"God, you're hard-headed. Come on. Do like Nike says and 'just do it.' You'll like this. Are you seriously going to make me force you to drive this thing?"

She slid into the driver's seat, mainly because he shoved

her there. Grant gave her brief instructions on where to find the controls. Jenny whirled the car around the parking lot a couple of times then gassed it onto the freeway. "Okay, it's a great car."

"Yeah." He laughed and leaned back in the seat. "Hey, where does David live? You want to go get *your* car?"

"So, you made me drive this and now you can't wait to get it back?"

Jenny had an epiphany at that moment. She'd known David a year and had never been to his house. Well, she'd been *to the house, but never in it*. He always came to her, or she picked him up and dropped him off. He never invited her in or asked her to stay. She didn't even know what kind of furniture he had. In truth, she probably knew more of that about Grant, than David, simply because Grant told her.

Did she want to go there and risk finding David with someone from the party? A part of her wanted to confront him. Find out for sure what this pseudo-relationship really was. Another part feared the outcome.

She deliberated briefly. "No. I'll worry about that in the morning. Can we just drop me off?"

"You sure about that? Aren't you gonna need the car tomorrow for work?"

"Yes, but—" She grimaced. "Look, I hate confrontations. I avoid them at all costs. I'm really not up for that right now. I'll come get the Mercedes tomorrow, or maybe he'll drop it by. It doesn't matter."

"It does matter. Or at least it should to you." He put his hand over the seat behind her and rubbed her neck softly with his thumb and fingers. Geez, he's got good hands. Damn good lips too.

When she pulled her neck away, the car shifted into the next lane briefly. A car honked and swerved to avoid them. "Don't do that," she said.

"Why not? You just sucked my tonsils out a couple of hours ago, why does it matter if I touch your neck?"

"I didn't mean to do that."

"The tonsil thing? Don't try to take it back, Jen. You meant it, or at least I hope so. Just like I did. Hell, I can still feel it." He brushed his hand over his mouth. *Don't remind me.* "In fact, I kind of like the fact that you don't want to go running looking for boyfriend Dave right now. I'm wondering if that means you might be interested in doing it again."

"No way. That was just an accident forced by the people around smashing us against the wall."

"Sure. Sure. Being with you is one accident after another."

"Look. I initially only meant to help you that day with your car—even though you were completely ugly about it."

"It wasn't you. I didn't mean to be that way but what did you expect? I was chasing a dog the size of a horse around the freeway, and then trying to change a tire in rush hour traffic. Both pretty life-threatening situations. Pardon me if I wasn't completely charming while trying not to get run over."

"You're really hard to get along with, you know."

"Really? I thought we were getting along pretty well earlier when your hands were pulling on my hair." *Did he have to keep referring back to that?*

"I wasn't."

He laughed. "Yes, I think you were. You're such a coward, Jen."

"I am not. Why would you say that?"

"You don't want to see what's going on with David because, well, you don't really want to know. It's easier to pretend he's a boyfriend than to realize that he's just using you to get what he wants, or where he wants. You and I both know he's not really into you. If he was, he wouldn't have deserted you the minute you two showed up at the party. You were his ticket in, once in, he didn't need you anymore."

"That's not really how it is, Grant. David's just easygoing. He likes to have a good time."

"Well, that I can vouch for. I saw him."

"Saw him?"

He opened his mouth, sighed, and then closed it as if to stop from saying more. Jenny raised a brow and he continued. "To be honest, I don't think you're really all that into him either."

"Of course I am. Don't think just because you planted a kiss on me in a crowd that I'm gonna dump him."

"I didn't plant the kiss. At least not that last one, and it was one hell of a frigging kiss."

Jenny whipped the red sports car into her apartment complex, killed the engine, and turned to drop the key fob in his hand. "Yeah, well. Thanks for the ride home, and for letting me drive. Love the car. Too bad for your ex. Maybe you should have planted a few of those friggin' kisses on her and it would have worked out. You know, you're kind of a coward yourself when it comes to taking the initiative on that. I wonder if those kisses would have even happened if you hadn't had a little help from the crowd."

She popped out of the car and started in toward her apartment. Heavy footsteps chased after her. He pulled on her arm.

"Are you telling me that you wanted me to? Even with a boyfriend lurking around somewhere, you wanted me to kiss you?"

Okay, how should I answer that? Yeah, I wanted to see if the first kiss was a fluke. If I wanted more. I wanted to see if you could make my toes curl up again or I was just over-stressed. And why my pulse knee-jerked when your hand was down my dress. Guess I'm more of a slut than I thought.

Jenny warily stepped against the doorframe of her apartment. "No. I didn't say that. I don't know. I just wonder if you'd ever make a move without another accident forcing you. You know, if there wasn't a boyfriend and I wasn't the girl."

She rotated away from him, pushed her key into the lock, and turned it. A warm hand brushed her hair from her neck. She felt his breath before his mouth touched her shoulder. *Gulp. Okay, that's a good move.*

He nibbled at her bare neck, stroking his fingers against her hair. When he clutched into the thick waves, he whispered. "But you are the girl and that's the tough part. What kind of move does a man make on a girl with a 'sort of' relationship with another man?"

"I'd say that would depend on what both of them expected out of it—what his motives were." Grant turned her into him. He ran his hand down her neck gently, and moved his lips toward her mouth. He hovered there, staring into her eyes.

"What if he's not really sure about that? He just knows there's something irritatingly interesting going on. Maybe. She's annoying, but there's a draw too. In a weird way." He closed his eyes and bent to continue trailing his lips along her shoulder. *Holy Guacamole.*

"My mistake. Guess you're not such a coward after all," she said.

He leaned toward her. His mouth just inches away, his thumb rubbing hotly against the nape of her hair. *Damn, he's sexy.* She leaned back against the door, trying to get balanced before she melted into the landing. His lips touched hers.

The door flung open from behind her hand. She fell backward with a thud on the carpet. Grant landed heavily on her, knocking the air from her lungs. She looked up dazed.

*

"What the hell?" Jenny leaned her head back and peered up to see Josh's lanky frame standing over her, grinning sheepishly.

"Sorry about that. I thought you were having trouble with the lock. I didn't know you were—busy."

"What are you doing in my apartment?" she demanded.

"Yeah, what are you doing in Jenny's apartment, Josh?" Grant repeated. He and Jenny untangled their arms and legs and rose to their feet.

Josh looked confused. Obviously, he hadn't considered the possibility that anyone other than Jenny would enter.

Jenny flicked on the overhead lights, smoothed the dress once to cover over-exposed bosom and restated the question. "Would you like to tell me not only *what you're doing in my apartment*, but also exactly how you got in?"

Josh shrugged. "You left it unlocked."

"I never leave it unlocked. Not ever. Try again."

He threw up his hands, whirled around and trudged to the sofa. "Okay! I may have tampered with the lock a little. That's why I thought you were having trouble getting in. I was worried that I messed it up." He dropped into the cushions and slammed his shoed feet on the table. He pointed to Grant. "What exactly are *you* doing here?"

"He doesn't have to tell you that, Josh. It's not like you're his boss," Jenny answered.

"No, but my *dad* is."

Jenny frowned and fisted her hands onto her hips. "You arrogant little turd. What Grant does for your father has nothing to do with you. Don't even insinuate that it does. Now, if you don't tell me what you're doing here right now, I'm calling the cops and turning you in for breaking and entering."

"She wouldn't dare. Would she Grant?"

Grant nodded. Jenny could see he was struggling to keep a straight face. She began dialing.

"I'm SORRY. Okay? I just wanted to talk to you. You said a lot of really crazy things earlier about Shilo. I needed to know where you heard all that." He glanced wide-eyed at Grant. "I can't talk about this in front of you, you'll tell Dad. I just need a few minutes with Ms. Madison and then I'll leave. I didn't come here to cause trouble."

Jenny recognized pain when she saw it. The kid was a mess. Kid. He was only four or five years younger than her. He was no kid. A college student struggling to become a doctor. All that studying and tension apparently took its toll. He looked downright haggard. "Grant, you can go home now. Thanks for the ride."

"I'm not leaving."

She touched his arm. "Yes, you are. I'll be fine."

"How did you get here, Josh?" he asked.

"I took Dad's Escalade. He never drives it, won't even know it's gone."

"I'm riding back with you. I'll wait outside." Grant tossed his keys to Jenny. "You can drive mine over tomorrow and we'll get your car at the same time." He opened the door, took a step out, and then turned. "I'll be right outside if you need me." He glanced at her mouth.

Jenny pressed the door closed.

*

"Okay, what's up?" Jenny moved to the chair across from Josh and slid into it.

"Look, Ms. Madison, I don't know what game you're trying to pull on me, but I don't like it. I have way too much going on in school to have some crazy lady pulling head games."

"What?"

"You know what I'm talking about. Where do you get off telling me that Shilo called you to pick up Mom—or all that crap you said earlier?"

"She did. And I don't know what you mean by crap, I'm just repeating what she said. She said you never listen to her. Wow, you really don't. You've completely tuned her out."

"Stop it." He gnashed his teeth. "You're a nut job."

"I most certainly am not."

"Then why the hell are you talking as if she's still alive?"

Jenny stared at him in shock. His eyelashes were damp. One puddled tear threatened to spill down his cheek.

"Still alive? Josh, I spoke with her tonight. There, in her room. She danced and jumped on the bed—and hid when you came in."

"NO! She did not. She's dead. Stop saying that. She died when she was five. That was eight years ago. I don't know what the hell you're trying to do to me. Or why either. But it's crazy and it's cruel. I want you to leave me alone."

"I don't understand." Jenny held up her palm and stared at it blankly. "She held my hand. She wanted to show me her room and show me the skit she did in her school play."

He dropped his head in his hands and started sobbing. "Stop it," he mumbled. "Just stop. Why would you do this?"

Jenny closed her mouth and pressed her fist against it to choke back the emotions welling up. Was she crazy? Did she just imagine all of that—maybe the drinks? She hadn't had anything in a long time but the thought that a couple of drinks would start her hallucinating didn't make sense either. "I'm sorry," she whispered. "I didn't mean to upset you."

"Exactly what *did* you mean then?"

"I don't—" She wasn't sure what to say, or do either. She sucked in a deep breath. What's the right thing to say? No idea. "Look, I didn't know. I must be tired or something and just thought—I don't know. So, what was she like? Shilo?"

"Don't try to get me talking about her." He crossed his arms over his chest. Minutes passed as he attempted to calm himself. A veil of anger closed over him. "I see what this is about. You're a social worker, aren't you? That's why you're involved. Why you're driving Mom around. Dad hired you, didn't he?"

Jenny observed his trembling hands as they latched across his forearms. He was a wreck. Should she persist that Shiloh had been with her? It didn't make sense to do so. It didn't make sense period. And she certainly had no desire to further agitate him.

"Uh, okay—you got me." What was the alternative? Tell him his dead sister has been haunting her? No way.

"God, he just won't give it up, will he? Look, I don't want to talk about it. It's over and I'm not going to get all touchy-feely and spill all my deep-seated problems and regrets to someone like you. So, just tell him to leave me alone." He strode toward the door.

"Good for you!" Jenny slammed her hands on her thighs and rose to her feet. She tugged up on the dress and followed him. "Now, that we've settled that, why don't you head home and go to bed. I'm tired and I'd really like to get out of this horrible dress."

Thank God, drama over. She yawned. It was late and she had absorbed more information than she could process. She wanted him out.

"Feel free to stop in any time you feel like it if you change your mind." Okay, she *really* didn't mean that. "So glad we had the talk."

She opened the door. Grant lurched off the stoop and surveyed them both. She shoved Josh to him and waved.

"Good night guys! It was fun. Let's not do it again." Bam. She slammed the door in their stunned faces.

What the hell?

Chapter 14

"I don't believe in ghosts. I don't believe in ghosts. I don't believe in ghosts." Jenny repeated the phrase over and over as she sprawled on the sofa with her hand on her forehead. When her cell phone rang, she nearly leaped off the couch.

"Ms. Madison?" A pleasant male voice was on the other end.

"Yes." *I don't believe in ghosts,* she continued in her head.

"This is Barry." She sat for a second. "Your new driver?" he said.

"Oh! Yes. Sorry. My mind was on something else. How are you, Barry?"

"Fine. I know you're off today and I'm not supposed to call but since there are some early customers tomorrow, I thought I should. I have a church thing in the morning around eleven and won't be done until the afternoon. I can't take the first two rides. I'm sorry but well, this is something I have to do."

She tapped the back of the couch. Church on Saturday? He must be Catholic. "No problem. I understand. Will you be able to work the rest of the day?"

"Absolutely. I'm just kind of doing a wedding so I have to be there."

"You're in a wedding? That's great!"

"No, I'm *doing it,* you know, officiating. I'm an ordained minister."

"Oh, wow." Well, that explains the overtly positive attitude and exceptionally nice but sort of creepy smile. "I didn't realize that. I mean you never mentioned. Uh, well, I guess that's not really something that comes up in a job interview but…" Open mouth, insert foot.

She heard him laugh a little. "It's okay, Ms. Madison. It always catches people by surprise the first time I tell them. Anyway, I should be able to get back on the road by four o'clock at the latest. I apologize for the inconvenience."

"No inconvenience at all. I'll be able to take care of the early calls. Most of the business happens later anyway. Thanks for letting me know." She hesitated. She didn't want to lecture, but it was part of her business plan. "Barry, you know you can't talk about that with the customers, right?"

"Yes, ma'am. I understand. I believe very strongly that certain things happen to you or around you for a reason. You just have to know when and then accept it and use it. This driving job was a calling for me. Just like the ministry, but I won't let one interfere with the other. Don't worry." He hung up.

She worried anyway. It's not that she had a problem with his religion. After all, she was practically raised in the church and her mom forced her to attend three times a week up until she was fourteen. Then it became such an argument that she finally wore the woman down and was able to skip it as much as she wanted. Still, her business was dependent on the principle that her customers were not given any grief over the need for a ride home. It wasn't her job to try to clean them up—merely to deliver them safely home without incident. God, she hoped Barry really understood that. She giggled. Does thinking that count as a prayer?

Okay then. Well, maybe the appearance of Shilo and then Barry were signs? She burst out laughing. Yeah, right. You are seriously losing it, girl! Your head is so screwed up. You're dreaming up ghosts, hiring ministers, kissing complete strangers in crowded rooms, wrecking cars, and carrying on conversations with said ghosts and considering them messages from a greater being. Anything else to add to that list? Her cell phone rang again.

"Yikes!" She dropped it and stared at the display. The device bounced around on the floor, vibrating and ringing. Nervously, she reached down and picked it up. "Hello? Barry?"

"No. Grant. Who's Barry?" She couldn't help but smile in relief.

"He's one of my drivers."

"Is he headed to your apartment too?" His voice was snippy.

"Of course not. He just called to say he needed me to take his early shift tomorrow. Why are you calling?" she asked.

"What are you doing to Josh?"

"I'm not *doing* anything *to* Josh. What kind of stupid question is that?" She pulled on the bottom of her dress. Patience with the fit and struggle of the dress was gone—it had to come off. She yanked the zipper down and stepped out of it. She scooped it off the floor, and headed to her closet with the phone to her ear. Grant's voice was practically booming.

"Why was he in your apartment? And why did he tell me not to tell his dad he'd been there?"

"I don't know. That's his business, not mine. What does it matter?" She pulled out her pajamas and struggled into them with the phone anchored between her ear and shoulder.

"Jenny, he's been through a lot. I can handle you messing with my head. I'm a grown man. I don't give a shit. He may seem like he's got it all together but he doesn't. He really took Shilo's death badly. They all did. Don't screw with him."

Yeah? Well, I kind of took Shilo's death badly too since I just now found out about it! Is he insinuating what I think he's insinuating?

"Are you really suggesting I'd go after a kid young enough for me to have babysat for him in high school? Do you think I would do that? That I *did* that?"

"No. I don't know. Hell. A couple of days ago, I would have said absolutely not. Now, after tonight, I haven't got a clue what's going on in your head."

"Grant?"

"Yeah?"

"Go to hell." She ended the call. Jenny's mom had always said she tried to find the best in even the worst people. Perhaps sometimes first impressions really are accurate and delving deeper doesn't help. He really was an ass.

*

The next morning, Jenny woke abruptly and padded to the bathroom, did her business, and started toward the kitchen. The sound of banging on her door brought her out of the groggy, half-awake stupor. She peeked through the hole to see Grant standing on the other side, two cups in his hands.

"What?" she shouted.

"I brought coffee." He held up the cups.

"Go away." She was *not* in the mood.

"I need my car. You said you had to work early so I thought we'd kill two birds with one stone and go get yours."

Her neighbor from across the hall leaned out and shushed him.

"Open up, Jen." He frowned at the neighbor, a scary look that sent her scurrying back inside. Jenny snickered at the old bag and opened the bolt on the door. As soon as the door opened, Grant breezed in. He handed a cup to her.

"I didn't know if you put anything in it or not." He reached into his pocket and pulled out some packets. "Here's some cream and sweetener if you want it."

She wasn't about to thank him after the ridiculous accusations last night. He needed to explain himself.

"Nice pajamas," he said. She pulled the shoulder of the T-shirt tight. "Put some clothes on and we'll get your car."

"Is this supposed to be an apology?"

"Apology for what?" he asked.

"For basically calling me a child-abusing whore."

He looked startled. "I didn't say that. I just—I was mad, I guess."

"No kidding. I never would have guessed. I suppose I'm responsible for that?"

"Yep. That's right." He sipped from his coffee.

"How so?"

He looked at her and laughed. "Your hair is sticking straight up in back." He patted a hand on her head.

Jenny jerked back and bared her teeth. "Wow, thanks. Be careful. I bite in the morning and I'm not going anywhere with you."

"Promises. Promises. Get dressed."

"So, that's the best I'm going to get?" She raised her cup and took a sip.

"What'd you want?" Grant asked.

"An explanation would be nice."

He just stared at her then plunked his cup on the counter. "Okay, I'm sorry. I really don't mean to be like that. I don't know why you get to me so much, but it brings out my worst. It's like I can't stop it and what comes out of my mouth isn't at all what I'm thinking. You kissed me and it was…unsettling." He shook his head, "I don't like the idea of that happening with someone else and it seemed so easy for you."

"Easy? As in with anyone, even a kid?"

"No. See, there I go again. I think one thing and it comes out totally different. Let's just go before it gets worse okay? I need my car and you need yours. Let's get it and be done with this."

She shrugged and plodded to her room to change.

*

Thirty minutes later they were in his convertible, breezing toward David's house. The top was down and wind whipped her hair back and forth across her face. She tried to get a grasp on what he'd said earlier. It didn't make sense. Unsettling? The sun toasted her cheeks with warmth. No wonder he kept the car. It was awesome to ride with the roof down, blue skies and sunshine above. This was what a sunny California day was supposed to be.

When they pulled up to David's house, her car sat in the drive. Not a scratch on it. Jenny realized when the tension loosened that she had worried about that. That car was her livelihood. One wreck was bad enough, but two would ruin her insurance rates. She couldn't afford any more expenses right now. She dropped her shoulders, relieved.

"Thanks. I appreciate the help." She closed the car behind her and stepped toward David's door to get her keys. Grant followed.

"You don't have to come," she said.

"I thought you might need some support."

"Why?"

He shrugged. Before they reached the door it opened and out walked David, followed by none other than tiara-girl. "Oh. Hey!" David said. A flush of panic crossed his face.

"What are you guys doing here?"

Crap. Guess that seals it. Jenny forced a smile.

"We came to get my car." She held out her hand for the keys.

"Her car?" The girl, who turned out to be too old to classify as a girl, asked. "I thought it was yours. Why are you driving her car?"

"Because he went to the party last night with me," Jenny explained. "Then apparently he ditched me for you. In my own car, no less." She couldn't believe how calmly she could speak.

Up close, the woman had to be ten years older than David.

Her makeup smeared down her cheeks. Ugh. Good thing she's famous because she's butt-ugly. Jenny's ego pumped a smidge.

"What?" The woman's voice hitched up. "Is this true?" She whirled around to face David. Her ratty hair was plastered stiff against her head.

"Uh. No! I borrowed her car because I don't really have one." He glared at Jenny. "I never drive. I don't drive. I pay people to drive me." *Ouch!*

"Well," Jenny smiled. "I am here to borrow it right back. Right now in fact, because I need to go to work. So, let's have the keys, *BABE.* "

She snatched them from his hand and turned. He started after her but Grant stepped in front of him. "Call a cab, dude. Or call a friend. Call anyone but you better not call her,"

Grant muttered before following Jenny.

She screeched the tires as she pulled out of the drive and floored it back to her apartment. Seconds after she killed the engine, Grant pulled up next to her and opened the door. He knelt in front of her, one hand on the car door as he closed her in. "You okay?"

She pushed the hand away and stepped out. "Of course I'm okay. Why wouldn't I be?"

One of the neighbors carried his trash out to the dumpsters. He waved a single brush of his hand in acknowledgement before going back inside. They both watched the man for no reason other than to avoid talking.

Grant cleared his throat to answer her. "Just checking. Well, good, then." He stood for a few minutes, shifted his weight from foot to foot, and watched her expression, then left.

Chapter 15

Never mind that she had spent the entire morning dealing with an appraiser on the damage done to the new car, nor that she had shuttled around three clients to the farthest ends of the city in the afternoon without a second in between to eat. Jenny was tired.

At 2 a.m., exactly one week from the party, she sat at a red light, ticking off last week's events. One super cute, blue-eyed, very selfish boyfriend (David) gone. Check. One hunkier but grouchy guy (Grant) on the "great kisser, but who knows" list. Check. One very youthful, free-spirited ghost in tow. Check. Ghost's big brother breaking into apartment. Check. New employee with issues. Check. Brand new car. Check. Brand new car crashed. Check. Insurance threatening to not pay. Check. Oh, yeah—one fancy party of elbow rubbing with California's super elite. Check. Quite the eventful week.

An apparently homeless woman sifted through the Salvation Army drop box that was placed at the corner of an empty parking lot. Jenny banged a hand to her forehead. Her dry cleaning was still in the trunk. Since she hardly ever dressed for success anymore, her trips to the cleaners were far and few between. In fact, this was the first one since she lost her job last year.

She thought it best to clear the dust from one of her business suits before she headed to the bank tomorrow to ask for money. She cringed at the thought. All this time, she'd managed to squeak by without help. She was proud she had held out this long on her own resources. It would be a cold day in hell before she asked her mom for help and suffer through the "I knew it wouldn't work" speeches.

But, now, she needed more vehicles and more staff if she intended to keep up with the onslaught of customers that were signing up. Expansion. The word sounded good, exciting even. It also sounded incredibly intimidating.

Jenny whipped the car into the lot, parked to the side of the drop box, and pulled the silk party dress from last week's fiasco out of the clean clothes. She handed it to the woman then jumped back into the car and drove off. "Good riddance," she said as the lady stared after her, dress in hand. Goodbye to the stupid dress that no self-respecting woman should consider wearing. Sure, it's hard to resist a man's request but that should have been her first clue that David wasn't her guy. In truth, he was practically pimping her out to get attention. If he cared about her, would he really do that? Okay, he's a man, sure he would. They're all so predictably visual. Thirty minutes later, Jenny carried the basket to her apartment, dropped it on the floor, and slumped into bed.

*

Jenny awoke to banging on the apartment door. What a horrible noise to start the day off. "I'm coming! I'm coming!" she shouted. She begrudgingly dragged herself to the door, stubbed a toe on the basket, and looked through the peephole. Two cups of coffee were poised in front of the hole with no view of the bearer holding them. She had a pretty good idea who it was though. She opened the door and stuck a foot behind it, holding it solidly in place.

"Good morning." Grant smiled. "Feel like some coffee?"

"Geez, what time is it?" Jenny ran her fingers over her hair.

He handed her a cup and turned his watch to read it. "Seven-thirty. Is that too early?"

"Yikes. No, it's fine. I have to be at the bank in two hours but there's plenty of time."

"Are you going to let me in?"

"Uh, I guess." She moved to the side and got a huge whiff of his cologne as he brushed by and sat at the counter in the kitchen.

Mmmm. Good way to start the day. Great smelling man and hot coffee. She followed and took the other chair. Maybe she'd even venture a grin later.

"I brought you something else too." He pulled a Starbucks gift certificate out of his pocket and slid it across the counter toward her. She smiled.

"What's up, Grant? Am I being bribed for something—or did you miss me?"

"No. Actually I needed to tell you something before you heard it from anyone else."

Jenny took a sip of the scalding hot liquid and spit it back into the cup. "Damn, that's hot!"

"Oh, I should have told you to let it cool a little. Here." He grabbed the cup, stood up, and ran a little cold water from the tap into it. "There, that should be better."

"Thanks, I think I lost the skin off the end of my tongue though." She spoke thickly which elicited a smile from him. And eye contact. Intense eye contact. "So, what did you want to tell me?"

"Hodge plans to sign David to a three-year contract. We're going to represent him."

"No kidding. Well, more power to you. He's good. His band needs some work, but I'm sure you know that."

"You're not upset?"

"Why should I be? It's business, right?"

"Yeah, but he used you to get to Hodge. I thought it might tick you off." More intense eye contact.

"It's not like I'm going to see him anyway. I don't travel in those circles. I went to the party because he insisted. Now that he doesn't need me, I doubt I'll run into him anywhere."

"You're taking this a lot better than I expected."

Jenny sipped coffee with one hand and twirled her hair between her fingers with the other. "What am I supposed to do? He's a vocalist in a band that will likely be famous someday. I'm just a glorified taxi driver for people who drink too much. It would be stupid for me to think he'd stay interested. I'm surprised he was in the first place."

"I'm not." He reached out and pulled the hair from her fingers. "So, I owe you an apology."

"For?"

"For what I said about Josh."

"About time. I'm not sure I'm over that one." She smiled.

He threw his empty coffee cup in her trashcan. "Hodge wanted me to ask if you had plans for Friday night."

"Just work. It's the holiday season; we're swamped. Why?"

"He's having a Christmas get-together for a small group. Nothing like the party a while back. Josh asked him to invite you."

"Josh? You're not going to make something out of that, are you? Is it supposed to be a date-like thing or what? You sure it's not going to be uncomfortable?"

"For me, probably."

"You're going too?"

"Yes, I'm planning the damn thing. When Lauren left him, I became the token party planner in lieu of a spouse."

"I don't know." She glanced at his mouth over her coffee cup, remembering the hot and heavy kisses. He twitched his lips into a grin.

"It's weird isn't it? This thing we have going on."

Yes, weird. Jenny looked around the room, settling her eyes on the clock above the kitchen sink.

"Uh-oh. I'm late. I have to leave for the bank in 45 minutes and I haven't even showered." She downed the remaining coffee, and then slipped off the stool to drop the cup in the trash. Grant stood as well and she got another whiff of his yummy cologne.

"You know, you didn't need to come all the way over here to tell me about David. A phone call would have been fine."

"Maybe, but I thought we owed you that much since we, or at least I, knew you first. You haven't said whether you're going to the Christmas thing Friday at Hodge's or not." He touched her forearm briefly.

"I'm not sure. I know I need to work that night. How long does it last? Maybe I could just stop by for a little while and then leave? It's not formal, is it? Will I have to wear a dress again?"

"No, it's casual." He shoved his hands into his pockets. "Jen, I hoped I could take you. Unless it makes you uncomfortable."

"You'll be busy planning and hosting, won't you?"

"Not that busy." He extracted a hand from his pocket and slid it across her cheek.

"Jenny."

"I can just drive myself. It'll be easier that way."

"No." He cupped her face with his palm. She couldn't look at him. Her stomach was doing back flips. He pressed his forehead against her other cheek. "I keep wondering what would have happened if Josh wasn't in your apartment the other night."

"You do?"

"Yeah. Now that the situation's a little…different, I'm even more curious."

"Grant. I really do have to get to the bank. I'm trying to get a loan to expand the business." Still, his thumb was rubbing against her ear lobe and the caress numbed her legs. She couldn't move if she wanted to. His breath fanned hot against her skin.

"You're not the least bit curious yourself?" he whispered in her ear.

Holy Shit.

"Please stop. I see what you're doing. I called you a coward. That threatened your manhood. Now, you have to prove yourself anything but that. I get it. You win. You made your point. You're definitely no coward. Not even close. So, you can drop all the moves. Now, can I have my face back?"

He laughed. "I think you are, Jenny Madison."

"I am what?" She swallowed.

"Curious. I'll pick you up at seven on Friday. Oh, and by the way—proving my manhood is the last thing on my mind. Being a man of any kind isn't something you prove, it's visible in what you do every day. Any guy can be a man, but not necessarily a good one. Maybe that scares you too."

He dropped his hand, pulled his forehead from her cheek and stood back. His jaw clenched just a tad.

"You know, sometimes things happen for a reason and you have to just trust that it will work out if you let it," he added, and then let himself out of her apartment.

You're the second person that's said that to me in a week. Yep, that's right, I'm scared.

Chapter 16

Jenny adjusted her rearview mirror into place after she pulled out of the bank parking lot. She had bumped the mirror with her head while thumbing through the papers they provided. *This is more homework than I did in college. I hope it's worth it.* Still, the loan officer was kind of cute. She grinned. No wedding ring either. Every basic business book says people should have a strong relationship with their bank in order to be successful, right? Of course, the pictures of kids on his desk were probably his children. Or perhaps nieces and nephews?

"You have to go to the party. It will be fun," a small, familiar voice said. The hair on the back of Jenny's neck prickled. *I don't believe in ghosts. I don't...*

"I know, I know," she said. "You don't believe in ghosts. What's a ghost, Miss Jenny?"

Jenny's rearview mirror showed a familiar youthful image. Surely if she's in the mirror, she's real, right? "It's someone that is no longer alive."

"Oh. Well, if they're not alive, then how can you see them? How can they talk and feel things?"

"Good point. I don't know. Maybe you could answer that for me?"

"Josh likes you." Shilo crawled up and leaned against the back of her seat. "You have to go to the party. He needs you to."

"Needs me to? I doubt that. He looks like he's got it together pretty well. Look at him—he's trying to get into med school. You can't get much more competent than that."

"What's comp…tent?"

"It means good at something. When someone's competent at something, they do it well."

"Oh, like I am at painting."

"Yes, that's right. Like Josh is at school." Jenny continued driving but avoided the rearview mirror.

"He doesn't think so. I heard him crying one night. He was talking to me but he wouldn't listen when I talked back. He said he doesn't think he can do it. He's not good enough. I told him he was. He ignored me. He said he's sorry. He can't help Mom or Dad any more than he could fix me. He said it was his fault, what happened. He just wanted to play and I was laughing at him and everything was great. He said he made me die. He didn't. The driver didn't see me. I was too little. Besides, look at me, I'm still here." *Yes, you are. Why?*

"He seems fine to me." Jenny answered.

"He's not. Look at his arms next time. He always wears long sleeves so no one notices. He keeps scratching marks in his arm. I can feel him thinking about making the holes deeper, making them go all the way through. He thinks if he does that I'll leave him alone. I can't, Jenny. Not unless he's okay. He's not okay."

"Maybe he's not okay because you're scaring him."

"I don't want to scare him. I just want him to see the reason he's still here. We all have reasons. He needs to see his."

"That's very smart of you. Do you really believe it?"

"I *know* it. You have reasons too. Everyone does. They change. When you get older, they get bigger because you're bigger. The reasons have more people in them then. He's going to save a lot of them."

"Why don't you tell him that, and not me?"

"Because you're part of it. He won't listen to me any more so you have to help before he hurts himself really bad. Besides, you're still working on your reasons too."

"You could just tell him what the reason is. You know, the reason he's still here. Surely that would make a difference, wouldn't it?"

"I tried to but he kept telling me to shut up. He's afraid people will think he's crazy for listening to me. Anyway, it doesn't really help—telling. He has to figure it out himself. Then he'll understand. So, you're going to help."

"What makes you think they won't think I'm crazy too?" Jenny pulled her car into the lot at her apartment and stepped out. Shilo followed her to the door.

"Who's they? I don't understand why whoever they are matters. He says that too. Walky has to save Mom and Dad. That's what he has to do."

"That's all? Shilo, they're adults—they can take care of themselves. What do you think he can do that they haven't already thought of?"

"I don't know. I was hoping you could figure that out."

Jenny unlocked her door and entered the apartment. She whirled around to ask further questions but Shilo was gone. She shook her head. *Okay, I'm officially crazy now. I've just become the freaking ghost whisperer.*

She peeked down the landing to the doors of her neighbors. Did anyone see her speaking to herself? The plants in front of her closest neighbor, Mrs. Ruth, sat still and unmoving. The giant "be quiet" sign on the door of her newest neighbor down three doors remained in place. It was a not-so-gentle warning to behave. She wondered if carrying on avid conversations with imaginary children constituted noise in his view.

Jenny remembered Mrs. Ruth advising her of a psychiatry student on the fourth floor.

Based on recent events, a trip to the fourth floor might be a good idea. Surely there was some underlying issue in her mind that was causing her to imagine Shilo? Say, a repressed incident of abuse as a child? Or perhaps some psychosomatic effect of losing two boyfriends and a job all in one year? Now that she thought about it, stress certainly makes people do weird things—like dream up ghosts. Of course! That surely explained it all. She needed to put the past in the past and stop dwelling on her failures. The future of her company was all that mattered. Having a love life is highly overrated and interferes with success, right?

*

Jenny organized the forms in order and began tackling the loan application process. Filling out the forms was easier than expected but she frowned at the number of lines she left blank. No collateral. No prior loan history. No business references—at least no good ones. The prognosis looked dismal. Still, she had to try, and, if successful, it beat asking Mom for money and getting the never-ending reminders of her inadequacies as a human.

She executed the last signature on the forms with ample time to shower and change for work. A quick rush to the bank to drop off the forms and she was on her way to her first call of the day. Triumphant that she had at least made the effort, Jenny spent the remainder of the day and night shuttling one person after another home from various celebrations. She looked at her notepad of lists and checked off 'apply for loan'. She wondered briefly if she should add "see psychiatrist" to the list, and then shook her head.

*

Wednesday morning brought more banging on the door, followed by a bark and some loud clattering noises. Fortunately, Jenny had risen earlier than normal and was sitting in the kitchen watching news on her tiny television. She inspected the landing outside the door through the peephole to see an unfortunately familiar frame carrying a box.

"This is getting to be a problem." She stood behind the door in her pajamas, a little embarrassed that they were the same ones he'd now seen each of the three mornings. "Go away."

"Why? You don't like to wake up early?" Grant grinned toward the door. She looked into the peephole and saw Bugsy's tail swish a pot from Mrs. Ruth's door. The pot clattered to the landing, spilling dirt and foliage. The dog didn't even seem to care or notice. Grant grimaced at the peephole. "Quick, let me in Jen," he said.

She opened the door partially and peeked out. "Why are you here *now*, Grant? Go bother someone else. Haven't you figured out that I'm *not* a morning person? I don't get home until really late, or on a normal person's clock, it would constitute as early. So, I try to sleep in."

The chain on Mrs. Ruth's door jangled just as Grant shoved the dog inside and slammed the door. Jenny arched a brow.

*

He shrugged and scowled at Bugsy. "Bad Dog," he reprimanded. The last thing he wanted was the woman across the hall to call the police on him. She'd threatened to do so the last time he showed up. It had taken four attempts to get Jenny to the door. In all honesty, he should have called first. Showing up was inconsiderate, he knew. Still, the fear that she'd run off to avoid him overruled good manners when it came to Jenny. Judging by the matted hair, he was pretty sure she'd had a rough night the time before.

This morning she was a little perkier. Her hair appeared combed and her face washed. Cute, in a healthy but brisk way. Is that possible? The pajamas were god-awful ugly. Not exactly the kind of thing a man likes to see a woman sleep in. Still, when she raised her arms to stretch, totally unaware that her stomach was bared, he felt a twinge of the want he felt when she kissed him at the party. The pants were loose and low across her hips, displaying the curve of her waist down to the slight protrusion of two inviting hipbones. Her belly button teased him to slide his hand across it then slip it down below the drawstrings. *Stop staring.*

Grant yanked on Bugsy's leash and commanded, "Sit. Stay." The dog begrudgingly complied as he darted his eyes and ears around Jenny's apartment searching for toys and attention. "We were just out taking a trip to the park and I thought I'd drop this off." He dropped the leash on the floor and deposited the box on Jenny's kitchen counter.

"You brought me a coffeemaker?" She passed a hand over the outside of the Keurig box as he opened the bag under his arm and pulled out the boxes of coffee.

"Yeah. Sorry it's not a coffeepot, but this seemed more appropriate. It makes single cups in, well, just about any flavor you want."

"Yeah, I've seen them. My friend Katy has one. Why did you bring it?"

"You didn't want a car," he answered. He filled the chamber with water then plugged in the device. He organized the flavors in front of her and gestured. "So, what'll it be today? Vanilla, Columbian Roast, Breakfast Blend, or Cinnamon?" He tapped each of the boxes and turned to her.

"Who said I didn't want the car?" she teased.

"I tried that once. It didn't work out so well. Besides, you said you wanted a coffeepot and I thought that seemed a lot less complicated, since we're not really involved. Plus it'd be more fun to stop here for coffee than Starbucks."

"So, am I to understand that you bought *me* a coffeemaker so *you* could drink it? Wouldn't it be easier to just keep it and make it yourself?"

He opened the Columbian Roast box. It took three attempts to find where she put the coffee cups. On the third attempt, he had to reach across her shoulder to get to the last cupboard. She pressed backward, her hands clutching into the countertop. The warmth of her face brushed briefly against his forearm. He retrieved a cup, set it under the machine and pressed the button to start it brewing. "What do you want in it?"

He liked her apartment. It was smaller than his but more comfortable. He'd only seen the living, dining, and kitchen area but it felt homey. It always smelled of some exotic candle that she must burn religiously. It sat on the table, the wax low and caved into a puddle surrounding the black wick.

When the scent of the brewed coffee filtered to Bugsy's nose, the mutt whined. "Okay, come here." He motioned and the dog rushed to his side. Drool threatened to fling on Jenny's bare leg but he reached down and swiped it with his fingers. Oozing, foamy slime covered his fingers and trailed down his wrist as he held his hand up and sped to the sink for a quick wash.

Jenny laughed. "He's such a great dog. He's a messy, huge clown. How many animals can love you with not only their eyes, but with nice, wet, lathery drool? You don't really give him coffee, do you?"

"No, but he has a great nose and recognizes that as time to go out. With the weather as nice as it has been, Bugsy wants to go out 24/7."

Bugsy reciprocated the affection by jumping up and placing both paws on Jenny's shoulders. He panted into her face, huffing boisterous dog breath that Grant could smell from two feet away. He panicked. Not exactly the impression he'd intended. "Down." He commanded. Grant grabbed the dog's paws from her shoulders and lifted back on them. Unfortunately, the dog's weight and clumsy moves caused him to overbalance and Grant fell into her, palms and paws placed ungracefully against her breasts. *Damn.* Not cool. Okay, felt good, but not cool. He cast the dog away and stood up to her.

"Sorry about that. He just doesn't realize how big he is. He loves to hug on people."

The machine finished the first cup and beeped a beckon. Grant slid the cup to the side and started a second. He handed the cup to Jenny and leaned against the counter while she added creamer and sweetener.

Grant thought he'd need to give Bugsy extra biscuits when they got to the car. The stupid mutt had helped him cop a feel. Not exactly the coolest of moves, he had to admit.

But hey, he was beginning to enjoy this accidental touch and kiss thing with Jenny. The only problem seemed that he didn't want it to be accidental anymore. Admittedly, he could think of little else on most days. It pissed him off. He would meet with clients and remember when they pulled Daniel over the railing. Or when the crowd pushed him into her, then she wrapped her hands in his hair and held on. He visualized her mouth constantly.

Bugsy pushed his wet nose into Grant's crotch and sneezed. Great. His khaki pants were now wet. Okay, the accidental thing had some drawbacks. Jenny's eyes crinkled but she contained the smile. It tugged at her mouth, only partially controlled.

The coffee machine signaled his coffee was ready. He pulled the cup and tasted it.

"Mmmm. Better than I thought it would be. What do you think?"

"Nice. You're not planning on coming here every morning for coffee, are you? 'Cause that's really not going to work for me. Most days I'm still in bed right now, especially if I've driven until 2 or 3 in the morning."

"It might do you some good to get a wake-up guest every morning but, no, I have no plans to use your apartment as a coffee shop." He looked around the kitchen. "You don't get the paper?"

"No. I watch the news."

"See. It wouldn't work anyway. I like to read the paper in the morning, with coffee and toast. Sometimes an English muffin. You probably don't have those either?"

"There's some bread in that cabinet." She raised a finger. He followed the line to the cabinet and opened it.

"You mind?" He pointed. She shook her head.

He pulled the package out and opened the fridge. He was pleased to see that she didn't have any diet butter in there. Only the real thing. He also noticed beer, cheese, and sandwich meat. It wasn't full of vegetables. He turned from the fridge, butter in hand and, without speaking, she pointed to another cabinet. He opened it and found the toaster.

Excellent.

When the smell of bread heating filled the room, he began to feel normal. Admittedly, he wasn't much of a morning person either. He forced himself to be, simply because the work required it. Bugsy put his head in her lap and gave her his best sad eyes. It usually bowled women over and she seemed to be no exception. She stroked his head and sipped coffee.

"So, how did your meeting with the bank go?" Grant asked.

The toast popped up and he buttered two pieces, slipped it on a plate, and then placed the plate in front of her. He added two more to the toaster for himself.

"Pretty good, I guess. I have no money, no loan history, and no collateral, but other than that, I'm peachy. Cross your fingers that they'll see the potential in my business and lend me the money. If we don't expand our fleet and add drivers, we won't be able to keep up with the calls. We're barely making them all right now with the three of us."

"Very few people would have the guts to do what you're doing. Go into business on their own. That should count for something. Most banks like to support small businesses, especially minority-owned ones." He took a bite of his freshly buttered toast and almost groaned. This woman bought sourdough bread. He loved sourdough.

"Well, I'm supposed to hear within the next two days so we'll see." She raised her crossed fingers and smiled briefly. "Change of subject. What's the story with Hodge and Lauren?"

"They're divorced. There isn't a story anymore. They were married for eight years. They had totally different ways of dealing with the loss of a child and couldn't seem to understand each other. Josh favors him more than her in looks, but his personality is more Lauren. He's a loner and a perfectionist. Doesn't accept mistakes. In himself or others."

"Do you think he gets that from living with a woman who has a drinking problem?"

"That's just a coping mechanism. She never did that when they were married. Shilo's death triggered different things in all three of them. Shilo was the spitting image of her dad in every way. She bubbled his enthusiasm for life through his friendly brown eyes. I never would have imagined those eyes on a girl until she was born."

"You've known them that long? I thought you only worked for him a short while."

"He's my uncle, my mother's brother."

"No kidding? But you're—white."

"You noticed that, did ya? Yeah, and my mother's black." Her face clouded over. He held up a hand. "My birth mom ran out on me when I was born. Dad remarried when I was a kid."

How do you explain a family that's nothing less than eclectic and a whole lot more than just what's seen on the surface? Grant had no idea. He stood out in the family and he knew it. Why? Well, to be blunt, he was white. Yeah. That's it. His mother was black. Or at least the woman he claimed as a mother. His Uncle—black. His uncle's wife, Lauren—black too. And they had been the tightest family he knew. The only family he knew.

Why? Hell, who cares? It worked. And maybe that was why it meant so much to him to save the business. It stood for something. Something that meant a lot more than just a financial statement or representing a bunch of egotistical rock star wannabes. It stood for *them* and that mattered.

Grant's dad and his *birth mom* got pregnant when she was eighteen—one of those hot and heavy, end of high school romances. His dad had never said it but he sensed that she never wanted Grant, *ever*. In fact, to date, he had not laid eyes on her but his dad said she was a pretty brunette that turned heads and hearts with icy reserve. He wouldn't know her if she walked past him on the street.

His dad, however, had been a surprise to everyone. Who would have expected a young high school guy with only sex on the brain to step up and take responsibility for an infant son, let alone two children? Apparently none of them did. In fact, Grant's own grandfather had tried to change his mind. It still marveled Grant that his dad had been the rock all along.

No wonder he fell for Geneva the minute he met her. They were two of a kind. She had been raised in a somewhat religious family. Her Friday nights were spent practicing for the church choir on Sunday. Unless, of course, there was a high school event which took precedence. She was tough and determined, but kept full reign on any possible wild streak that she may have felt. She intended to go to college and make her family proud.

That was the case until her brother's voice, a phenomenon across three counties, caught the attention of a fairly well known blues singer.

When Hodge was offered a contract to go on tour with the singer's band, his mother laid down the law. There would be no devil influence on her son that corrupted him from the good man he was intended to be. She dared not squelch his dreams but she certainly put a collar on his wild streak by strapping Geneva to his coattail. If Hodge went, Geneva went. Geneva was the bulldog that kept everyone in line and she especially kept an eye on big brother. If anyone wanted to corrupt Hodge, they'd have to deal with her first. She became a legend in the music industry as a result, and so did Hodge.

Grant's dad met Geneva while they were on tour. Out with a group of friends to see the opening performance, he had no idea the sultry woman sitting at the bar was attached to the musicians. She never let on until the final song. By that time, he'd already made up his mind that wherever she went he intended to follow. She laughed him off and sent him home, telling him to "get his big league pants on if he intended to see her again." William Tucker had never backed away from a challenge in his life, and that had certainly been the best one he'd been offered. Second, of course, to raising his son. His theory was that a good challenge makes a great man.

William "Billie" Tucker doggedly pursued Geneva until she finally accepted that he intended to stay. They married in her hometown church because she refused to allow anything else. They had dated less than a year and were inseparable. It worked well for them because she understood him in a way that many women didn't.

Grant vaguely remembered sleeping in the smoky rooms behind stages when he was four. He also remembered riding in tour buses occasionally, which for a six-year-old had been a dream world. He didn't know it at the time because they all made it feel so incredibly normal.

Not once in the entire twenty odd years that Billie and Geneva were together had the color of their skin been mentioned. Except by others. They were the same, the two of them. They had deeply rooted needs to be responsible and do the right thing. They were strong in character and mind, both going on to get music degrees from a performing arts academy between gigs on the road. They were good people.

Grant can't remember when he started calling Geneva "Mom." It just happened. Sure, he sometimes noticed the strange looks they received, but it didn't matter. They found it amusing. In truth, Grant had never known any other mother and she had been the best. She showed up for everything he did in school, even when no one spoke to her. If he'd been more concerned with his image, maybe he would have been embarrassed. But he wasn't. Since his biological mom deserted him at birth, he felt incredibly lucky to have Geneva in his life. She loved him like his genetic mother didn't. Not to mention he wouldn't dare detract from his dad's happiness.

His college graduation had been the culmination of a family goal that brought tears to both his parent's eyes. Not only did he graduate, but he'd ended up in the top 5% of his class and had a job offer with a tech firm in New York. It was everything they had planned for him and, because they were a very detailed and organized family, a good plan mattered. It was the pathway to success.

Hodge had started his fledgling talent agency while Grant was in his sophomore year at college. There wasn't a lot Grant knew at the time as his mind was on…well, partying, sex, and cramming for tests. It had taken a crisis to make him understand the importance of what Hodge wanted.

Grant remembered vividly when Hodge called to tell them that Shilo had been injured. It was a Tuesday night, two weeks after he'd walked for commencement. He was due to move to New York the following month.

The whole scenario had stuck in his head because Shilo had been exceptionally charming the weekend before. They'd gone to Hodge's new house for a Sunday afternoon cookout, just family, and he'd carried her around on his back. He'd pretended to be a horse and she'd laughed like crazy. She was the cutest little girl. So joyful. When she'd finally worn out and taken a nap, Grant lounged in the study and listened to the family talk business. Lauren was there and her excitement at some of the new talents they'd snagged was infectious.

Theirs wasn't just another talent agency, and they didn't represent any performer. They had vowed to keep it small and stick to people they could trust. Ones that had the strength of character to handle fame and fortune without imploding. Ones that didn't enslave themselves to drugs, alcohol, or any other vice that reflected poorly on the business. Grant heard them talk and felt the passion in his mom's voice when she proudly boasted that they may someday be the most reputable agents in the business if they actually pulled it off. Shilo's death changed everything for all of them.

Grant finished off his toast, put everything away and made himself another cup of coffee.

"I have a marketing degree. When I graduated, I worked for a while in New York. Hated the cold, loved the city. I moved back after two years and fumbled around looking for something.

"When Shilo died, Hodge was a mess. Lauren folded in on herself and spent days in the fish room staring at the fish and drinking. When she surfaced, she'd clean the house and bitch at him constantly about everything from the bad side of his business to his distance the day she died. He was out of town when it happened. He blamed her; she blamed him. I felt bad for him. Both of them really. He tried to hold it together, the business, the marriage, being a father to Josh."

"I kind of thought there was some pretty extreme drama going on there when I spoke to Josh, you could tell."

"Josh is fine. He's the one who has handled this best. He threw himself into school and excelled. He should have no problem getting into med school. He's a teacher's dream." Grant sipped the fresh brew, burning his tongue. He gulped it and felt the scald as it went down. "Anyway, when Hodge and Lauren couldn't look at each other anymore, she threatened to run back home to her family and take Josh with her. Her parents live in Colorado and he wasn't about to lose another kid. He bought the house she's in, which is close enough that he can keep tabs on them.

"Then he offered me a job as a personal assistant. He doesn't call it that, but I know what it is. If it were anyone else, I would never have considered it. I felt bad for Uncle Hodge. His daughter died, his wife tanked and took his son. He needed a support system. I needed a job."

"You don't mind doing things like this?" She pointed at Bugsy, who had slithered to the floor and sprawled himself lazily across her dining area, leaving little room to pass. His eyes were closed and his tongue drooped out. Looking at the beast, Grant had to smile.

Did he mind? Sometimes. But he knew the experience far outweighed the downside. How many people his age could say they assisted in the management of some of the top talents in the entertainment industry? Surely that would aid the job search when it became necessary.

"That's the easy part. You should see him at the park." Grant's phone buzzed and he looked at the display. One of their clients. "Well, time to get to work. Thanks for the breakfast and coffee."

He pulled Bugsy unwillingly to his feet and answered the call. Lifting the cup to salute Jenny, he let himself out of the apartment. A pile of half-folded laundry covered her sofa by the door. He smirked at the jeans skirt on top, its pocket boldly embroidered with the words "bite me." Yeah, that's Jenny. Looks sultry. Like someone you want to have against you at night, but tough and angry when she talks. A defense mechanism, maybe? Underneath that bite-me attitude, she was a pretty decent person. That's what Josh liked about her. They were similar in that respect. They have issues but they have goodness too.

Chapter 17

Grant glanced back through the email from Hodge with disdain. Quonna Lynnaid wanted to issue a press release that she was seeing an up-and-coming Rock Star named David Keith. She also wanted to rearrange her schedule to appear at his next performance.

David hadn't weighed in on the request yet. Grant had learned enough about him in the past two weeks to know he had potential to be a big hit. He also had potential to be his own worst enemy. Too charming for his own good, combined with an addictive personality, spelled trouble. They could usually work around it, but something about David didn't feel right, and it had nothing to do with Jenny. Although, he admitted, that didn't help.

Grant and Hodge were meeting that morning to discuss how best to handle the new "relationship" that had developed since the party. He also knew Hodge would want to evaluate each member of David's band and start reviewing potential replacements for at least two of them. Their drummer was offbeat periodically. It was slight and only happened a few times but it was still noticeable and detracted from the professional performances.

As much as he liked several of their clients' personalities and enjoyed working with them, Jenny was right in her assessment that Grant didn't fit this lifestyle. He would never have envisioned it for a career. Catering to spoiled stars of screen and music, as well as controlling their public images, was a lot less noble than he would've chosen. Still, it had some perks, most of them financial. Hodge was one of the best and very careful to stay away from the people that could damage his reputation and business. Human nature often ruined a lot of celebs. While Hodge was no angel himself, he was a shrewd businessman.

"What do you think of our Keith?" Hodge asked after David left the meeting. The meeting hadn't gone as Quonna expected. David seemed pretty excited about the prospect of getting his name in the gossip mags but less enthusiastic about a potential strong link to Quonna. No surprise. He was keeping his options open.

"In what respect? Talent or overall?" Grant asked.

"Both, I guess."

"I don't mind answering that but, more importantly, what do *you* think? You're the boss."

"I think his voice is strong. It's unusual in that raspy, sexy way women go for. He's got a good look, friendly, charismatic. Looks like someone you want to know. There's something else though, that I don't really have a grasp on yet. He's hiding something. I'm not too concerned about his relationships. That happens all the time. Quonna's a little old for him but would certainly boost him into the big time a little faster if we linked them up. It won't last long though. You and I both know as soon as his name starts headlining, he'll have a string of women around if he wants to."

"Yeah, so far I'm with you."

"There's something else that doesn't quite fit."

"Like what?" Grant asked.

"Well, he did something odd at the party," Hodge said. He got up from the table. Thank God. They'd sat there for over an hour with David, and Grant's ass was throbbing from being planted on hard wood for too long. Hodge walked out of the room, obviously expecting Grant to follow, and headed to the fish bowl. Inside, he flipped on the neon blue lights then went to the bar. "Too early for scotch?" He pulled the bottle and a glass from the shelf. Grant recognized that it was never too early on Hodge's clock and shrugged.

"Sounds fine." Grant nodded.

Hodge dug both glasses into the icemaker to fill them, dispensing with the ice tongs on the counter. "Water?"

"Please."

Hodge handed the glass over, taking a long sip from his. He walked to the tank, standing with his back to Grant in front of it. He admired the slow movement of the octopus for a second then spoke.

"He saw you across the room, you and Jenny. I would have thought it'd make him mad. That he'd go sailing across the room to punch you out. I guess I've been around too many hotheaded, territorial musicians and actors. He just watched with a shit-eatin' grin on his face. Almost like he was glad. Then Quonna caught his eye and he focused in on her like a guided missile. The earlier grin—when he saw you two—was almost eerie. He turned on a completely different charm for Quonna. If I didn't know better, I'd think the guy had a history that might be a problem for us."

Grant wasn't sure how to react. "What kind of history?"

"I don't know, maybe the criminal kind, definitely a bit twisted."

"Just because he didn't care that his girlfriend was kissing someone else?"

He assumed that with the crowd, Hodge didn't know about the incident with Jen. They'd done a background check on David as with any new client. It was prudent to know what you were getting before you sealed a contract that practically married you to a person for a few years. His background wasn't too bad. The guy had some addiction issues but he appeared to have it under control.

Hodge turned to face him. "That was pretty wild, by the way.

You and Jenny. Not like you to be into PDA. Definitely not to the point that you forget you're in a room full of people. What the hell is going on with you two?"

"Nothing. It just…happened. Sort of an accident."

"Fuck that. Nothing accidental about it. She would have pulled your hair out if I hadn't called you. Scary woman—nice, but scary."

Grant laughed. "Scary," he repeated. *Wonder what he'd think if he knew I'd had breakfast with her twice this week…or at least coffee.* He downed the scotch and set the glass on the bar by the bottle.

"You really want to get involved in that? David's—"

"None of your business, H." Grant glared briefly at Hodge. "I need to get to the bank and take care of some things. I'll go by and check on Lauren and Josh also, then make sure the caterer's all set for the dinner tomorrow. I won't be back this afternoon."

Hodge raised a glass. "No problem. See you then."

One thing Grant hated about working with family was their constant need to interfere in a man's private life. He refused to call the guy Uncle Hodge on the job. Had to keep it professional. That didn't seem to keep Hodge from sticking his nose into *his* life. The man summoned him when Jenny was entrenched in the kiss. Was Hodge protecting him—or her?

Chapter 18

Jenny reached into her closet for the black dress then shook her head. If she had a talent at all, it was the ability to read people. Grant Tucker. Not very many confused her, but he certainly did. He seemed like such a klutz, so completely messed up in every way. And so terribly angry. If she hadn't seen him at work, she'd think him bashful and unsociable. Yet, in the glitzy atmosphere of the party, he fit. He looked like one of them. He looked drool-worthy and perfectly at ease in the party scene. She frowned as she dropped her shorts and T-shirt to the floor. She looked in the mirror at herself, clad in bra and panties. She'd lost some weight over the past few months. Her work had taken a toll. Her hips were slim and tapered to legs in a smooth litheness she'd prayed for a year ago. Her waist actually was there. The result pleased her.

Tonight she'd turn on the charm and see what happened. After all, Jenny convinced Barry to take her calls for four hours while she attended the dinner. It was a trade-off for her taking his calls on Sunday. What could possibly happen in four hours over dinner? Absolutely nothing. She removed the bra and slipped the black dress over her head. The thin straps felt cool and smooth against her skin. She pulled her hair into a loose knot at her neck, added some makeup and earrings, and then poured herself a glass of wine.

When the knock on the door came, she was ready. She only needed to slip on her heels and grab her bag. Her breathing quickened as she realized she was nervous. She opened the door and stared into dark eyes filled with surprise and, she thought, admiration.

Grant loudly took in a breath as he sized her up, and then strode past her into the room. "That suits you much better than the dress you wore at the party."

"Was that supposed to be a compliment?"

He grinned. "The other dress had its…advantages, but it looked like the rest of the room. This one is more you, but I did say it was a casual thing, didn't I?"

She sighed. "I'm still not sure whether you're paying a compliment or throwing an insult. Yes, you told me casual. Still, according to my socially expert girlfriend's rules, one can never be overdressed for a dinner. Underdressed, however, can be brutally embarrassing. Casual, for me, is a pair of shorts and a T-shirt or maybe jeans if it's cold out. I seriously doubt that would fly at a dinner party at Hodge's. Since you're wearing khakis rather than jeans, this is probably good. If you don't like it I can change."

"No, don't. Don't change a thing." He slipped a forefinger under the strap on her shoulder and rubbed the cloth between the finger and his thumb. "I like it. Very classy. You look great. Better than great."

Jenny felt the flutter of her heart against her ribs when he dropped the hand to stroke the bare skin below the strap. "Thank you," she murmured. She trailed her tongue across her lips, tasting the gloss she'd applied earlier. Why did he make her so uncomfortable? She needed distance. Fast. Jenny stepped back only to wedge herself against the top of a chair.

"You have a habit of trying to plaster yourself as far away as possible Jen," Grant said, his voice husky and smooth. The hand on her shoulder slipped behind her and strained her toward him. "That's not going to work this time. No accidental kisses tonight and no accidental touches either."

He stroked fingers across the hair on her forehead. "And no intruder to interrupt. Just us. You," he pressed a finger to her collarbone, "and me." His finger felt warm and inviting on her skin, his eyes challenged her to move.

Jenny rose to the challenge. "You don't scare me, Grant Tucker."

She flipped her hair back and stared straight into those smoky dark pupils. A slight upturn of her lips was meant to further the provocation. He promptly wiped it away by crushing them with his own. The hand on her back swept up to clutch into her hair and hold her to him as he greedily opened his mouth to explore hers further. Bold. Then he hesitated. For a moment, she sensed him retreating, holding back. Softly, with gentleness, he meandered his lips across her face, her eyes, then back to her lips.

"You are such a beautiful person," he whispered against her neck. "You could wear anything at all and still be that." Grant leaned his head back and looked down at her moist lips.

She studied his face, acutely aware that she had slipped her hand inside the buttons of his shirt and her fingers were entwined in light hairs just above the thudding heartbeat.

"You clean up pretty well yourself for someone who pretends to hate it. That's odd because I've never seen you in anything but business or dinner dress."

He quirked a smile. "Does that infer that you want to see me in less?"

Gulp.

"I—" He captured her lips again, staving off any response. Lord, this guy had some hellacious tonsils. Or maybe it was the tongue. No, the lips. Definitely the lips. Or the hands? Crap. Who the hell cared? She'd take them all. She wrapped arms around his neck and pressed her entire body into him, shifting the balance from him to her. It wrenched a small, hungry grumble from Grant, who moved a palm from the small of her back down to the hem of her dress. Fingers trailed gently, softly up her thigh then higher yet to her hip.

"Jesus," he breathed against her cheek. "What are you wearing under this?"

Jenny shrugged. She couldn't speak. She couldn't breathe either. Obviously Grant had made an art of touching and kissing women. She realized how badly she'd underestimated him. Sure, he seemed brusque and clumsy, but what a ruse that was! This was methodical, seductive, and passionate. *I'm in trouble*. She opened her eyes.

"What kind of trouble, Jen?" Grant mused as he surveyed the flush on her cheeks.

"I said that out loud, didn't I?" She slipped her fingers out of his shirt and tugged the shoulder of the dress up where it had fallen off to expose her skin. He nodded. "The kind that can't get involved with someone on the fly for no apparent reason."

"Since when did reason have anything to do with seduction?" Grant asked.

"Ah, you admit it then." She dropped her hands to her sides with a quick tug to pull the dress in place.

"Admit what?" He frowned. "Wanting to seduce you?"

"Yeah."

"Kind of hard not to. Look at you, Jen. You're practically exotic in that thing. Bare shoulders, long legs in all that silk. You may be grouchy as hell but your body is made for a man to touch."

"You're such a romantic, Grant." She slipped past him and grabbed her bag from where she'd dropped it. "We're going to be late to a party that you're hosting. Shouldn't we get moving?"

"Romantic." He sighed. "The woman wants romance. Okay, let's go, but don't forget my spot." Grant touched a finger to her wet lips. "That spot, right there."

He strode to the door, took her hand and guided her to the landing. She searched the parking lot for his Audi. A whirring sound caught her attention as the sleek lines of a black limousine stopped in front of them.

"Your chariot has arrived." Grant grinned as he opened the door for her.

Jen's mouth dropped. She glanced from car to man. "Are you serious? A limo?"

"Sure. Why not?" He shrugged.

"For a casual dinner party?"

"It was that or the subway. My car's blocked in at my apartment. Hodge picked me up earlier and I've been at his place most of the afternoon. The limo was there already so I took advantage of it."

Jenny slipped in and settled back to the leather seats, noting the champagne cooling nearby. Out the window she observed the curtains of an apartment slide into place as her nosy neighbor backed from the glass.

Grant smiled. "Romantic enough for you, Jen?"

She patted a finger to her cheek. "It's a good start."

*

Grant handed a glass of champagne to Jenny, letting his fingers slide in a caress against hers. His mind focused on the smooth feel of her hip that these same fingers had skimmed along earlier. He considered the remote possibility that she was interested in taking it further. He had shelved it in the back of his mind when he started out for the evening, but after the earlier kiss he could think of little else. "You didn't answer my question, Jen."

"What question?" She sipped lightly at the champagne.

He knew she had to go back to work afterward, so he doubted she intended to drink much.

"What exactly are you wearing under that?" He pointed at the lower portion of the dress.

Jenny met his eyes. "I'm not answering that question, no matter how many times you ask." She ran a finger along the rim of her glass. "You'll just have to save that thought."

135

The car slowed and turned into a parking lot. "Why are we here?" she asked, regarding the familiar surroundings of his apartment complex.

"Well, I hate to burst the bubble but I need to change and Dennis was just going to drop us off to pick up my car. Surely, it's not still blocked in." He surveyed the parking lot, noted that the Buick that had earlier prevented his departure was gone, and nodded.

"It's not."

*

"Give me ten minutes to clean up," Grant said as he tossed his keys on a table and headed to the shower. He strode down the hall, pulling off his shirt on the way. Her feet tumbled after him on their own, she had zero control. Fortunately, he hadn't noticed and the door clicked into place two steps before she reached it.

Jenny waited in the kitchen with a glass of water while Grant showered.

*

"I like your style." She waved a hand at the décor when he returned.

He didn't feel like acknowledging that was the one thing about his ex that remained. He could care less about art on the walls, or the color of the curtains or pillows. She had been pretty good at that though.

"Ready?"

She whirled to him and smiled. He hadn't anticipated what she looked like when she was relaxed and enjoying herself.

Stay. The word popped into his head again, almost a scream. He didn't want to lose that expression just yet. He reached out a hand and stroked a cheek, returning the warmth. "Amazing."

"What?"

"You."

"Um, thanks."

"Come here." A quick jerk of his arm was all it took to break her balance on those heels and send her against him. She let out a small "ugh" at the contact with her upturned face. He worried he'd hurt her for a second, but then the feel of her against him took over. He didn't hesitate.

"Just in case you wondered, that was not an accident," he said.

"Good to know."

"Neither is this." He threaded his fingers into the knot at the base of her neck and gently forced her mouth to his. From the first time they'd accidentally touched lips, he had sensed the electricity of Jen's skin and wanted her. There was little reasoning. She was just a woman. Not even an agreeable one. Yet it popped into his head at the oddest times. Kissing her brought the urgent desire to have her hands in his hair, his shirt, and on every inch of him.

"You're really on the full court press, aren't you? At this rate, we'll never make it to dinner." Jenny broke the kiss, her breathing noticeably stilted. He smiled. They'd miss him but he didn't care. His mind was still focused on the dress, the skirt, the legs and her kissing him.

"If only I could be so lucky," he grinned, "and we had all night to ourselves, but I like the way you think." He pulled her hand from his neck and led her outside to his car.

*

The smell of the Christmas pine tree met them when they entered the house. A pleasant, welcoming scent that always beckoned the festivities of the season.

Hodge's house had turned to panic in his absence. It never failed to confuse him that a man twice his age could completely crumble in minutes when the slightest slip of schedule or unexpected change occurred. Wasn't he hailed as the mature one? Something had gone wrong with the meal, Grant didn't know what, and it was a major deal.

"Dad's freaking out," Josh told Grant the minute they entered the dining area. "You'd better get in there." He nodded toward the kitchen.

"I'm sure it will be just fine. There are only eight of us. Hodge always orders twice as much as needed, so whatever's not working…we just leave it out."

He missed the time when Lauren took care of this part. He wasn't much of a cook, and kitchen emergencies didn't constitute a critical upheaval in his book. He left Jenny in the company of Josh and followed one of the catering staff to investigate.

The staff stood lined up beside the counter watching Hodge pace across from them with a pile of food between.

"I want to know who did it and I want to know right now." Hodge's voice boomed in a threatening rumble. "This is unacceptable. Completely disgusting." He pointed at the food.

"What's going on, Hodge?" Grant asked.

"Look at the food!" he spat. "Look. One of these idiots has completely ruined every dish."

"How so?" Grant glanced at the food, all pleasantly displayed in white china. It appeared fine.

"It's intentional. Which one of you thinks that's funny?" Hodge continued.

Grant leaned closer to the food and evaluated each dish.

"Oh," he said when seeing the opposite side where a piece of turkey had been pulled out as if to taste. The dressing had a finger swipe through it and was missing a bite-sized chunk. The mashed potatoes matched the dressing with one added flare—a large smiley face drawn in. Apparently all done with someone's finger. Grant tried to contain a grin. The Jell-O mold was the clincher. At one time, it had been a beautiful red wreath with fruit inserted at all the right places. Now, it had large open wounds in two spots and the strategically placed fruit no longer showed. Yes, it was unacceptable in a catering staff, but so like what a family member would do in anticipation of the big meal. He raised a brow and surveyed the faces standing opposite him. Not a guilty face in the group, he surmised. Someone is either a really good faker or none of them were culpable.

"Are you sure it wasn't Josh?" Grant asked.

"Josh has been at Lauren's. He had classes until an hour ago. He walked in a couple of minutes before you, after the damage was done."

Grant shrugged. Time to improvise. "Well, I'd recommend someone reshape the potatoes and dressing, then cut the turkey up in here and take it out in slices. The Jell-O mold's toast—no way to fix that. The rest can be salvaged if you just leave these guys to do their jobs."

"That's not the point. Someone trailed grubby hands through all our food. Now we're going to just pretend it didn't happen and eat it? That's gross."

"Yeah it's unsanitary, Uncle Hodge, but how many times did your own kids do this over the years? Come on, I remember Josh with pudding all over his face the time Lauren made that wonderful custard for your birthday. His entire chin was dripping with it. And let's not forget what Shilo did to her birthday cake before we even got a chance to put candles in. In fact, it looked a lot like those mashed potatoes there, didn't it?"

The silence between them served to punctuate the fact that Shilo would never be able to eat cake again. Hodge sucked in his breath, squinted glistening eyes, and shifted his gaze out the window toward the back yard. He nodded.

Grant continued. "It doesn't matter. It's not like it's going to kill any of us. At least the damn dog didn't get to it. Let's just get out of the way and let these guys clean it up. We'll sit down and act like nothing happened and I promise you, you'll survive. We will *all* survive."

"Okay. Okay," Hodge agreed. "I just wanted it to be nice. I wanted it perfect. Lauren's gonna be here in a little while and I—"

"You want her to see how well you're doing without her." Grant finished his sentence. He understood more than Hodge admitted. Lauren had done everything for him. When she fell apart, he'd picked up and gone on. He threw himself into making sure the business kept going. In fact, with Grant's help, it flourished. As much as they succeeded, though, Grant knew it wasn't enough. Hodge needed her to think he was surviving without her in order to muffle the pain.

She had chosen another mechanism to deal with her loss, and it was almost as if he wanted her to see *the right way* to handle a loss. Where she drowned herself, he did just the opposite. He had not had more than a single drink a week since the accident. Lauren had completely given up all responsibilities, especially the ones at which she'd been exceptional. Hodge had gone from leaving all the details to her and others, to being consumed with controlling every tiny thing. Grant wondered if their complete opposite personalities and lack of understanding for each other cultivated much of their breakup.

He leveled his gaze on his uncle. "Maybe you should concentrate less on making Lauren see how well you're coping, and more on the experience itself. Just enjoy yourself, Hodge.

Stop trying to orchestrate the day and go with it." He grabbed the man's arm, turned him to the door, and ushered him out.

"See what you can do," he said over his shoulder. "We'll all be in the other room having drinks. Won't we, Hodge?"

"I don't—"

"Yeah, today you do," Grant admonished.

Lauren stood outside the door, her arrival had occurred during the commotion. "And I don't," she finished. "How are you sweetie?" She hugged Grant and smiled, then gave a questioning glance at Hodge.

"Good to see you, Lauren," Hodge muttered.

"You too, babe." She smoothed her red silk blouse. "The house looks nice. You've done a good job with it. Thanks for inviting me."

*

Awkward was the only word that came to Grant's mind. The first thirty minutes of Lauren's presence in the house was totally that. Awkward for all but Josh, who had lived with her through the issues. He'd been there for the breakup, the arguments, the drunken binges, everything. He'd been a rock. Where Grant had tried to support Hodge, Josh had done the same for Lauren. Grant knew there was a toll he'd paid internally, but still, the boy had matured into a good man—a strong, intelligent, capable man who would soon be a doctor. If anything good had come from the accident, Grant could honestly say Josh's success was it. There was anger under the surface—misplaced anger at Hodge for not supporting Lauren better, and at Lauren for giving up. Still, Josh channeled everything in a way that had positive dividends. They were all proud of that.

"Everything okay in here?" Speak of the devil. Josh's hesitant voice came from behind Lauren.

Hodge frowned almost undetectably before changing his demeanor and flashing his manager-like smile. "Yeah, superb. Almost ready but we should get out of the way and let these people do their jobs. Everyone into the fish room." He thrust his hands in a pushing gesture toward Lauren and Josh to shoo them out. Grant turned to the kitchen crew with an apologetic smile before leaving to find Jenny.

Chapter 19

A sit-down Christmas dinner that looked like something out of *Home for the Holidays.* That's what popped into Jenny's head when she observed the table they approached.

Dishes overflowed with food. Ruby red glassware graced each place setting along with sparkling silver utensils. The scent of various flavors mixed together, making her mouth water in anticipation. A beautiful family affair so different from her own celebrations. Normally, Jenny and her mom ate something simple. No turkey, ham, or anything remotely like this. Since her dad passed away, her mother had completely quit celebrating anything in a big way. Jenny always went to see her, mainly because she had the time off and nothing else to do. And she loved her mom. One little problem—Mom had never let go of Dad, even though his death was nearly eight years past. Visiting her was creepy and depressing.

Grant pulled out a chair and patted the back, motioning for Jenny to take it. A whiff of his cologne caught her as she slipped into place. Mmmm. Her stomach grumbled and she was pretty certain it wasn't caused by the food. He took the seat to her left as everyone else claimed a spot at the table. Bugsy curled up in the corner of the room and sighed loudly. Jenny smiled at the noise. The dog couldn't have spoken his displeasure at being excluded any better.

"Unky Grant's good looking, isn't he Miss Madison?" Shilo's voice was in Jenny's ear. Jenny lifted a hand and swatted at the ear as if to shoo a fly away. *I don't believe in ghosts.*

"Yes, you won't say it but he is. Better looking than that other guy that throws rocks at cars…your friend, David."

Throws rocks? David?

"I like to follow Unky around when he's here. He's funny. He used to give me rides on his shoulders and sometimes he'd let me sit on his lap at the table. He helped me paint the door. Well, not really. Mom did most of it. But I wanted a flower and he helped me put one on there."

"Really?" Jenny glanced at Grant.

He stopped spooning dressing and raised a brow. "What?"

"He likes you too," Shilo whispered.

Jenny shook her head.

"Really what? What's wrong—you don't want me to eat this?" He motioned at the food.

"No, that's not—" She shrugged and reached for the bowl he had in his hand. "Give me some of those."

Shilo moved to the other side and sang in Jenny's ear. "Jenny and Grant sitting in a tree—"

"Stop it."

Josh's eyes shot up and met hers, then looked past her.

"Stop what?" Grant asked. "Who are you talking to?"

Jenny smiled weakly. "Myself. I'm telling myself to stop taking so much of this great-looking food." *Okay, it was stupid, but what else should she say? I have a ghost talking in my ear about you? And it just happens to be your niece?* She passed the bowl to Josh.

Grant rolled his eyes. "You're strange."

"Yeah, tell me something I don't know."

Shilo slapped Jenny on the shoulder. "See, he likes you! And he wants to kiss you. Blah." Shilo squealed and ran to the corner where Bugsy sprawled snoring. She launched herself onto him and wound her arms around his neck. The dog bolted up and looked around, letting out a soft *whoof.*

The entire group turned to Bugsy as he bolted his head around, then lowered it to the floor and huffed.

"I swear that dog is deranged." Hodge shook his head. "He does that all the time. It's really disturbing."

"I'll put him out." Grant slid his chair back and walked toward the drooling beast.

I don't believe in ghosts. Not even ones I can see petting a monstrous dog and that whisper in my ear.

"I don't either," Josh mumbled. Jenny shot a concerned look his way. *You saw it too?*

"What?"

"I don't eat them," he smiled and pointed to the carrots, "but thanks."

"Oh."

He passed the bowl that hovered in her hand on to the next person. *I'm losing it! I'm totally wigging out here. What gives? I'm imagining a ghost talking to me right in the middle of dinner. I'm carrying on a conversation with her.*

Grant dropped back in his chair and reached under the table to pat Jenny on the leg.

"It's okay, Miss Madison." Shilo grinned from the other side of the table behind Josh.

"You're not wigging. Your hair's fine. You look nice."

"Leave me alone," Jenny growled. "I don't want to do this right now."

Grant yanked his hand from her leg. The group at the table all turned and stared.

"Everything okay over there?" Hodge asked.

Not you! Oh God. "Yes, we're good." Jenny smiled. Josh snickered and stuffed a spoonful of mashed potatoes in his mouth. She turned to Grant. "I'm sorry. That's not what I meant."

Thump. Thump. Thump.

The noise caught the attention of the entire group. All turned to the door. A thunderous noise followed—a freight train approaching. Jenny swore the floor rumbled under her chair and the plates on the table rattled.

A tennis ball bounded into the room, followed immediately by a tangle of flailing legs and slobbering dog. The three men rose from the table and shouted in unison. "Bugsy, no!"

Lauren reached to help herself to the cranberries, ignoring the approaching beast. Bugsy chased the ball behind Lauren's chair, his feet slipping and scratching to gain traction on the unforgiving marble. His awkward movements sent his back hip heavily against her chair legs. He didn't even notice Lauren teetering dangerously backward as his efforts concentrated only on the play toy bouncing away.

Hodge's face turned raging red, then almost purple as he stopped breathing. "I thought you put that damn dog out!" He pointed a shaking finger at the beast.

"I did. Someone must have left one of the other doors open. I put him out through the kitchen."

"Oh shit!" Lauren yelled. She dropped the bowl of crimson colored berries to the table. Jenny jumped to reach for her. Josh lunged over the table grasping toward Lauren's hands, which flailed helplessly for something solid. She clutched the tablecloth that did nothing to keep her from falling backward. *Crash*. She landed hard on the floor, the wind knocked from her lungs, her eyes blinking in shock. A fraction of a second passed as mashed potatoes oozed across her chest from her dinner that tumbled from the tablecloth. The turkey from her plate lay plastered to her neck.

Bugsy glanced briefly at the disarray, not to be deterred from his target. He lunged under the corner of the table and picked up the tennis ball with his slobbering jowls. His tail swept through the air, sailing across the table. The movement swooped the tip of the cranberries, frothing his tail in red juice. The juice flew around the room like blood spurting. Splat. It painted a line across the wall. Splat. It painted a trail along Hodge's pant legs. Splat. The red continued to swash the room. And the bowl tumbled too. Straight to Lauren's crotch.

She shrieked. Bugsy padded to her and dropped the tennis ball into the mashed potatoes, then lowered to haunches with drool stringing between the ball and his lower lip. Mashed potatoes on her boobs (messy), turkey on her neck (funny), and a red oozing crotch (gross). She looked like a food sundae with a yellow cherry on top. Everyone stared in shock as her chest started shaking, then heaving. Lauren reached up to grab the tennis ball and burst into laughter. She laughed until she cried.

Jenny couldn't help but join her. What else could she do? After all, it did look ridiculous. The whole mess was something straight out of a movie. In moments, all of them were straddling chairs or lying on the floor clutching their stomachs. Even Hodge gave in and chuckled.

"Oh my God! This is fricking hilarious," Lauren rattled when she could finally breathe again. Tears were streaming down her cheeks. "Look at me. I'm completely covered in goo."

To punctuate her statement, Bugsy licked the mashed potatoes from her chest. Grant grabbed the leash and hauled him to the door. Hodge slipped over the food on the floor and reached a hand to Lauren, who took it with laughter still rolling inside. He pulled her to her feet as food slipped to the floor in blobs.

"I'm sorry, Lauren," he said.

"It's okay. It's okay. In fact, I'm glad it happened." She smiled up at him devilishly.

"The only thing that could have made it better would have been if *you* were the one covered in food." Without warning, she slid her arms around Hodge and hugged him to her, plastering potatoes, gravy, turkey, and cranberries into his Prada shirt and pants.

"No, you didn't," Hodge growled.

"Yes, I did."

"My clothes are ruined."

"No shit. So are mine." Lauren grinned. The two seemed locked in a moment. Jenny waited for an explosion. None came. Hodge eased into a laugh and hugged Lauren back crushing potatoes into his chest and red juice into his crotch. *They still love each other.* Jenny smiled as Hodge stuck a finger between them to scoop potatoes into his mouth.

A tinkling sound of childhood laughter reached Jenny's ears. She glanced up to see Shilo thoroughly enjoying the scene, an expression of satisfaction smugly plastered to her pale face. She clapped her hands in small short raps. Jenny was stunned. She noticed movement out of the corner of her eye and glanced sideways to stare solidly into Josh's eyes.

Chapter 20

Grant decided Jenny Madison was either one hair short of a lunatic or going through—something. But what? He'd never seen her act so strange. Hodge's dinner was over—a disaster, but not at Grant's hands. Hodge and Lauren had slipped out of the room, laughing hysterically. They mumbled something about needing a change of clothes but Grant was pretty sure a lot more was going to change than just clothes. They never returned. Sure, Jenny was beautiful in that dress. No one could deny that. Sexy as hell, and his fingers certainly twitched to touch her. He hadn't missed the way the man at the table next to them stared at her, the greasy bastard. The guy's eyes seemed plastered to her cleavage, which he had to admit, was hard to ignore.

He didn't mind Lauren and Hodge ditching the dinner. He had always hoped they would work things out. He loved Lauren, almost as much as he loved his uncle. Now, he was stuck in the uncomfortable position of dealing with the beautiful crazy woman he had kissed earlier—the one who couldn't stop talking to herself. She had twitched around like a nervous cat at the dinner. It was damn uncomfortable for everyone. Even Josh had noticed.

They sat waiting for the lasagna she'd suggested when the decision to give up on the dinner was made. The enticing smell of garlic filled the room, like it would in any good Italian restaurant. The place was nice and warm with a view that overlooked the Pacific, and the cold froth of the waves rolling onto the beach. A fire burned behind her in an open stone fireplace. The orange and white flashes flickered an enticing sparkle over her shoulders. He squirmed nervously, waiting for her to start talking to the walls again.

"Jenny, is everything okay with you?"

"Yeah, fine. Hold still." She wadded a napkin around a finger and dunked it into her water glass. She raised the wet cloth and rubbed it across his cheek then down his neck.

"You had cranberry sauce on your face. It looked like you just walked off the set of a slasher movie."

He chuckled nervously. The perfume on her wrist reached his nose and it instantly set off a hard response. Shit, he hated being so attracted to her. She was obviously very messed up. Why hadn't he seen the delusional side before?

"Why do you ask?" She placed the napkin back in her lap and waited for his response.

"Ask?"

"If I'm okay."

"You were really acting strange back there."

"I was? In what way?"

"You're kidding right? Christ, you were talking to yourself—and the walls. You would look around like you expected someone to jump out at you. It scared the hell out of me."

He reached for his drink and took a sip. "If I didn't know better, I'd think you were on something."

"No," she said.

He swore her face went pale. Was she going to deny it? Her Adam's apple bounced as she swallowed. An accompanying thrust of her chest up and down stirred another burn deep in his groin. *Shit. What the fuck is wrong with me? This woman is a complete nut case and I'm wondering about kissing her again. About getting her alone.*

"Look," she said, "I guess my imagination was just playing tricks on me—seeing things."

"Seeing things? What kind of things?"

"Nothing. Okay, I know it sounds stupid. Forget about it. I'm fine. I'm sorry."

A fog of steam rushed to cloud the space between them as the waitress dumped plates of food down on the checkered cloth. His face heated. They both picked at their meals. Jenny held her head back and tossed her hair, adjusting the bangs out of her eyes. A small yellow hue remained on her forehead. *Ahhh.*

Grant paused his fork. "Did you go to the doctor after your car accident?"

Jenny nodded as she sawed a piece of lasagna free and scooped it. She held it in front of her mouth and blew. "I was taken to the hospital afterward, then discharged with nothing but a moderate concussion."

"Were you supposed to go back for a checkup?" he asked.

She slipped the food into her mouth and started chewing in a motion that, somehow, turned him on. "Yeah, but I skipped it. I was already back at work and there wasn't time. Besides I'm fine."

Right. She played with the napkin in her lap, rolling up the corners then pushing them flat again.

He frowned. The seductive movement of her mouth had him speechless. And frustrated.

"Stop staring at me like I'm a freak, Grant. I'm fine. Really, I am. I'm sorry if I scared you." She turned her head toward the television over the bar, then lowered her eyes to the guy behind the counter and motioned to him. A few seconds later, the waitress reappeared and Jenny ordered a draft.

"I think I need a drink. What about you?"

He nodded and she held up two fingers to the waitress.

"Does it hurt?" he asked.

"My head? No." She ran a finger over the yellow spot. "Not at all. Which is why I didn't go back. *I'm fine.*" The last word came out a bit strong.

Grant considered the faded bruise and the completely erratic behavior from earlier.

"You need to go for a checkup."

"No, I don't."

"Yes—you do. Monday morning. I'll come by and pick you up. I know a guy who can fit you in without an appointment. We'll go before you head out for work and it won't interfere with anything else you're doing."

She started to argue but he held up a hand and turned his head as if to squelch whatever came next. *God, she's cute. A little crazy but definitely cute.*

"Subject closed." He smiled and pointed his fork at her lasagna. "Eat."

"You're annoying, you know."

"Yeah, so I hear."

"You're growing on me, though. Kind of like that stupid monster dog of Hodge's. At least you don't slobber on everyone."

"Not everyone, but I probably would drool under the right circumstances. Certain kinds of food, too much beer, or thinking about what you have on under that dress." He raised a brow in question. "You're not going to tell me, are you?"

"Nope."

"Can I take a peek?" He reached a hand to her knee under the table, half-expecting her to yank away like she did earlier. She didn't. She laughed. *That's a good sign, right?*

"Nope."

"Is that a nope, not right now—or a nope, not ever?" She slipped another bite in her mouth and started chewing. Seconds passed.

"I'm not sure yet, but it's leaning toward the first one. I'm waiting to see what happens next. You don't have any more accidents planned, do you? Say another dog or wayward musician forcing you to cop a feel, or a crowd rushing the room and pushing us into the wall, crushing us together? Or maybe something more dramatic?"

"Look, I know it all seems pretty damn convenient how all that worked out, and I can't complain. It turned out pretty well from my perspective, but that's not how I normally do things."

He thought for a second. How, exactly, did he handle things with a woman? He wasn't sure. There wasn't really a *modus operandi*—he just went along with whatever happened, whatever seemed right at the moment.

"How do you *normally* handle things then? Because this has been a real show. If I were a suspicious person, I'd say you have an odd way of being very forward."

Grant grinned. "I never thought about it that way, but forward is not something that most people would use to describe me. So back to you and the nope thing." He rubbed a thumb across her knee, admiring the softness of her skin. His fingers barely extended far enough to touch her. He reached down and grabbed the bottom of the chair and yanked on it. There was a screeching of wood on the tile floor as the chair slid toward him so that he could cradle a knee between hers. The family in the booth across from them glanced their way. He flashed them a smile. "Is there a timeframe on the 'not now'?"

Jenny shrugged and dropped her fork. "Not forward? Really? I'm done."

"Does that mean time's up?" He was getting a good feeling about this.

"Don't get your engines running just yet, buddy. I have to get to work tonight, remember? I only had a few hours off, and that time *is* about up." *So much for the good feeling.*

He made a *tsking* sound, and then signaled for the check. He kept his hand up and looked for their waitress until she noticed him from behind the counter and nodded. "Speaking of work, how did things go with the bank? I forgot to ask. Have you heard back yet?"

"Not yet. I don't have a lot of confidence though. I have zero credit so the chance they'll approve us for a loan is slim. I should hear back on Monday. Keep your fingers crossed." She held up two entwined fingers.

"I could help you with that, you know."

"No. I'm not asking anyone for money. Besides you don't even know me, why would you want to take that kind of chance?"

"You helped me. I could help you."

"There's a huge difference between giving someone a ride and giving them money."

"I have no intention of *giving* you money. Investing in your business, maybe. I don't really give money away for no reason. I'd be broke if I did that. I'm not Hodge. I have enough to invest in something if I have a reason to do so, but not enough to just throw it away."

"So, what would the reason be?" She arched a brow.

"A peek at the panties?" He grinned. It was worth a try.

She met his gaze with a strange look. "What panties?"

Shit. With a lump in his throat, he grabbed her hand and pulled her out to the car. She shouldn't have said that.

*

She didn't want to admit it, but Jenny found Grant's insistence to go to the doctor sweet, and in odd conflict with his normal caustic temperament. Maybe she did need a checkup. Perhaps Shilo really was a hallucination brought on by head trauma—or at least that would certainly be a nice way to explain it. What other logical reason would explain her talking to an imaginary person?

Jenny slipped from Grant's car as soon as they reached her apartment and clipped off to her door in the heels she couldn't wait to ditch. He trailed quietly behind her. She turned and caught his eyes on her behind.

He shrugged when he saw her watching him. "I'm a guy. You can't tell me something like that and expect me not to think about it."

"Yeah, I'm a little surprised that you think money would help you with that. I don't need the loan bad enough to prostitute myself for it."

"What? I never—" His mouth dropped. His face turned crimson. "You may think me pretty awkward, Jen, but I've never paid someone to have sex with me in my life. In fact, there've been plenty of opportunities, and, so far, I can't recall anyone complaining about how I've treated them. Just because I find you interesting in some stupid, hate-me-love-me way, it doesn't mean I need to buy your attention." Grant's brows furrowed as he turned to leave.

Jenny panicked. Sometimes, she should just swallow her tongue. There's nothing wrong with *thinking before you speak.* In fact, most people consider it a very wise practice. But no, she had to just blurt out whatever came to mind. How stupid. "Wait."

He turned back to her and jammed his hands into his pockets, a very safe two feet between them. She thought about it for a second—what to do? Let him leave and maybe not talk to her again? Ask him in? No, she had to work. Just say she's sorry? Nix that one too; she wasn't good at apologies, never had been. She'd also never been one to admit she was wrong. Still, she wasn't ready for him to leave. Especially angry.

"What, Jenny?" His voice held a hint of exasperation.

Okay, he wants to know so I'll show him. She turned sideways, looked over her shoulder at him as she put the key in the door, and lifted the hem of her dress from behind. Lifted it very, very slowly. Inching it higher over her hip until the indention at the curve of her spine was partially visible. She thought she heard a soft expletive but her ears were ringing just a little from the way he stared. When he stepped toward her, she smiled. And slipped inside and clicked the door shut behind her.

Chapter 21

"Go away!" Jenny shouted at the banging as she pulled the pillow over her head. "You've got the wrong apartment," she added before pressing the fabric and fluff to her ears. More banging. She lifted the corner and peeked at the clock. 8:30. She vaguely remembered setting the clock for 10:30 when she pulled herself into the bedroom at 3:30 this morning. What a night. Her last customer had puked all over her door and tire. Luckily, she pulled over fast enough that he didn't erupt inside the car. Still, she'd had to stop on the way home and hose it off at the car wash. Nothing worse than letting that nastiness crust on the paint of your car. Yuck.

More banging. She thought she heard a voice, too. "All Right! Dammit! I'm coming." She already knew who it was. No one else in their right mind would think of waking her at this time of day. He seemed to enjoy it. It really pissed her off how much he glowed when he needled her. Monday morning. He could have at least called first.

"Get up, Jenny!" His voice boomed from the landing outside. Yep, that was Grant. She opened the door at the same time as the neighbor across the hall.

"Good morning!" She waved at the woman with her face screwed up in knots. "Don't you just love Mondays?" Jenny swung the door wide and gave the woman a syrupy grin as Grant passed into the living room. With a loud "humph" old lady Margaret slammed the door and Jenny closed hers too.

"Are you genetically incapable of calling before you show up? Just once, it would be great if you'd give me a little warning before you bring your irritating smiley face to my door." Her voice raised a bit. "My neighbors would probably appreciate it too. This was a pretty quiet floor until *you* started stalking me."

"You're not ready." He ignored her tirade and frowned.

"Ready for what? For you to bang my door down? To go buy new hinges since they're getting loose from your pounding? What the hell?"

Grant chuckled. He chuckled! This guy had the nerve to blast her out of bed after the worst night ever at work, and then he laughs? She couldn't help it; she lunged at him, fists clenched.

"Whoa, hang on there now." Grant clasped his hands around her wrists and twisted them behind her back, which forced her against his chest. "You're going to the doctor this morning, remember? I told you Friday night I'd take you." He was inches from her face and, dammit, he smelled good. Clean and…oh, hell. Jenny wrestled a hand free, grabbed his shirt, and yanked him down to her mouth. *That'll teach you to get me out of bed. How do you like kissing morning breath?*

"Is that supposed to scare me?" he asked when she finally let go of him. "A toothbrush might be nice, but I can stand it if you can." He laced his fingers into her hair and smoothed it back from her face, catching in the tangles.

"Hey, if you can't bother to give a girl warning, you deserve what you get. I only wish I'd had garlic on my breath or something else equally disgusting."

"So, this is punishment then. Hmmm. Okay. I like that idea." He pulled her back to his mouth. "Punish me some more, woman."

Well, that backfired. He kept his mouth against hers until she inched her lips open a bit, then he worked his tongue into the mix. *Damn.* When he finally let go, her breath was coming in short spurts. One of her knees had involuntarily inched up his leg and her ankle was wrapped around his thigh. How did that happen? She shook her head.

"Punishment over," she said. "It doesn't seem to work with you."

"Oh, it worked. It worked just fine." He slid his hand up the leg that was coiled around him until he met the fabric of her pajama shorts. He paused only briefly before slipping his fingers under the fabric and continuing up. His hand splayed across her rounded hip and he pressed her against him.

Jenny backed up. Or at least she tried to. Grant didn't let go.

"You can't just flash me your entire backside and then run off for two days without expecting me to think about that, you know."

"I didn't flash you my entire backside—just one hip. And barely that."

"Yep, that's the right word. Barely. Barely anything covering it from what I saw. Barely anything covering it now, too."

"Okay, stop. I need to get cleaned up."

"Not on my account," he teased, but he let go and headed toward the kitchen. "Want some coffee?"

"No."

"Want me to help you clean up? You know, wash your back or something?"

"No!"

"Okay, grumpmeister, go take a shower. And hurry, I told Josh we'd be there by ten."

"Josh? I'm going to see Josh?"

"Sure, why not? He's pre-med. Almost as good as the real thing. Besides, when I talked to him yesterday, he said to bring you by. He thought you were acting a little weird too. When I told him about the car wreck and you not going to your follow-up, he offered. If you need to see a real doc after, he'd be able to get you right in."

"I distinctly remember that you warned me off him a while back."

"I figure he's seen me kiss you enough he wouldn't dare let you near him now, even if you tried."

"You're convinced I won't still try?"

"Nope, but I'd like to think you've moved on to more mature subjects. In some respects, it's none of my business anyway." He pulled a steaming cup from the coffee machine and held it up. "You really don't want any?"

"Okay, okay. If you're going to put it in my face like that, I guess I'll take it." She grabbed the cup and started toward the bathroom. "Give me thirty minutes. Oh, and if you ever come to my door without calling again in the morning, I'm not answering. Not even if you cave in the damn door." She heard him grumble a response just before the door clicked closed.

"That was a long thirty minutes," Grant said when they pulled in the driveway at Lauren's house. *This is awkward.* She was going into a customer's home to get a checkup by her son. Weird.

"Yeah, well maybe if you called first, I'd be ready when you show up. I happened to get into bed around 3:30 this morning so I'm entitled to sleep past 8. I work nights, remember? Did that ever cross your mind? I'm beginning to think you have some sick desire to scare me out of bed in the morning."

He snickered. "Sorry about getting you up so early, but you're right about the sick desire thing. I like your pajamas... and I like pissing you off."

"You're kidding, right?"

He shook his head and stepped aside for her to pass.

*

The minute Jenny walked into Josh and Lauren's home, the tone changed. What is it about people in the medical profession that causes them to lose their sense of humor? Is that

a prerequisite to med school? Oh, you're going to be a doctor—
bam, you can't make jokes anymore and definitely no sexual or
physically inspired banter.

Josh greeted her and gave her an almost sickly pasted-on
smile. He took her vitals, asked her a bunch of questions,
studied her every move, and wrote a bunch of crap on a white
pad of paper. When he pursed his lips and frowned, Jenny
couldn't contain it anymore—she cracked up laughing. Josh
was so startled he jumped. "What?" he asked.

"Did I do something wrong?"

Jenny muffled her amusement before answering. "No, not at
all. In fact, just the opposite—you've done everything exactly
RIGHT. I just can't get used to you with such perfect manners.
It's so *awkward.* "

"Why?"

"Because I knew you before." Jenny shook her head,
pressing her lips together to stop the pending chuckle. "It's
weird. Sorry."

"So, why are you here then? Grant said you're seeing things.
Is that true?"

She analyzed the best way to answer the question. The
truth would likely put her in the psychiatric unit of the nearest
hospital. Josh was writing something on the pad in front of him.
The sleeve of his shirt caught briefly on the rigid edge of the
clipboard showing the skin of his wrist.

"Not to change the subject, but how did you hurt yourself?"
Jenny asked. She pointed to the red mark barely displayed
under the cloth.

Josh dropped his arm. "Excuse me?"

"How did you get the red mark on your arm?" She stepped
off the counter that served as a pseudo examining chair and
grabbed his wrist. Lifting it in the air, she slid the fabric down
with one swift movement. "Oh my God." She tried to say it

without gasping. He had at least six red scars, two of which were scabbed over. The others looked older. He yanked his arm from her grasp.

"This isn't about me. I'm here to help *you*. Answer my question."

"Josh. We need to talk about that. Don't pull away," Jenny pleaded. "I think that constitutes more of an emergency than my headaches."

Josh slammed the pen onto the clipboard and slapped it on the counter. He sighed and turned his back to her for a brief moment.

"I don't need to talk. It's old news. I hurt myself some time ago. It's nothing. It's almost healed." Josh's back gave little view of his emotions as he pulled his sleeves down and buttoned the cuffs tighter.

"Look, I'll make a deal with you—I'll answer a question for you if you answer a question for me." She laid a hand on his shoulder urging him to turn around.

"There's nothing to say, Ms. Madison. I've been poked and prodded by every mental health professional within 40 miles. I'm not interested in talking to anyone else. Just leave me alone."

"She said you'd been hurting yourself but it didn't make sense at the time."

"She? Who's she?" He turned and focused on her face. Jenny realized her mistake.

"I'm sorry, I was thinking out loud."

He hesitated. Josh's eyebrows tilted down into a frown. "Okay. I'll answer one question and you'll answer one. Deal?"

"Deal."

"I get to start though," Josh said. He leaned back against the counter and crossed his arms.

Jenny shrugged. She looked out the front window to see Grant pacing the lawn with his phone pasted to his ear. He had a hand up and was gesturing as if to convince the listener. She smiled.

"Do you see Shilo too, or does she just talk to you?"

Jenny snapped her eyes back to Josh. "Huh? What?"

"You heard me. I watched you and I think I know the answer but I want to see if you intend to be straight with me—or take the normal 'mental health professional' route."

She shook her head, reaching up to twist a section of hair between her fingers. "I'm not sure what you mean."

His eyes bore into hers. "Yes you are—I know you hear her. I've heard her for years. I used to tell people about it—over and over. Everyone thought I was hallucinating. Mom and Dad sent me to one professional after another. They put me on all sorts of medications to end my 'mental health issues.' It didn't work. None of it did. At one point, I was so drugged that all I could do was sleep. Still, she talked to me—in my damn dreams."

"Josh, maybe you're hearing her because you were there. You saw it happen and have it imprinted on your mind. That's a pretty traumatic event for a child to go through." She broke his gaze and looked back out the window at Grant, wishing he'd return.

He rolled his eyes. "Yeah, right. Look, I'm not in pre-med for nothing. I need to understand why I still see this—and what the doctors could have done to save her. I owe that to her. If it weren't for me—"

"Don't tell me you're blaming yourself for what happened? You were just a kid yourself."

"It was supposed to be me, not her."

Jenny's mouth dropped open.

Josh's face clouded over and water puddled in his bottom lids. He pursed his lips. "Well, that was way more than one question for both of us. Guess this health check is over. But you still didn't answer mine. Do you see her too?"

The door opened with trepidation and Grant paced into the room. "Well, how's the patient? Do we need to head over to the ER and get a CAT scan or something?"

"No." Josh shrugged. "She's fine. Just needs to take it semi-easy for a while."

*

Grant wasn't convinced. Josh's expression told him there was more to know. He'd been around the kid all his life; pretty much grew up with him. Albeit Grant was several years older and in college when Josh was in junior high, still he'd been there through most of the family's big events. He knew when Josh was lying and he was definitely over that line now. Jenny wasn't much better. She wouldn't look him in the eye—damn nervous as hell.

"You're shitting me, right?" he asked, raising his brows.

Josh shook his head. "No, of course not. Why would I tell you otherwise if she needed to be checked out? That would risk her health. As a person with a respect for the medical practice and one that hopes to take a 'first do no harm' oath, I don't believe in doing that."

Jenny looked over his shoulder out the window at something for a couple of seconds then grabbed her bag. "Okay then. I guess I'd better get back and work on some paperwork before my shift. Thanks for taking the time for me Josh." She reached out to shake Josh's hand.

Something's not right, Grant thought.

Jenny turned and headed to the door with a quick goodbye. She didn't look back, just went straight out to his car. There was little Grant could do but follow.

He slammed the door and buckled up. A high-pitched voice like a ventriloquist stated,

"Your phone is ringing, moron."

He suppressed a desire to laugh and shot a scowl across the car. The voice repeated itself as Jenny scrambled in her bag. "Nice ring tone."

"Sorry. Katy put that on my phone and I keep forgetting to change it. Do you mind if I take this? I think it's about my loan."

He nodded his approval and she answered the call as he pulled the car away from Lauren's house. Her voice took on the same tone it had when she first met Hodge. He clenched the steering wheel as he realized the flirtation behind the conversation. When she ended the call, her face was flushed and smiling. He turned the music up in the car to block his thoughts.

"Well, I have good news and bad news. Which should I tell first?"

Grant shrugged. "Your choice."

"Okay, start with the bad and end with the good. My loan was denied." Strange that she would be somewhat cheery when saying it.

"You don't sound too disappointed. I thought you needed the funding."

"I do. I do. And I have no idea what I'll do now. I guess go to another bank. I could ask my mother but there's no way in hell I'm going to do that and suffer through any more lectures on how ridiculous it is for me to have such a business."

"Your mom doesn't like what you do?"

"She lectures me about everything. You name it. Since my dad died, she's increased the pressure tenfold."

He frowned. That made a lot of sense. "Okay, so tell me the good news."

"I have a date." It startled him. He cast a narrowed glance sideways, not sure whether to react or not. A slight tick of his jaw was all he showed as he gritted his teeth together.

"With the loan officer. He wants to meet me for lunch and give some advice on what to do so that another bank would be interested in approving the application. It's not really a date—just a business thing." She turned her arm and looked at her watch, then frowned.

Yeah, right.

"I'm supposed to meet him in thirty minutes. It's twenty minutes to my apartment and another fifteen back to where he asked to meet me. Do you think you could just drop me at the restaurant?"

Is she really asking me to escort her to a lunch date with some asshole? No fricking way. Do I look like the big brother type?

"Why don't I just go with you? I haven't eaten either, and you may need some help. I'm pretty good with Hodge's bank." He didn't look at her when he spoke, simply kept his focus on the road and swiftly maneuvered the traffic.

Jenny ran her hands over the legs of her pants, clearing her throat as if to consider whether it would be appropriate for him to be there.

Awkward.

"I can handle myself fine. I don't think—I mean, I'm not sure." She glanced at her watch again. "Okay, fine."

He smiled. "Don't worry, Jen. I'll behave." *Maybe.* "Where are we going?"

She gave directions and his frown returned when he realized the guy was taking her to Amici's, a nice, romantic Italian restaurant with low lighting, very plush and private booths, and fantastic food. For lunch? Really?

"You're interested in this guy?" he asked when they pulled into the parking lot and waited for the valet to appear.

"He's my banker. It's simply lunch and for a business purpose. Besides, don't think just because you kissed me a couple of times, you get to decide who I eat with and where I go."

"I never said I did. If it bothers you that much, I'll sit at another table and you can pretend you don't know me. Would that make you happy?"

"Oh, God. Don't get testy now. That's stupid. I'm not going to make you sit by yourself." She put a finger up to his face when he held the door for her to enter. "But don't you dare screw this up for me."

He gave her his best devious grin. *Now why would I want to do that?*

*

Grant forced himself to maintain a pleasant smile. She had introduced him as a business acquaintance, slipped into the booth across from him with Banker Boy next to her, and started the most saccharine-sweet conversation on earth. He'd lost his appetite. *This is how she conducts business?*

"Excuse me a minute, I need to make a phone call." He recognized a momentary twinge of guilt as he slipped from the booth and stepped to the lobby. Yes, a quick phone call to his friend, Jeff. *After all, it is in her best interest.* She wouldn't like that he interfered, which was why he told the bank's president to keep the whole thing confidential. No need for her to get worked up about this. Her success was important to their business. Or at least that's what he told Jeff.

Now, he felt like eating again. He smiled cheerfully when he returned and finished his lunch in silence. He said goodbye to the schmuck when it was over and even told him to "treat Jenny well" in a teasing manner. He hummed all the way back to her apartment and waved as she exited the car. Her face in the rearview mirror looked confused.

*

Grant spent the remainder of the day working on the schedule for their latest client's tour. Hodge had entrusted him to do this one alone—a huge opportunity. Hodge was incredibly anal about these things so the confidence in his abilities was an ego booster. One Grant realized he needed after a few weeks of pent up frustrations surrounding Jenny. He wanted to get the tension out of his system. Only one way to do that.

He thought it'd be easy until lunch. The way she went after the guy in his presence made it evident that he overestimated where things were going with her. After all, they only kissed a few times. For him, that usually led to one of two things: sex, or the realization that the person wasn't interesting or interested. Maybe his assumption of the former came in direct conflict with her thinking the latter? No, not likely. She had been as into it as he was. Hell, her hands were all over him. He remembered the feel of her thigh as he ran his hand under the black dress. Damn. His body tightened with the nagging urge to finish the exploration.

Grant shook his head and started making the calls to book spaces and equipment. He needed to forget Jenny and stay on track with work. There wasn't time for sexual fantasies. He continued reminding himself for two more days. His temper grew.

Thursday night at 2 a.m. he woke to the sound of his cell chanting at him on the stand by the bed. He pulled his hand to rub his eyes and looked at the clock. No one calls at this time of night. Probably a wrong number. On the fourth ring, he rolled to his stomach and lifted the phone to see the display. Hmmm. Jenny. He must still be asleep. He vaguely remembered thinking about her with her tongue sliding down his throat, then his chest. Another ring.

"Hello?" His voice was hoarse. He cleared his throat and said it again.

"Grant. Thank God you answered. Are you awake?"

"Yeah, sure. Are you okay?"

"Oh, uh, sorry about that. I tried everyone else I could but my other two drivers are on jobs, and none of my girlfriends are answering the phone. What are you doing right now?"

I was having some pretty intense dreams that involved you and my shower, then you and my couch, oh and don't forget about the kitchen counter. Grant stroked his hand over his face. "Not much. What's up Jen?"

"I need your help."

*

Less than an hour later, he was standing next to her wearing a crumpled T-shirt and shorts watching a tow truck pull away with her car. A flat tire and a flat spare.

"You know, between the two of us, we're almost on a first name basis with the tow truck service here. In your business shouldn't you be more conscious of the status of your tires and everything else? When's the last time you had this car checked out?"

"I know. I know. I had it on my list to get tires and an oil change, but I just have been so focused on the loan and everything. I let it go too long. At least I was on my way home when it blew and didn't have anyone in the car with me."

"It probably would have been safer for you to have someone there."

"Maybe." She shrugged. "But really bad for business."

"So, you keep a to-do list? What else is on the list?"

"It's on the dash, and it's a mile long." She waved a hand toward the car as it disappeared down the road. The wind swept a strand of dark hair from her face as she turned to him. He could smell her shampoo.

"You hungry?" he asked.

"Are you?"

"I asked *you*."

"Okay. Yeah, I guess."

"I'll fix you something."

"Oh, I thought you meant go eat somewhere."

"Not much open other than gas stations. I don't know about you but this late at night, everything you'll find is left over from the day before and that doesn't sound too great." He held the door and motioned for her to get in the car.

"I don't have any food at home. Haven't been to the store in a while."

When they were moving again, Grant said "I have a full fridge if you don't mind stopping by my place first."

She gave him a wary look.

"Just to eat, Jen. Unless you had something else on the brain? Not sure I'd feel comfortable with that right now considering the circumstances." He wiggled his eyebrows.

"What circumstances?"

"Well, you're interested in Banker Boy for one thing…and I can't kick you out after since you don't have wheels, so it'd be pretty damn awkward, don't you think?"

"Ah, your true nature rises up."

Damn right about that. He grinned. "But hey, if you're curious, we could skip the food and go straight to your place."

"Yeah, right. I'm not curious. And suddenly food sounds good—and safe."

*

At his apartment, he liked her sitting on the counter, popping potato chips while he fired up a skillet. "How about fajitas?" He slathered spices on the chicken.

"Sounds great." She threw another chip into her mouth. He noticed the crumbs on her shirt and smiled. He pulled out a package of pre-cut peppers and onions from the freezer and dropped some into the oil. The explosion of popping and fizzing caused him to lower the flame. He added the chicken a couple of minutes later. Once he'd poured some white wine and broth into the pan, he covered it and let it sizzle. The pile of crumbs on her belly had grown a bit.

"You're mainlining chips." He wiped the crumbs from her shirt into his palm. "Put out your tongue." He held the chips over her head and waited. When Jenny closed her eyes and opened her mouth to receive the salty crumbs, an urge overtook and he dropped the crumbs on her face, dusting her in the shards. He couldn't forestall the laughter that surged inside.

"Hey." Jenny retaliated by dumping a handful of chips into his T-shirt and subsequently smashed them against his chest.

"Nice." He laughed. "Real nice." He pulled the shirt away from his skin. Crumbs spewed on the floor. "And itchy." He pulled the shirt over his head and handed it to her.

"Go ahead, eat 'em. It's obvious you have a potato chip addiction. I doubt you'll want those to go to waste. I wouldn't recommend eating the ones on the floor though. Bugsy's ass was there a few days ago."

"So I like chips. It could be worse, you know. I could be a chocoholic, or an alcoholic, or a shopaholic."

"That's a lot of holics."

"As I see it, I'm pretty low maintenance compared to those types."

"Low maintenance? For whom? You're talking to a guy you just pulled out of bed in the middle of the night to help you with a flat tire." Grant rubbed his eyes with a thumb and forefinger.

She shrugged while concentrating on picking crumbs from his shirt and, yes, she ate them. Strange, though, she put her mouth right up to the cloth. The smell of garlic and onions filled the room as the spattering sound of the chicken browning served as their background music.

"You said you were awake. Oh, I forgot to tell you, my loan was approved!" she said.

"Good." He wasn't surprised. "Guess your lunch with Banker Boy proved successful in convincing him."

"You say that like I tried to seduce him into giving me the money."

She had finished with the T-shirt, dropped it on the counter, and returned to the chip bag.

Grant lifted the lid and turned the chicken over. "Wasn't that the plan?"

"No—like that's really gonna work anyway. Look, he didn't even approve it. He doesn't have the authority. I got a call later that day from a lady named Karen Cross. She said there was a mistake and that the loan wasn't processed correctly. She's taken over the account and will be my contact going forward. I'm supposed to get the check next week."

Good. Exactly what he had asked of Jeff. He didn't make a habit of using Hodge's influence for personal gain—hopefully Hodge wouldn't find out this time. "So, how is Banker Boy? Have you seen him since then?"

She pointed the bag at him. "I don't see that's any of your business. He is kind of cute though, don't you think?"

Grant shrugged. He stirred the chicken and put the lid back. "No grown man wants to be called 'cute,' and you're not seriously asking me to answer that, are you? Jesus, Jen. You had your tongue down my throat less than a week ago. You really want me to give you my opinion of his potential date-ability? That's kind of shitty."

"I did not have my tongue down your throat…and, you had your hand up my skirt too, as I remember it. Besides, I seriously doubt you're concerned about it. There's a Christmas card taped to your wall that's signed, 'Love you always, Gracie,' so you don't seem starving for attention. It's not like we have anything going on here." She waved the bag from him to her.

Grant turned off the fire under the chicken and snatched the bag from her hand. There were less than half a dozen cards taped on his wall, mostly from business associates.

Interesting she noticed that particular one.

The loud paper crackling startled her as he crumpled the bag closed and tossed it into the pantry. He turned back and faced her with two paper plates in one hand and a bag of flour tortillas in the other. Should he explain? Obviously it bothered her so perhaps he should. "Gracie's my sister," he said as he measured her reaction. Nothing.

Grant put tortillas on plates, filled them with the chicken mix, added some cheese and pushed one into her hand. He liked that she noticed the card and maybe even that it bothered her.

"Smells good. Thanks."

"Welcome." He watched her take the first bite. A piece of cheese trailed the corner of her mouth and she flicked her tongue out to scoop it in. The simple action sent a surge of lust through him. He looked away and leaned against the counter. *Get a grip, dumbass.*

"Aren't you going to eat?" She motioned at the plate sitting untouched.

"I think I disagree with you, Jenny."

"About what? Eating this stuff?"

"No, there *is* something going on here. I'm not really sure what the hell it is, but it's definitely going on."

Jenny looked at his stomach. "You have chips on your belly."

Grant blinked twice and looked down as she laced her fingers out and brushed them across his naval just above the zipper on his shorts. It sent a shiver across him and he suddenly became very conscious that he was no longer wearing a shirt. He sucked in his breath and grabbed her wrist. Shit, that felt good. He closed his eyes and rested his head on her shoulder. He was tired. His mind clouded. Was this just a different version of the same dream he'd had the last two nights?

"Grant, you okay?" she whispered.

"Yeah, yeah." He yawned. "How about you? Long day? Tired?" He glanced over her shoulder at the clock. It was blurred but he thought it said 4:37.

"A little. Let's take this to the couch." Jenny nodded at the food. She grabbed the two plates and headed to his new leather furniture.

It didn't take much to entice him to follow since she'd moved out from underneath him, his only prop of stability. Just the thought of sitting for a minute sounded nice. He yawned again and sank into the cushions next to her. Damn, her leg felt nice against his.

He leaned his head back and closed his eyes. "Did you get enough to eat, Jen?" he mumbled.

"Yeah, it was great. You were great." He thought that's what she said and he smiled. He knew she liked it.

"You were too. Damn, you feel good. Okay. Yeah, touch me there," he whispered. He thought she giggled. He wasn't sure, then he was dreaming again and she was taking his pants off. *That was new.*

Chapter 22

Jenny drooled on slick, supple leather. She sucked in the wetness and licked her lips. The smell of leather was fabulous. She once had a leather jacket that her mother gave her as a birthday present. This was the same smell. Musky, strong, and so rich. She rubbed her cheek along it—along the smoothness of it. Then suddenly there was warmth against her hip. Against her leg. She turned over and light blasted her in the face, a blinding white glare. Pulling both hands over her eyes, she cupped her hands to block it out and groaned.

"Oh, sorry about that," a voice murmured next to her. She heard the sound of curtains closing and when a comfortable darkness engulfed her, she slipped her eyes open to small slits. Grant.

"You're awake." She raised her hands in a long, luxurious stretch. "What time is it?"

"Eight." He stroked a finger down the bridge of her nose. "I'm sorry I fell asleep."

"It's okay." She smiled, remembering how he'd spoken in his dreams. Crazy, rambling words that were almost seductive. "It was late. You needed rest. I'm sorry I had to bother you. I know it makes it hard to get up and go to work after a long night like that." She sat up.

"You want some coffee?" He placed a mug into her palm, no answer expected.

Jenny scooted further up and pulled the cover over her legs. After she laid him out on the couch earlier and covered him, she had slipped off her jeans and wrapped herself in the blanket from his bed. She wasn't about to take over his bedroom so she draped her blanket-clad body across the loveseat positioned adjacent to the sofa he was on, and dozed.

The cover she'd thrown over him during the night had slipped and barely covered his torso and she had spent any number of minutes rehashing what he looked like below it. His hair ruffled up above his ear in a loosely tangled flip. She smiled and ran a hand over her own. "You passed out."

"Yeah, sorry. I'm not used to staying out that late, and I haven't slept too great lately."

"I'm sorry. Give me a minute to get dressed. Do you have time to drop me by my apartment?"

"No."

"Oh, uh, okay. I'll call a cab."

"No. You'll go back to sleep. I called in and let Hodge know I'd be late. He's okay with it. You need rest. Your friend Katy called earlier trying to find out if you were still stranded on the side of the road. I hope you don't mind that I answered your phone. It was right next to my head and, well, she wasn't going to give up. I was tired of being called a moron by your ring tone."

"She probably was a little panicked."

"Yes. She was."

"You told her I'm okay?"

"Yeah, and I answered a lot of questions. Damn, she's nosey."

Jenny smiled. "She's just making sure you're not a bad guy. I've had a couple near misses lately."

"Close your eyes. I want you to sleep a couple more hours then we're going to get your car."

"I need to get moving."

"No you don't. Today's your day off."

"How did you know that?" she asked.

His leg was against her. She could smell him again. He'd handed her his T-shirt full of crumbs earlier and the scent of it, with his cologne solidly ingrained, was addictive. She'd held it up to her face and breathed in the muskiness. He probably thought her crazy.

"Katy told me when she called."

"That girl has a big mouth."

"Yeah, but I like her." He lifted her legs and slid back into the couch, draping the sleek skin across his lap. "Go back to sleep." He rubbed her legs softly until her eyes drifted closed. When she thought she couldn't get more comfortable, she felt him slip his arms under her and lift. Seconds later, her head sank into the softness of a wonderful feather pillow filled with his musky cologne. A blanket draped over her shoulders and she fell asleep, dreaming that Grant was spooned against her. His lips trailed down her shoulder, pushing the fabric aside. She sighed and arched her neck to give easier access.

"Jenny," he whispered against her neck, "we're not going to do this while you're half-asleep."

She groaned and pulled him into her. "I'm not asleep." She thought he laughed softly.

"Yeah, you are."

Okay, maybe I am, but keep doing that.

Hours later, she blinked her eyes open to find her nose smashed against Grant's Adam's apple. She sucked in an enormous gulp of his scent then sighed. He was warm. Fantastically warm. And she was in his bed, wrapped up in blankets.

Wait! She was WHAT? How the hell did that happen?

"Hey, it's okay. It's okay. It's just me, Jen. You're fine."

"I'm fine? I'm in your bed with no pants on. What the hell?" She shoved against him, sat up, and pulled the covers against her.

"I had nothing to do with the pants. You took them off yourself. And all we did was sleep. Both of us. We slept." His eyes bore into hers. "You remember me carrying you in here?"

She looked away. "Yeah."

"Okay then. We slept." He sat up too. "Nice panties though."

She peeked under the blanket and saw the turquoise cotton with black lace that covered her hips. Silently glad she had on something fairly nice, she suppressed a grin.

"Yours aren't too bad either." *Sure, I looked. I'm not stupid.*

He put a hand out and rubbed her arm with his thumb. His hands were warm, big, and a bit on the rough side. "So, you were checking me out on the couch? Jenny Madison, you're a bad girl."

"Yeah, well that makes two of us," she teased. She could barely see him in the darkness. He had drawn the blinds so the dark engulfed them like a hotel room into pseudo-night.

"God, I hope so," he whispered. His grip on her arm tightened and he yanked her against him. He was an early morning person, she realized. In many ways. He was up, really up, in the morning. She used to be like that but with the new business, now, her internal clock had flipped its axis. *Who cares?* He could be from a completely different planet and she'd still want him—right now. The guy was gorgeous. Okay, maybe gorgeous wasn't the right word for a guy, but she wasn't sure what else to use. Not cute, apparently. All she knew was that every pore in his being was against her and the feel of it was just about to drown her. She gulped a breath then trailed her lips against his neck. Did he kiss her forehead? Did he really whisper against her ear, 'Jenny, you are so damn beautiful'? Was that his tongue flicking against her ear…grazing her lips, her eyes, and her nose? This was so out of control. She was sleep-deprived. That was it.

"Jen, I've got to touch you. Really."

Did he say that or did I imagine it? She shook her head.

Grant drew back in the dark. The scent of him pulled away too.

She clutched her fingers into his sides. "No."

"No?" He was asking.

"I didn't mean no, don't touch me. I meant no, don't pull away." She hesitated. "Am I asleep? Wake me up, dammit."

"No. God no. Don't wake up. Just keep going. I like this dream. I want it. Holy shit, I *need* this dream, Jen." His mouth smothered hers, sucking her lips until they felt chapped.

Then, he did the strangest thing. He sank his head down to her belly and rested his face against her stomach with his lashes fluttering on her ribcage. It tickled. And it turned her on. His arms wrapped around her waist in a cocoon. He groaned into her skin, a hot rush against the coolness of the sheets. He started lifting the fabric of her shirt and pressing lips against her skin.

Jenny wasn't sure when or how it happened, but a few moments later her shirt was on the floor, along with the black lace of the bra and panties. She thought she remembered muttering, "Oh hell" as she threw them there, but maybe that was him. The black boxers she'd stripped him to during the night joined her garments, wrapped together as if they wanted to be permanently attached. He still had potato chip fragments tangled into the hairs surrounding his naval. Sexy was all she could think of. Jenny couldn't form a lucid thought. Was she still asleep? Did it matter? Damn he was hot, and his kisses melted into her collarbone as he ran a hand down her neck and trailed it along the underside of her breasts.

"Jen. I can't—" He sounded pained as he spoke into her cheek. She ran a hand down the feather sprinkling of hair that lined his torso, brushing the crumbs aside, and reaching deeper still. Grant moaned a long, painful exhale. "Don't make me—"

She drew back. "Don't make you do this?" she asked incredulously.

He laughed. "Don't make me stop. Please don't make me stop." He grabbed her hand and steered it where he wanted her to go then he laced his fingers along her thigh, then up to where she ached for him to touch. He worked his fingers gently until she shuddered. The spasm came suddenly. So suddenly that she stopped breathing for a second. Lights exploded in her peripheral vision as the first wave hit.

"Holy shit! Holy…lightning…hell!" *Did she really say that?* She rose off the bed and clutched into him as he touched and caressed. He stared into her eyes. Or at least she thought so. It was too dark to really tell. She felt his hand on her backside, squeezing into her skin as his mouth worked over her neck, her jaw line, and her breasts. Then, he lifted her to his lap and hugged her tightly to him, skin on skin. He was warm and engulfing in his embrace.

Grant murmured something against her collarbone but she didn't grasp it, then he eased her onto her back. She could hear his stilted breathing. She probably should be glad for the dim light; it hid any imperfections of her less than perfectly sculpted curves. Unfortunately, she wasn't glad. She wanted the lights on. She wanted the blinds open. She wanted to see his face and know what he felt. He took care of the protection thing then slipped into her, a thrusting motion that glued them deep together.

"Stay with me Jen," he whispered. As if she would do anything else. His hands splayed hungrily across her back. She couldn't help but work with it, rocking into him as he moved. And he moved. God, did he move. He lifted up and cradled into her neck with his forehead. She rolled her head back and let him take her with him into the deep pit of his pleasure. His fingers dug into her hips as she cascaded in rhythm with his body. She arched toward him.

Was she really doing this? His lips licked and sucked their way over her neck and down to the dip between her breasts before returning to her face. In rhythm with his thoughts, his touch, his mouth, his never-call-it-cute body. When the wave hit him, she was right there with him. Every muscle in his smooth, hard body strained to enjoy the moment as much as she did.

"Damn, Jen. Holy…lightning…hell, you're beautiful." He repeated himself and was practically panting when he said it.

They lay quietly for a stretch before he said it again. "Jen, you're beau—"

"It's completely dark in here, Grant. Everyone looks good in this light." She sucked in a gulp of desperately needed oxygen and turned to roll onto her stomach. She lifted her feet to cross them at the ankles.

"Come on Jenny, don't do that shit." He took advantage of her position and lowered his head to pillow it in the small of her back. As he trailed fingers lightly up her spine, he added, "Don't try to ruin it for me. I know what I see."

"You see nothing."

"I see you. And everything about you. I don't need the lights on to know the details."

She started to argue. "You can't possi—"

Grant groaned and snaked a hand up to the back of her head. He palmed her hair like a basketball and shoved her head straight down into the mattress, muffling her words.

"Can't you just let me enjoy this for a few more minutes before you start throwing barbs at me?" he asked.

"Okay," she murmured into the pillow-top.

He let go of her head and returned to her back. Jenny decided words weren't necessary. He was doing just fine without them. Really fine. Holy. Lightning. Hell. Fine.

Chapter 23

Sleep deprivation, no matter how it comes about, always catches up with a person. Maybe it wasn't the lack of sleep. Jenny had lived with that for months now without problems. Had to be the sex. She was out of shape.

"Man, I need to get to the gym," she mumbled with one eye open. The room was still dark; she had no idea what time it was. They'd both drifted off this time. His head was cradled against her spine. She could feel the soft breeze of air from his open mouth on her skin. Regular little sighs. He rolled off and bear crawled to her side.

"I never pictured you for the gym type," he said. "Especially after seeing the way you inhaled that bag of chips."

His mouth pressed against her shoulder. It was damned intimate and made her uncomfortable. She wasn't very good at the intimacy thing. What was it he said about kicking her out after?

Jenny reached to the end of the bed and tugged the sheet until it rested gently below her chin.

"It's a little late to cover up, don't you think?"

She couldn't see him but she knew he was grinning. She sighed. "I'm cold."

"Yeah, and I'm a radiator." Actually, that part is true, she thought. "It's time to go get your car. If we don't get moving, they'll be closed."

"Really? Good grief, what time is it?" She slid her feet onto the floor, wrapped the sheet around her three times, and padded toward a light under the door. Bam. She hit her shin on something and cried out. Grant laughed. The flicking sound of a switch echoed after his chuckle, and a light by the bed gave her the visibility needed to find the bathroom, which, by a woman's standards, was pretty nasty. She looked in the mirror and panicked. *What the hell am I doing? This isn't me.*

Chapter 24

"I really appreciate what you did for me," Jenny said when they stopped at the tire store. Her car sat out front, waiting. He grinned.

She backhanded his arm. "Not that! I meant coming and getting me. Helping me with the car. It was nice."

"Nice," he mocked. "Right up there with cute. Not what a guy wants to be called by a woman he's just burned the sheets with."

She raised a finger. "Stop. Can we just not talk about that, okay? It's bad enough I had to call you for help. I'm probably not going to live it down. You don't have to rub it in that I—" *I attacked you. I was half-asleep.*

"You yell out 'Holy. Lightning. Hell' in the heat of the moment?" Grant teased. "I like it. I like it a lot. In fact, I think I'm going to start saying that all the time now. I like it so much." He yanked on her hair.

"I don't usually do that."

"No kidding? Then I like it even more." He grinned. "And no, we can't just not talk about it. You're not getting off that easy. Okay, maybe you did, but—"

She backhanded him again and stepped out of his car to the store. A warning frown let him know she didn't want to hear another word. She expected him to drive off. After all, she had her car now. He didn't need to stay. Instead, he parked and followed her. When she finished paying, he tossed her his keys and slipped hers from the counter.

"I'll drive it to your place," he said over his shoulder as he pushed out the door into the afternoon sunshine. "Just to make sure everything's okay. You can take mine and follow."

"You're really going to trust me to drive your convertible?" She squinted into the brightness.

"Sure. Why not?" He hesitated as if questioning the decision. "You follow me. Okay?"

"Got it." As soon as they hit the freeway, she zipped into the passing lane, gassed it and took off.

*

By the time Grant arrived at her apartment, Jenny had backed the audi into a nice spot and was sitting on the hood with her arms around her knees. *Nice car. No wonder he kept it.*

"What happened to following me?"

"I'm not too good with orders or following."

"Yeah, I see that." He walked around his car as if checking for scratches and stopped in front of her. "You're crazy."

"So are you."

"I guess so. Good thing your car didn't break down on the way here." He grinned.

"What are you doing with the rest of the day?" He slipped his hands into his pockets and kicked the tire.

"Why do you want to know? Haven't you got something to do?"

"As a matter of fact, I do. I'm supposed to be in the bar at the Beverly Hilton in an hour to meet with a client. You want to go? We could eat dinner after."

She slipped from the hood and moved around him toward her apartment. "I'm still wearing yesterday's clothes, and I look like I've been run over by a truck."

"You look fine." He started to close the distance she tried to put between them.

"Word of advice, Grant. Remember how you said grown men don't like to be called cute or nice? Well, while we're schooling each other on terminology, grown women don't like to be told they look *fine* either. That's just a polite way of saying 'you look like shit but I don't mind'." She posted her hands on her hips and frowned.

"That's not what I meant. Look, if you want to go in and take a shower, feel free. If you want to change clothes, knock yourself out. I don't really care what you wear—I'm sure you'll rock it whatever it is, and everyone will wish they were me. But me, I just want you to go. Personally, I like the way you look right now, mainly because I know why you look that way. It's a man-thing. We need to be on the road in," he looked at his watch, "twenty minutes tops."

They were on the road in fifteen. She wore the black dress again, and she thought what he said was nice. Oops, not nice— sweet. She was fairly certain he wouldn't like that either.

*

Grant's client meeting didn't happen. He'd half-expected that since Ms. Lynnaid was adept at standing people up. It frustrated him to hell, but that's the way a lot of these ego-driven people are. No consideration for anyone else. They think the world revolves around them, and until they get too old to perform and fall out of the limelight, that was pretty much true.

A month ago, he would have gone home and worked his anger out by putting in a few more hours on the computer. That was a month ago. Now, Ms. Lynnaid's rudeness was a fricking godsend. He had been concerned about her interaction with Jenny anyway. He scanned the glitzy bar with its mirrored walls and neon blue lights.

"Grant, who's your new talent?" Hal, the bartender asked, as he sprayed tonic water into a glass. He gave a nod in Jenny's direction.

Grant circled an arm around her. His hand clutched into the slinky fabric as he pulled her forward. "Jenny, this is Hal Guthrie. He's worked this part of the hotel for as long as I remember."

"Ten years." Hal offered a hand to Jenny. "When will I see you on the screen, honey?"

Grant shook his head. "You won't. She's not a client."

Hal put two wine glasses on the counter and filled them. "No? Could have fooled me. Try this. It's new. Italian. Chef says it's pretty good, and I know you like the reds." He winked, then caught himself and cleared his throat. "Red wines, that is."

"You must see all sorts of famous people, Hal." Jenny said before lifting the wine to her lips. Grant couldn't help but stare at her mouth. She'd added lipstick.

"A few. This place has some pretty strict rules so the wild ones usually go down to one of the places at the beach or near the studios."

"I guess that means Grant's not one of the wild ones?"

"I can be wild," he interjected. "Just not when there's business to discuss." He tapped a finger to the top of the wine glass. "Tell Chef this one's a winner. Hal, do you think you could get us in tonight? I didn't call ahead for a reservation. I thought I was meeting Quonna for a bit, that's all. Jenny's never been here."

"We're booked—but sit, sit." Hal motioned to the barstools near them. "I can get whatever you want right here. Wait, no— take that booth over there." He pointed to a quiet spot in the corner near the window that had just been vacated.

The booth faced a picture window that overlooked the city. Due to the way the hotel was situated, they could see all the way to the beach in the distance. Jenny started to slip into the bench seat opposite him, but he grabbed her hand. "Over here." He tugged on her arm and she fell in beside him. "You can't see the sunset from there."

"And I want to be blinded by the sun at the end of the day?"

She tries so hard to be caustic, but it doesn't work. It comes off funny. He put his nose into her hair and whispered, "I vaguely remember that you didn't see the sun until a couple hours ago, so you're behind on your quota of vitamin D for the day. Besides, maybe I'm trying to impress you."

"You already did."

He looked at her. "A different kind of impression."

"Hey, anyone that is willing to come get me when I call them in the middle of the night makes a pretty damn good impression. But you thought I meant something else, didn't you?" She poked him in the side with a grin. "Don't overestimate yourself, big guy."

"Thanks for bursting my bubble."

"You wouldn't expect anything less, would you?"

"Tell me about your parents." He slid his back against the wall and draped an arm across the back of the booth so that he could face her. "They live here?"

"My dad died eight years ago in a car accident."

Damn. Shouldn't have asked. He slipped his fingers to the back of her neck and rubbed. "Sorry."

She continued. "My mother took it pretty hard. In fact, she still seems driven to meet his expectations. It's really awkward to go back because we have so little to talk about. Dad was an attorney and he hoped I'd go that route too. Law school would have meant two more years. I was just finishing up my bachelor's when he died. It broke her heart that I didn't do it, but I didn't have the money. I couldn't. I applied for some scholarships and grants but my grades weren't good enough."

"I can't see you as an attorney."

A waiter dressed in full whites, right up to the piped hat, appeared and slid two plates in front of them. Compliments of the chef, he advised. Grant thanked him.

"You don't think I have a knack for arguing my point?"

"Arguing, yes. You've got that down. I'm not so sure you'd be comfortable wearing those suits and high heels."

"I'm wearing heels at the moment." She smiled. "Not that I'm a big fan."

He leaned toward her. "You're not wearing them but since this place has a very strict, 'no shirt, no shoes, no service' policy, I won't tell." He had noticed when she hooked the end of both with her toes and let them slip to the floor. One bare foot was tucked under her hip, the other rested next to his leg on the carpet, within a hair's breadth of touching him. The hem of the dress hiked to her thigh and he found himself wanting to slide his hand along it.

"Okay, I'm not big on the formal clothes thing, but not because I don't like to dress up. Every girl does. It's just that I don't want to spend all my time worrying about it and being uncomfortable. I threw away that dress I wore to Hodge's party for that very reason. I spent the whole night wrestling with it. You've missed the point though. I'll wear whatever it takes if I'm doing something that matters to me."

"You did seem pretty preoccupied with covering yourself that night. I don't know why you bothered. Especially now that I've seen you."

She lifted her hand to punch him, but he grabbed the wrist and ran a thumb down the pulse point. "Jenny, you're going to have to stop hitting me. Someone might think you're abusive and call the cops."

"Another reason I'd make a shitty lawyer." He released her wrist. She dropped it to the neck of his shirt and twisted the material between her fingers. "I'm a little too aggressive. My mother thought I'd grow out of it—sort of a maturity thing—guess not."

"You pretend to be all gruff and tough but I know you would have a hard time with the compromises an attorney sometimes has to make. Too much gray area. Does your mom work?"

"Yes, she worked in Dad's office as a legal assistant. That was how they met. She's still there but she keeps talking about retiring. She's upped the ante lately though. One of Dad's friends and partners died last year of a heart attack. I think that was a pretty unsettling blow for her."

"How old is she?"

"Fifty-six. I don't think she can afford to retire yet. Doug keeps encouraging her to stay."

"Who's Doug?"

"One of the other partners. Nice guy. He's only been there about six years. He's a widower too and has been a good friend. I see him sometimes when I go home. I think it's nice for Mom to have a friend that didn't know Dad first. It kind of takes sympathy out of the friendship."

"So, they date?"

"What? No! He's just a friend. They work together. She's not interested in him. He's not at all her type."

"I don't think anyone has a type. Sometimes things just happen and it works. Wow, taste this—it's fantastic." He slipped his fork into the colorful food in front of them and lifted it to her mouth. He found it interesting that she tried so hard to be what her mother thought she should and her mother apparently did the same. In reality, they had both moved on with their lives since her dad died. She wasn't a lawyer but rather something much better—a business owner. It fit her personality and, of course, helped the people she served. Doubtful she'd ever admit it, but why else would someone do that? The hours sucked, the income couldn't possibly be too exciting, and it played havoc with her social life.

"Mmmm. Yes, good. I can't believe I let you feed me like a baby," Jenny said as she chewed on the melting splendor of Brie, toasted pecans, and cranberries.

"This bothers you?" He held up the fork.

"It's kind of demeaning, don't you think? Spoon feeding an adult."

"Fork feeding," Grant corrected.

"Whatever."

"It's like forcing one of your children to eat their vegetables when they clearly don't want to."

He shook his head and dipped the fork back into the dish. "Sometimes the way you think surprises me. Sharing something you like, as in food, is like sharing a moment. Something special." He swirled the morsel on the tongs around in the red jellied sauce and lifted it for her to see. "And you like it so much that you just have to share it, preferably with someone you hope will enjoy it as much as you do." He swished the fork back and forth in front of her mouth, holding his hand under it to catch loose drips should they stray.

She parted her lips. "How can you make something as simple as that sound so temptingly personal and sexy? That's not quite fair." She leaned toward the bite, opening further. He wanted those lips. As she took the bite into her mouth, he leaned after it and kissed her, tasting the sweetness of the sauce.

"It *is* sexy. Tell me, doesn't it taste good?" He brushed her lips again, feeling her leg rest solid against his thigh. She nodded. He looked at the remaining food and said, "I hadn't thought about it being personal but I guess the fact that you let me do it must have been big for you. Here. Your turn." He set the fork on the plate and pushed it toward her.

"You want me to feed you? Seriously?"

"Yeah." He waited. For such an argumentative person, she sure had some strange walls to get past.

"I'm not going to feed you, Grant. Pick up your fork. I'm not your mother." She let out a sigh and slid her glance to the window. He shrugged and took the plate back. The last two bites disappeared into his mouth in seconds.

The rest of the dinner was spent talking about his sister and parents. She didn't ask many questions but he told her anyway. No questions about Hodge. Not one word, in fact, and that pleasantly surprised him.

Almost everyone that knows his business wants to find out as much as possible about the great Hodge Larson. That was an eye-opener when he dated Emma. Beautiful woman—the kind he thought was his type—but she was really only interested in what he could do for her career. Obviously that didn't meet expectations. In fact, if he really thought about it, very little in that relationship was what he'd hoped for either. Emma barely noticed the little things he did for her, and certainly never returned the favor. Other than the one time she'd thrown a birthday party for him at the apartment and invited Hodge and most of his clients. He hadn't even fussed about the cost. He thought she wanted to please him. Funny thing was, that's how she met his replacement.

The sun lowered over the ocean, first to a golden glow, then a fuchsia fan over the horizon, and finally a pink and blue haze that reluctantly left them alone in the dark booth. Jenny stifled a yawn and thanked him for the dinner.

"Time to get you home, Cinderella," he said.

She was groggy as they walked out of the bar. He threaded his fingers through hers to guide her through the gathering crowd. Hal slid him a quick thumbs up when Jenny was well past. He nodded.

Chapter 25

Thursday morning, Jenny shook her head as she sipped tea that she'd made with her new brewer. It was damn confusing to think about. This thing with Grant made no sense. She wasn't a glitz and glamour girl and that was his world. She wore ripped jeans skirts and shorts most of the time and her idea of going out involved beer and pizza, not champagne in a fountain made of sculpted ice.

It had been almost a week since he dropped her back at her apartment after the day spent in his much nicer quarters. Well, only five days actually, but it felt longer. Contrary to what he'd said, he didn't kick her out. In fact, she almost felt like he wanted to stay when they ended up at her apartment after dinner. He walked her to the door and just stood there, hands in pockets, acting all awkward. When she didn't invite him in, he just kissed her on the cheek and ambled off.

She must have misconstrued though. No word at all the first four days. When she finally left the apartment yesterday, there was a cup of cold Starbucks sitting on the ground. She assumed he'd left it. No note or anything. He could have at least knocked. Okay, well, maybe she'd told him to call first, but if he was there, he might at least *say* so. There was always texting. She had monitored her phone religiously, nothing.

Karen, the loan officer, called just before five Wednesday and needed her to come sign the papers. They agreed on a time Thursday afternoon since it was her day off. Jenny filled a bowl with cereal and opened the fridge.

"Damn." An empty milk carton was lodged in the door along with a carton of sour cream that had a date of July 22.

She tossed them both in the trash and stared into the empty fridge. She really needed to get groceries. "Today's the day," she muttered to no one.

Jenny dressed and grabbed the keys. An hour later, she'd filled the cabinets with cans and chip bags. She'd also gifted the fridge with milk, cheese, and a few pieces of fruit and veggies. She even added a nice wrapped steak, which she intended to cook for dinner on Thursday to celebrate her newly achieved debt. It would go nicely with the bottle of wine she intended either to toast herself with or drink herself into a nice slumber.

Jenny opened the last bag, unwrapped the new coffee cups she'd purchased on a whim, and placed both by the new pot from Grant. She turned them so the front faced forward and smiled. It had been a stupid buy. She turned them again to hide their labels before dodging out the door for her first job of the day.

She dragged herself back into the apartment at 1 a.m. and crawled into bed without turning on a single light. Though exhausted, she did remember to lock up and set the alarm. She was tired but not stupid.

Her phone started calling her a moron around nine Thursday morning. Jenny groaned at the clock. Scrambling for the cell, she knocked the tea from yesterday's breakfast over. Luckily, there were only small drops in it and they clung to the inside of the cup.

"You have someone at your door." Was that her neighbor's voice? She'd never called before.

"Excuse me? Who is this?"

"Maggie from next door. Your boyfriend has been sitting out here waiting on you for an hour."

"I don't have a boyfriend." She heard a *humph* on the other side.

"Yeah, well, if you don't get out here that may be true. He brought me a plant and I think I might just keep him." The woman said something to the person with her then returned. "Oh, and I drank your coffee. It was getting cold."

Jenny opened the door to find Grant sitting at the little table by Maggie's door sipping Starbucks and reading the paper. *Nobody reads the paper anymore; they use iPads, Nooks, or Kindles.* He stood, thanked Maggie, and entered without saying a word.

"That's pretty lame," she said.

"What is?"

"Using my poor neighbor to get me to open the door." She pulled her hair back with both hands and twisted a tie around it as she shoved the door closed with her foot.

"I didn't intend to but she felt sorry for me. I'd sat there on the steps for a while and she came by twice. Once to take her dog out, and another time to go to the store. I was getting up to leave the second time when she said she'd call."

Jenny smoothed her T-shirt down over her shorts and strode into the kitchen. "I don't suppose you want more coffee?"

"Damn fine idea." He smiled. "Thanks for asking. So, what's the plan for today?"

Jenny put the coffee in to brew and slid the new cup under the spout, then pushed the button. "You say that like you're planning on staying."

"No, I just came by for coffee. I have to work. Big meeting this afternoon and a party tonight."

"Ooooh. Big party man." She held up her hands and made quoting gestures. The acid tone did not go unnoticed.

"What's the matter, Jen?"

Oh, let's see. We spent the night and day in your apartment and I haven't heard from you since. The smell of the coffee hit her nose at the same time that it beeped ready. She pulled the cup out and handed it to him. "Nothing's the matter. Here's your coffee. Better get going." She waved him away in a mock good riddance gesture.

Grant held up the cup and stared at it. His mouth dropped. "You bought me a coffee cup." The bright yellow G was unmistakable on the blue surface.

"Yeah. Two days ago." She fixated on the cup to avoid looking at him.

"You bought me a coffee cup." He set it down and rounded the counter toward her, backing her against the cold tile.

"You already said that. I thought it might be better than the throwaway ones you always use. Besides, you seem to be into the grand gestures." She placed her palm between them to maintain distance.

"This is a grand gesture?" He lifted a brow and pointed at the cup. She nodded.

"For me, but don't make a big deal out of it. It's just a cup."

He shook his head. "No, it is a big deal. You have a cup with my initial on it at your apartment. That's almost *personal*. Kind of like feeding someone with a fork. What do you think Banker Boy will think of that?"

"He's not going to see it. Besides I thought you'd take it with you—it's one of those car cups. Look at the bottom, it's made to fit in a cup holder."

Grant lifted the cup up and surveyed it. "So it is." He kissed her, a hot liquid kiss that made her stomach rumble. "I like it. A lot."

"It's just a cup."

"If you say so. Jenny, you're off today, right? Because I thought maybe you'd go with me to see Josh. He asked about you last weekend. I have to pick him up for the thing this afternoon."

"He's going to your meeting? I thought he was a student."

"Hodge asked for it. Apparently, they have something planned for the weekend after Christmas and want everyone in town. My parents are coming too—a family thing of some sort."

"Your parents? They're not there now though?" She did *not* want to meet his parents.

"No, just Hodge's family—you know, Josh, Lauren, him."

"Why do you want me there?"

"*Josh* wants you there." Now, she understood. He really didn't want to be here at all, it was all about the job. Hodge had sent him. In fact, if it weren't for Josh, he probably wouldn't be here now. And she'd given him a stupid coffee cup.

"Okay, look, I want you there too," he said.

"Doesn't really sound like it."

"You want me to beg?" He drank the coffee. "I like my cup. Thanks. So, you're probably mad at me."

"Why would I be mad?"

"Because I…we—"

"Had sex? Why would I be mad about that? It seemed to work okay for both of us."

"I'll say." He drank again. "You're mad that I didn't call."

"Why should you? It's not like it really meant anything. It just happened. It's over."

"Mmm, hmmm. Over." He nodded.

Jesus, put the damn cup down. She wanted to throw it against the window and watch it shatter into a million shards. "I wasn't expecting anything."

"I was in Texas and then New York. I left Friday and got back Tucsday. We're launching David's band and they start touring next month as the lead-in for Quonna. Their first concerts are in Texas. I came by yesterday but then I remembered, you said not to come by without calling, and I wasn't sure if you—"

And they don't have phones in Texas or New York? "It doesn't matter. It's not like we owe each other anything anyway. And I've been working."

"Okay." Finally he put the cup down. Unfortunately, that left both hands free to wrap around her. *Damn.* He slipped one into the back of her T-shirt and fisted her skin just enough to tingle. "Jenny. It was nice of you to buy me a coffee cup and I'm sorry I didn't call. Did I ever tell you I had a fantasy that involved you and my kitchen counter?"

Gulp.

"Tell me about it."

Chapter 26

Confetti and streamers adorned the entire entrance of Hodge's house when they arrived, a rather less ostentatious décor from the formal affair of a few weeks earlier. Still, it was beautifully warm and celebratory. The type of party Jenny preferred.

"So glad you could make it," Lauren greeted them at the door. "We have a kind of fun surprise for you, or at least I hope it will be."

Jenny still had a twinge of discomfort with the fact that her client was also quickly becoming a friend. She'd always thought it was bad business to mix friendships and work too much. It eventually led to disappointment or disagreements.

Jenny also felt a pending panic attack as she remembered the last time she'd been at this house. A peek upstairs at the hallway that led to the flowered door served to increase the tension. She glanced around the room, half-expecting a small form with mounds of dark curls to bound toward her. Nothing. *Thank God.*

Grant put his hand against her back and slid it under her hair to rub against her neck. The unexpected touch along with the current surroundings made her jump. A frown crossed his face as he dropped his hand back to his side.

"Hopefully a good surprise, Lauren." He dropped a peck on her cheek. "How are you?"

"Time will tell. Time will tell. But every day gets better and today's no exception. Come on in." She motioned for them to follow her as she led them to the fish room. Jenny had begun to understand the importance of the room. It was where historical events occurred in this family. Big decisions were made. Deals were struck or killed. Partnerships formed. This was where they took everyone when whatever occurred next required a calm and level head. With the supporting calmness of the liquid blue lights, and the fluid, serene movements of the fish, the atmosphere tended to make a person at ease with whatever they announced or planned.

Jenny lowered herself into the sofa cushions at the back of the room, placing herself outside the quorum with a full view of the pending action. Grant went to the bar and retrieved two bottles of water before returning to sit next to her.

Josh entered and sat near the edge. "Anyone else coming?" he said.

"No, just us. The core family. Plus one, of course." Lauren smiled at Jenny. Hodge strode in, flipped some background music on the speakers overhead, and rubbed his hands together.

"Okay, a little announcement for everyone." He grinned. "Lauren and I are going to have a little ceremony the weekend after Christmas that you will all be involved in. Jenny, we won't put that pressure on you just yet, but we certainly want you there."

"What kind of ceremony, Dad?" Josh said. His expression did nothing to hide his skepticism.

"A wedding ceremony." Hodge held his hand out to Lauren. "Don't worry, it's just the family—not a big production. It's time to put the past in the past, forgive ourselves, and start living again. That's what Shilo would have expected of us."

Chapter 27

The phone blared at Jenny as she waved goodbye to her customer. She always seemed to think of changing the negative ringtone while driving or doing something else.

"Hey, Boss." It was Barry and he asked to meet her somewhere nearby for about thirty minutes.

"Is there a problem?" she asked.

"Sort of." He hesitated. "It's something I need to talk to you about, personally. Don't be alarmed; I'm not planning to quit or anything. I have some other commitments that I really have to discuss with you though, related to my, um, other job."

"You promised you wouldn't let it—"

"I know, I said it wouldn't interfere…but it's the holiday season and our big Christmas show is coming up. I can skip it, but everyone expects me to be there."

Dead silence. Oh great. She hadn't even thought about the fact that a minister should attend his church's celebrations. All she thought was that he intended to start preaching to the passengers. Boy, did she feel stupid. Way to jump to conclusions, idiot.

"Okay, I'm at Beach and Caroline. Meet me at the Starbucks in say, thirty minutes?"

"See you then."

She really needed to stop thinking the worst. At what point did her entire life start to reek of cynicism? Especially when there were so many people around her that made it difficult to dislike them.

The meeting at Starbucks was brief. A schedule was put in place so the church would have its minister in attendance at all but the rehearsals and Jenny even promised to attend the service on Thursday night. A moment of weakness for sure, but still he was doing a great job and she didn't want to lose him. A small sacrifice to make.

Her phone chimed again as she headed back to the car to leave. "Hey Jen, how's your day going?"

Grant Tucker. Sex God. Tall, dark, and…okay, only grumpy at times now. Definitely dangerous, though—and still hanging around. She hadn't scared him off yet, and she couldn't figure out why.

"Fine. We're just planning how we'll handle the holiday time off. What's up with you?"

"Just the subject I wanted to discuss. Are you going anywhere for Christmas?"

"We're still working up through the day before Christmas Eve. Then I'm going to my mother's. Why do you ask?"

It's not like they were a couple or anything, and needed to spend the time together, was it? Was he going to ask her to spend time with him?

"I just wanted to let you know I'm going to my parents for a few days. I didn't go last year so I owe it to the family to be there this time. They'd never let me get away with missing it twice."

"That sounds nice. So, your parents and your sister will be there?"

"Yes, and a slew of cousins, grandparents, aunts and uncles, all that. Hodge and Lauren too, for a while."

She couldn't remember the last time she'd been to a celebration that big. His family seemed to really be into them. Compared to the small affair she expected to attend, it sounded overwhelming and exciting at the same time. Jenny wondered if his sister had the same dark hair and eyes, the same dry sense of humor.

"Jen." He hesitated. "Call me over the holiday, will you?"

"Sure, but it sounds like you'll be pretty busy."

"Not too busy to talk."

They both hung up. And she realized only two more days of shopping and she'd bought nothing, not a single gift! *Crap.*

*

Jenny forced herself out of bed at 9 a.m., somewhat disgruntled that a man hadn't awakened her at her door. It was hard to admit she enjoyed the interruptions, even though she pretended not to. By 10, she was furiously shopping with the other 9,000 last-minute shoppers. By noon, she was exhausted and had only three hours before her first call.

She ticked all but one name off her list and frowned. Maybe it was too soon—he probably didn't expect to get anything from her. She wouldn't even see him anyway since he would be gone tomorrow and not back 'til afterward.

What do you get someone who runs in those kinds of circles anyway? Anything too glamorous probably wouldn't come close to what he was used to. Tickets to a concert would be a waste since he probably got into them for free.

She walked into Macy's. The clearance corner caught her eye: a big wicker beach hamper with wine glasses, corkscrew, and accessories for two seemed to beckon. Yes. Perfect. A nice romantic dinner for two on the beach.

Wait. She pictured a huge dog trampling through the celebration right at the moment they sat down. No. Scratch that last part.

She bought the beach gear and left. Mission accomplished. It wasn't anything fancy like a car or anything but she hoped he liked it. If he didn't, she'd throw it at him—or maybe keep it for herself now that she was better at channeling her anger.

Jenny let out a quick giggle at the thought. She arrived back at her apartment, quickly changed clothes and headed out to work.

*

Crawling back to her apartment at 3 a.m. felt like dragging two concrete blocks through quicksand, her feet were so heavy. As she approached the door, she noticed a lump of blankets piled at the base. She started to kick them aside then noticed two feet extended from the corner. She prodded the pile with her fingers and it wiggled. A groan was expelled as the bundle moved and a head emerged from the pile. A dark head of rumpled hair and two sleep-filled eyes. "Hey, you're home." Grant smiled and rubbed the side of his face.

"What are you doing lying on the floor here? You could get mugged or trampled or something."

"I brought you something." He pulled out a box. "Merry Christmas."

"You laid there all night just to give me this? It looks like you used it for a pillow." She took the package with a heavy dent in the top. She regretted the words as soon as she said them. They sounded too harsh.

"Uh, I kind of did. Sorry."

Jenny unlocked the door, tossed the smashed box on the couch, and picked him off the floor. "Come on, sleepyhead. Let's get you inside. Where'd you get the blanket? Did you plan to camp out here all night?"

"No, Maggie gave it to me a few hours ago. I guess she felt sorry for me. Take it easy with the gift. It's breakable."

"You know there's a key hidden inside the butterfly pot by her door. I'm surprised she didn't tell you. You've got that old bat wrapped around your finger now. She'll probably never talk to me again when you stop coming around. She'll think I did something horrible."

"Wouldn't that be a shame? I'm tired, honey. Can I lie down? Have to be at the airport tomorrow at ten." He rubbed his eyes. "Wanted to see you."

He teetered with his eyes half open in her living room, then without hesitation staggered to her room and dropped on the bed. He was sound asleep making that soft huffing noise in seconds.

"Sure, make yourself at home." She registered the name he'd called her as she eased him from his clothes and tossed a blanket over him. Poor guy, he was getting good at crashing at her apartment. She was getting equally good at undressing him.

She snuck into the kitchen and quickly wrapped the basket, or at least wadded paper around it. The shape was so non-uniform; it was impossible to make it look nice. It was exciting to think about, really. The thought of exchanging gifts with a guy. She hadn't done that in a long time. She crawled into bed next to him and fell into a slumber with her back snuggled against his rib cage. Without even waking, his hand went to her hair.

Then the dream came. She had thought it was gone—a product of the bump on her head. The car, the boy running in front of them, the girl screaming. This was different though. This time, she wasn't driving; she was a passenger. And she was screaming too. *Daddy!!!!*

"Jenny! Wake up!" Her teeth clinked together as she felt her head bobble back and forth. She battered her eyes open.

"What?" she breathed. She was shaking uncontrollably.

"You had a bad dream." Grant stroked her hair from her face. "Are you okay? What was it?"

"Wow. Sorry. It's nothing. I keep dreaming about the wreck."

"When you banged your head a while back?" he asked.

"Yes. Uh, no—not that wreck. This one had a little boy in it. He ran in front of us and I—we—swerved to miss him and hit a post. But it wasn't just a post. There was a little girl screaming."

"It was just a dream. You're fine." He hugged her to him and stroked her hair. "You're not getting enough sleep." *Probably not going to sleep after that.*

*

When Jenny woke at nine, he was already gone. He'd left a note that they'd open gifts on Friday. He signed the note, "Stop dreaming about wrecks and miss me." That was all he said, but she remembered him calling her honey when he was tired.

He had grown on her. She wasn't sure when it happened, but somewhere between all the dog slobber and accidents, things changed. It wasn't just because he looked hot without a shirt on. Or with it on, for that matter.

He was a lot like her. He used sarcasm to keep people at arm's length, but once past it, he was a great guy. Thoughtful, kind, and overly generous.

*

Grant's flight was smooth. His sister Grace met him at the airport. His parents would have been there too, she said, but they were tied up getting Grandma settled in. The thought made him smile since his grandmother was the most ornery person he knew. She hated fuss and wouldn't allow anyone to make one over her. So, it boiled down to the fact that they hated the drive to the airport and the traffic on the freeway. He was fine with that since the drive back with them would have been more than painful.

Where Hodge was glitz and glamour, his parents were nothing close. It amazed him that his mom and Hodge had the same parents. She was so down-to-earth and straight-laced with a quick wit that edged on sarcasm (wonder where he got that from) and Hodge was driven to prove himself—so much so that he often didn't even know what others were thinking, nor did he care. He had heard they were more alike in younger years, but his dad and made a big impact, softening her. She had been a big part of the business up until he reached puberty, then she'd ditched the glamour world for mom duty. Said she could only handle one troublemaker at a time and Grant needed a woman's softening.

Maybe that was the difference between women and men? No, if that were the case, Jenny would be less caustic and more like his mom. He grinned at the thought. A horrible one. He knew it was all a camouflage, her protection mechanism. She had something well-hidden underneath all that gruff and grump. He couldn't place a finger on it, but he knew it was there somewhere. And, whatever it was, it likely explained why she always held him at a distance. The physical distance was breached last week, but the emotional one still needed some work.

"Are you going to answer me? Are you seeing anyone?" Grace asked. Her tone suggested it wasn't the first time she'd asked. She stared at him, a female version of himself. He hadn't told Jenny that Grace was his twin; that would have made her uncomfortable. It normally did. For some reason, people always found it a little strange.

"As a matter of fact, I am, but it's early."

"Anyone we know?" She grinned.

"No, but ask Hodge and Lauren if you want the details. They know her."

"Oh, is that how you met?" Grace looked surprised. As if he'd never let them introduce him to someone. In truth, they didn't—or at least they didn't mean to. Lauren had no clue that he was there the night Jenny picked her up from the Halloween bash. He didn't have the heart to tell her because she had been such a mess, she'd never want anyone to see her that way. And as he watched how Jenny talked to her and treated her with respect, it melted him.

Until they left together, he'd thought her another pretty, high-maintenance girl, like so many he'd met. Like the one he was stupid enough to live with. The fact that she didn't treat Lauren like an obnoxious drunk impressed him. Knowing she was exotically beautiful didn't hurt either.

"Not exactly. I ran into her a couple times on the freeway. Not literally, of course. She helped me with a flat tire and things just kind of went on from there."

Grace smiled. He hated that look. It was one of those *oh, you're hooked* expressions. Why is it he can fool everyone else in the family, but not her?

"I'm happy for you, brother. Why didn't she come with you? I'm sure everyone would love to meet her."

"No way. She doesn't hate me yet and I'd like to keep it that way for a little while, if you don't mind. The minute I take her home, you'll all start telling her every gross story you can think of about me and it'll be a matter of seconds before she drops me like a hot rock."

Grace laughed. "Well, it's not like we'd be lying to her, you know. I can't help it if you're such a gross specimen of a man."

"Yeah, and don't forget that I can tell a few stories about you too—so watch out." He glanced out the window as they drove down the street to their parents' house. "What about you? You involved with anyone?"

"Ha, that'll be the day. I am definitely *not* wasting my time on men. No offense bro, but you guys are just a huge distraction in life. I have bigger plans."

She was telling the truth about that. Grace had graduated a semester before him—one of those determined, serious girls that had a plan. In fact, she talked about that plan almost every Christmas. It consisted of a series of one-year, five-year, and ten-year goals. So far, she had her life so planned out, he wondered if she'd penciled in a husband and kids somewhere. He doubted it. Still, to some extent, they were very much alike—driven to be best at whatever they pursued. Or at least, that was the case until Shilo died. For Grant, that was when he realized all those goals and plans were irrelevant in the overall scheme of life…and life sometimes had a different agenda.

"Bigger plans. Sometimes the biggest things have no plan involved, girl, but they end up being the most important parts of your life. Don't get so wrapped up in your goals that you forget to have a good time getting there."

Goals were something he'd left behind when he took the job with Hodge, yet now he wanted to make some. His thoughts went back to black lace and the way it had slid off Jenny's hip the night he'd helped her with the flat tires. The night everything changed between them. She wasn't a first for him, nowhere near that. Still, something about Jenny was hard to leave alone. Something he wanted to go after.

"And sometimes hard work *is* a good time. I like what I do, Grant, don't lecture me about enjoying life because you don't."

He frowned. She had a point.

"I enjoy life."

"Do you? I'm not so sure. I know the only reason you're working for Hodge is because you feel like they need you. They're all so screwed up that you had to step in and glue them back together."

"Not true." After a second's hesitation he added, "Someone had to be there. It was easy for me since I needed a job anyway." He was glad when they pulled into the drive and he could escape the interrogation. Why did she *always* do that? Make him feel like shit about his decisions.

"Yeah, and easy for them to let you give up your own life to accommodate theirs."

Grant had already closed the car door when she completed the sentence. He pulled his bags out and headed inside for more of the same from his parents.

Yippee—home for the holidays.

*

To Grant's surprise, Jenny did call. While he was celebrating Christmas Eve with his family and he missed it. He'd left his phone upstairs in his old room. When he went back up and saw the blinking message light on his cell, he thumped a fist on the nightstand at his stupidity. Great. Tell a girl to call then don't answer. He dropped onto the bed and dialed her back. Plumping the pillows while he listened to the rings, Grant hoped she wasn't working.

"Hey." *Love that deep, sultry voice.*

"Sorry I missed you." He mused that here he was in his old room on the phone talking to a girl, wanting to be with her—just like he had growing up. The only difference now was that he wasn't *afraid* to talk to girls. Or was he? "No problem. I just came in. Slow night."

"Everyone's celebrating with their families, I guess."

"Yeah, probably. How's things there?" She sounded good.

"Good. It's nice to see everyone. I'd forgotten how nosey they are though. Too many questions and advice." He decided not to say the questions were about her and the advice somewhat related. She laughed softly.

"That's what families are for."

He was glad to hear her voice. They talked for almost an hour; Grant didn't really care about what. His legs were cramped from bending to fit the bed. When did this damned bed get so small? A twin. He hadn't slept in a twin since— he laughed—this one. Memories of growing up in this house, experiencing puberty, first kiss, first call for a date (in that order), first beer. And even though his parents would have a fit, his first experience with sex happened right here in this room. What a far cry from the experience with Jenny last week. What a different person he was now, with a new appreciation for what human contact should be.

"Jenny, I want you to meet my family sometime. You'd like them," he said. Dead silence. Okay, that was probably too much. "You still there?"

She coughed. "I'm here. Yeah, that sounds nice."

"How are things with your mother? Everything okay with her and Dougie?"

She laughed. "Now that you mention it, they are doing fine."

"Fine?"

"Okay, better than that. I guess you were right about them. I don't know why I didn't see it before. He was here for presents and for dinner, but then he left to see his kids. He has three and he said next year they'd come too. So, I guess that means something, right?"

"Yeah. Be happy for her, Jen."

"I am. It's just hard, that's all. I don't even know this guy." She yawned. "It's late, Grant. I'd better let you go. Merry Christmas."

"Yeah, you too. Merry Christmas."

*

Grant returned home feeling as if he'd been gone a month, but it had only been two days—two very long days. As much as everyone thought Hodge and Lauren were ruining his life, the truth couldn't possibly be farther from their perception. By delving into their lives, he'd stopped dwelling on his, which allowed him to enjoy whatever happened more. It's easy to find fun at something that you don't have any heavy investment in. Not so easy when your future depended on it and every move you made should be one that furthered your success. Grant was never happier to take life less seriously.

Even though it had been on his mind since he stepped off the plane, he waited until almost at his apartment to call Jenny. As he pulled into the lot, he changed his mind and veered back to the freeway while dialing. He listened to the rings and they didn't come fast enough. "Hello there." She knew it was him. Had she added his number to her phone? Or just recognized it?

"Hey. Are you back yet?"

"Of course, got here this afternoon. I have to work tonight, remember? Although, right now there aren't any calls so I doubt I'll be doing much. I guess everyone's with family."

"So, you're home then?"

"Yeah. Why?"

"I'm pulling up right now." Maybe it was a little foolish to come here before going home, but after being around his family for so long he'd been a little sentimental. He started toward the door but she was already there in a green T-shirt and that funny jeans skirt.

Chapter 28

It was awkward standing on the doorstep, watching him walk up as if she'd been waiting for him. Still, her stomach knotted and she gave him a smile. With all that stubble on his face and his hair falling to his eyes, she assumed it was a long trip and tiring flight back. Still his eyes were warm when he smiled. Warmer yet, when he slid a hand around her waist and dropped a quick kiss on her mouth.

"Did you miss me?" he asked, looking into her eyes.

"I, uh…"

He laughed. "Better not answer that."

"I did, actually. I slept late everyday and no one woke me by beating down the door."

"That's it? You didn't miss my hellacious hands or boulder-like body?" he teased.

Well, I did think about that a few times BUT… "You wish."

She opened the door to her apartment smiling as his hands never left her waist. Inside, he shoved the door closed with a foot and picked her off the floor to kiss her solidly, wetly, until she clung to him.

"Hmmm." He spoke against her mouth. "I missed *that*. Thought I'd imagined it. Thought I'd imagined this." He slid a hand up her leg as he buried his head in her hair.

"Well, let's just not waste any time now, Grant," she said sarcastically. They'd been in the door less than a minute.

"Okay, let's not." He picked her up and carried her down the hall, dropped her on the bed, and covered her with his weight.

"Hey! I was kidding. I meant it sarcastically."

"I know. Don't say what you don't mean though. Someone might take you seriously." He eased his hand up inside her shirt, pressed his mouth against her lips and melted his weight into her. She thought the shirt was coming off until he very gently dug his fingers into her skin—and tickled her.

"Stop it! Don't do that." She shoved hard against his chest, pushing him on to his back.

"What? Too personal for you? I was just trying to make you laugh. Why can't you just let go and enjoy yourself?"

"I can enjoy myself. I *do* enjoy myself. I just don't like being tickled." *It reminds me of...* "Dad used to do that to me all the time. He wouldn't stop until it hurt and I was doubled over and kicking him to stop."

He frowned. "Sorry."

"How would you know?" she said.

Grant pulled himself to a sitting position and laid a hand on her leg, stroking it with his big fingers. He stood and held out a hand, the frown still implanted on his features.

"Let's go get those gifts," he said.

She'd ruined the moment she knew it. His face closed up like a steel trap.

"I did miss you," she said as she grasped the extended fingers.

"Yeah. Yeah. You missed having me bang on your door for coffee every day. I get it."

She tried to catch his attention but he just looked away into space. "No." She slid a hand up his T-shirt and rested it against his abdomen. "It wasn't the coffee I meant."

That caught his attention. His eyes came down to meet hers, his lids half-closed.

"So, it *was* my boulder-like body then?"

She laughed and kissed him hard on the mouth, wrapping her arms around his neck. She pulled back. "Sure. Of course. That and you're wonderful personality."

He kissed the line of her neck up to the earlobe and looked back at the bed.

"Gifts, Boulder-man, gifts." She pulled him toward the kitchen.

"Okay." But he kissed her again, pressing her into the wall halfway down the hall, his tongue lazily delving to mesh with hers, persistently pushing her brain into hot lava mode.

Who cares about gifts anyway? Jenny had always been somewhat of a control-monger. She realized that one of the things about Grant's touch that differed from other men was her lack of need to steer it. Before him, she'd always wanted to lead things a certain way, as if she had to prove herself. Or maybe it was just a need to feel more than she thought she had inside. A need to feel *something at all.* She felt every little contact now and the clarity of that made her giggle.

Grant pulled his head back. "Now you laugh? I tickle you and it makes you mad but this is funny?"

"No! Not funny. It's just that I feel it. I'm not trying to force things. I just want—"

"What? You want what, Jen?"

"This." She stroked a hand down his neck and rested it on his collarbone. "You said you wanted me to enjoy—"

He didn't let her finish. He put a finger to her lips and shushed. Then gently he lifted the green cotton from her body and slipped the denim "bite me" skirt down her thighs, letting it drop to the floor. She followed suit by shrugging his shirt up his chest to his armpits and when he lifted his arms and pulled it over his head, she fumbled for the zipper of his pants.

They slid to the floor in a pile of clothes and she made love to him on the carpet in the hall. Or maybe it was the other way around, he made love to her, and it was exactly what she'd wanted it to be. *Yes! I feel that. I feel it all.*

When she opened her eyes, his were boring down on her. He'd obviously recovered a little faster and though his heart was still racing against her chest, his breathing had returned to normal. "You didn't say it."

She looked puzzled. *I'm not saying THAT. I don't know you that well.*

"Holy, lightning, hell. I was waiting for it." He grinned.

"God, what an ego you have. If I could have said any words at all, that would probably have been the ones to say." She sighed. "Thank you."

"For what? This? You're thanking me for touching you? Surely you're kidding."

"No. Just for being here. It's good. You're—" He hugged her so hard, her face was planted against the dampness of his chest, muffling her words.

"It really *is* good, isn't it? Not just the sex, but all of it. You're not trying to be something else and neither am I."

Yeah, that's exactly what I was thinking.

He stood up and pattered to the kitchen without even looking back. His naked backside rippled as he moved. She reached for clothes and slipped on what she could before attempting to rise.

"Don't get up," Grant said as he came back around the corner with the packages from the kitchen. "Let's open them now. Right here."

"Can I get dressed first?"

He smiled and yanked on the T-shirt that was over her neck. "No." He tossed it toward the bedroom door where it hooked the hinge and dangled.

He slipped to the floor leaning against the wall opposite her and handed her the box, complete with head indention. She lifted it to shake but he grabbed her wrist and shook his head. "Don't. We're lucky I didn't break it the other night. I held my breath when you tossed it on the couch just waiting for the sound of crushed glass."

She ripped the paper. Two bottles of the Italian wine from the restaurant and two wine glasses. "That must have been a pretty uncomfortable pillow." She arched a brow then caught herself. "It's perfect. Let's drink it tonight."

"I was hoping you'd say that."

"Your turn." She lifted the bulky, poorly wrapped package to his lap. He ripped the paper off in seconds, admiring the basket.

"A picnic basket." He surveyed it. "Awesome." He leaned forward to kiss her but she put a hand to his chest.

"Open it."

When he lifted the clasp and looked inside, he grinned. "It really is true then, that great minds think alike. You gave me this, I gave you that." He waved a hand at the wine. "It all goes together as if we meant it to."

"Together." She couldn't remember the last time she'd used that word. Probably when she and her mom and dad were just that…together. Now, there's no such thing. Never will be. She picked up the torn papers, wadded them, and carried them to the trash bin.

Can't possibly be another family together moment. Not after that, not after watching and knowing she could do nothing to stop it. No, she'd not do the together thing anymore. When she reached to grab her remaining clothes from the floor, he wrapped fingers around her wrist.

"What's wrong?"

"Nothing's wrong." She gently pulled her hand from his grasp and slipped back into the skirt, then went to retrieve the T-shirt.

"Liar." He sat naked and cross-legged on the floor staring at her. "You didn't like the gift."

"No! I loved the gift. It was great." How could she explain? He had a big family, everyone around him at this time of year. She had her mother and the new boyfriend. She didn't belong anymore, anywhere.

He stood, dressed, and took the items back to the kitchen, disappearing from view.

"We're using them now," he called out.

"What do you mean?"

"Just let me handle it. I'm good at this. Go take a shower or something. Or come talk to me."

Curiosity got the best of her and she rounded the corner to find his head buried in the fridge. He was pulling out all sorts of things and dropping them on the corner while talking to himself. *Yeah, that...and that...oh, this will work.* He lifted some cheese and surveyed the package.

When he looked up, he gave her a dazzling smile. "Picnic on the beach, okay?"

"It's kind of cold for that, don't you think?"

"We'll take a blanket."

"I might have to work."

He pitched an eyebrow at her. "Really? On the day after Christmas? If you get a call, I'll go with you. We'll take your car just in case."

She opened her mouth to protest but he started slipping things into the basket. The wine. The cheese. Sandwich meat, crackers, bread, and cookies. He opened the pantry, grabbed a bag of chips, and held it up teasingly. "Gotta have these. I know you can't resist them."

"Okay, you got me there." She remembered the crumbs on his chest and navel. Jenny changed clothes, grabbed a blanket, and they were on the way. *Together*.

Chapter 29

Jenny had only been inside the door five minutes for the wedding and Grant swore she intended to ease right back out. The look of panic as she attempted to melt into the wallpaper was almost humorous, or pathetic. He excused himself from his family and headed straight to the doorway, intending to intercept her before she got a toe through. She shook her head at him and mouthed the word, "no." He nodded and mouthed back, "yes.'"

Grant pursed his lips and stepped up the pace. He slipped an arm over her shoulder, palm against the wall, and leaned forward to whisper in her ear. "Don't you dare bale on me, Jen. It's just a damn wedding, and it's not like they haven't already been here once before."

"I know, but I don't know anyone. I shouldn't be here." Her eyes were almost terror-stricken.

"You know me. And Josh. And Lauren and Hodge. It's just a family thing anyway; there's hardly anyone else here." He grazed his fingers down her arm and entwined them with hers.

"Grant, your family is here."

"Yeah, so what? Don't tell me that scares you." He made an exasperated tsking noise.

"They'll think…"

He waited for her to finish but she didn't. What was she afraid of? That they'd think this was serious? Or that she'd like them?

"They'll think I'm all wrong for this."

"I don't know what the hell that means but I seriously doubt anyone looks at a wedding guest and thinks, 'Oh, that person is all wrong for this wedding. Send them away'."

"I meant they'll think I'm all wrong for—"

"Me? Who gives a shit? It's none of their business."

"I've seen your ex's pictures." That caught his attention. How? He'd thrown out all the pictures at his apartment. Hodge maybe?

"Then you've seen the antichrist. You should know they all hated her. So no matter what you do, they'll like you." He knew he was right about that and not simply because they thought anyone could be better for him than Emma. Jenny may overdo the dry wit sometimes, but she was genuine.

"They hated her?" He thought he saw her Adam's apple almost eject from her neckline. "Then I should really make an impression. You have to know I'm not good at pretending to enjoy this type of thing. It…it's annoying."

"Then be annoyed. Be totally pissed off. Be whatever the hell you want to, just be it *here*." He pulled her away from the doorjamb.

"You don't mean that. You know you don't want me to embarrass you."

He laughed. "The day I let you or anyone else embarrass me hasn't come yet. Embarrass yourself if you want to, but if you leave, I'm not the one who'll be upset. Hodge and Lauren are. Okay, maybe I would be, but this isn't about me. Lauren thinks of you as a friend for some reason." He knew why but didn't say it. *You're the only person that liked her at her worst without knowing who she was.* "Come on, chicken." He pushed her in front of him and started guiding her toward his family.

"I don't understand why everyone's getting wedding fever right now. After all this time."

"I'm guessing someone else you know is getting married. Don't worry; I've been immunized for that."

"I wasn't talking about you. I don't even *know you* and frankly I'm not into all that anyway. Remind me to send my mom to your doctor though." *Oooh. Now I get it. That's a relief.*

"So, Mom and Dougie decided to take the plunge too?"

"Doug. And yeah. Stop calling him Dougie. It makes him sound like a kid and he's about as far from that as can be."

Just as Grace stepped forward to open her mouth and talk to Jenny, Grant pulled on Jenny's arm and yanked her back to him. He stared into her eyes. "I don't blame you for being mad about it. You still miss your Dad and Dougie…Doug is no prize it sounds like. Still, it's your mom and you want her to be happy, right?"

"Right. I guess."

Grace tapped him on the shoulder. "That was rude, brother. What are you doing, warning her about us?" Grace pushed him aside and held a hand out to Jenny.

Here we go, he thought. "Jenny, my sister Grace. And my mother and father." He pointed to each and waited while they all shook her hand. Or at least, all but his mom. She jumped up and forced a hug, which made Jenny totally uncomfortable. He didn't miss the pained look that crossed her face as she glanced at him over Mom's shoulder.

"So, you're the pill." Grace smiled.

Nice way to start out, Sis.

"What?" Jenny asked, looking from one sibling to the other.

Grant held his hands up in defeat. "I didn't say that. I swear."

"I meant the pill that's going to cure him of that horrible fame-chasing girl he dated last year. What a mess she was. Thank God Grant finally found his brain…and found you, of course. I understand you're a business owner?"

"That's right. He told you?" Jenny asked.

"No. *He* didn't tell us anything," Grant's mother interjected. "We had to get that from Lauren and Hodge. In fact, Grant's said very little at all."

There's a fine line here that is hard to identify. What's too much and what's not enough? Tell your family and suffer the endless questions and snooping? Or not tell them and then she thinks she's inconsequential?

Grant groaned loudly before he realized everyone heard him. "Maybe I didn't want you to start grilling her before she's had a chance to get to know me. That's not exactly a good way for a guy to start out, is it?"

"Well, I don't see the big deal." His mother huffed in return. "We're just being friendly."

A loud gong sounded, signaling the beginning of the ceremony. "Ah, saved by the bell," Grant muttered into Jenny's ear. "Let's get out of here." He steered her to the front and took a seat behind Josh. The ceremony was short and simple. No one stood with them and they explained that during their vows. It was only the two of them together for now and always. Less than twenty people attended. Once the ceremony was over, they all spilled into cars and headed to a reception where simple became non-existent.

*

The reception was the most grandiose affair he'd seen and Grant was thankful he'd had nothing to do with it. Lauren planned the whole thing.

Around 300 people milled around; the noise level grew steadily as more arrived. Grant clung to Jenny's hand, not letting her get away, although she tried several times. As soon as they'd made their round of greetings, they snuck out and retreated to his apartment. She barely spoke.

"That was strange—and cool," she uttered when the door closed behind them and she had slipped her shoes off.

"Why?"

"Not the wedding. It's just odd seeing your face on a woman. I would never have imagined it." *Oh that.* "Why didn't you tell me?"

"That I was a twin?"

"What else would I mean? Of course. Were you afraid I'd have a problem with it?"

"I didn't think it was important. She's my sister. It's not like we read each other's mind or anything. And, regardless of what you might think, we don't tell each other details of our sex lives either." He shuddered at the thought of it. Grace had always been pretty adventurous with men and that was one part of her life he had no interest in hearing.

"She knew about me, didn't she? You must've said something because she knew I existed."

"Jenny, this is starting to sound like there's an argument coming and I don't have a clue why. Yes, she knew about you. When I went home she asked me if I was seeing anyone. I told her I was but it was early and I didn't want to talk about it. She was happy for me. That's all. Does that make you mad?"

Jenny's phone started up, calling her a moron. Grant grabbed it from her fingers. "I hate that stupid ringtone. I'm changing it." He found the recorder and spoke into the phone, "Jenny, someone wants you." He pressed a couple of buttons and handed it back. "There. Much better. Not near as abrasive. Look, I don't know why this is bothering you. It doesn't mean anything. My family lives three states away, it's not like you have to see them."

"It's just so personal—meeting someone's family."

Oh, THAT again. "And you don't do personal. I get it. This is all too personal for you. Kind of like feeding you with a damn fork. Only this is worse because you might actually like them, and then that would be even more fucking personal, wouldn't it? It's okay to know every inch of someone's skin but what's underneath it is off limits?" He pulled off his jacket, tossed it on the couch, and loosened the tie at his neck. "I hate wearing these." He turned his back and went to the kitchen to pour a drink.

"I'm sorry," she mumbled.

He stepped back around the corner and narrowed his eyes. "What? I missed that."

"I said I'm sorry. Yes, it's too personal. Way too personal for me. I just don't want to s—"

"Stay? You don't want to stay. Fine, then go." He flung a hand toward the door and took a lengthy draw from the glass.

"No. That's not what I was going to say. You have a really annoying habit of finishing sentences for me." Jenny stomped into the kitchen, took the glass from him and tossed the remaining contents back with one swallow. He watched in amusement as she coughed and pounded her chest. "What *was* that?"

"Scotch."

"Holy crap, it burns! Blah." She stuck her tongue out and wrinkled her nose. He wanted to laugh but he was a little too pissed off at the moment. After shaking her head a couple of times to clear the taste, she spoke again. "I just don't want to see it all blow up. I'm not good at this type of thing."

"That makes two of us." *She* was afraid it would blow up or get too personal? Emma was fine with it being personal as long as it had advantages for her. Jenny didn't want personal. She had one foot out the door before she even came in. She didn't want to get attached. In a way, he understood. Maybe she was afraid he'd do the same thing David did. Ironic, since they both had that same fear.

"I think I'm going to throw up." She held her hand to her mouth.

"Seriously?" He reached out and stroked her cheek with his palm.

"Maybe. How can you drink that? It's nasty."

Now, he could laugh. "According to Hodge, it's an acquired taste."

"Pardon me if I don't acquire it then. Gross. Can I get a water now?"

"You said you were sick." He lifted a brow.

"The feeling has passed." She sounded unconvinced. "I think."

Chapter 30

Scotch, Cheez Whiz, crackers, and shrimp cocktail. What a combination. Jenny opened her eyes in the dark and the tastes surged back. "Oh, my head." She groaned and palmed her forehead. She looked around trying to get her bearings.

"Want some aspirin?" Grant's voice came from beside her. He flicked on the light by the bed and she discerned that she was in his room. He sat up, bare back in full view.

"You're naked," she said.

He nodded. "Yeah, so are you." He looked over his shoulder briefly as she glanced under the sheet. "Pretty fun way to get there too. I think I'll have some of that aspirin myself." He stood and padded toward the door.

"Wow," Jenny muttered. *He really is a fine looking man.*

"What?" Grant asked, leaning one hand against the jam.

Jenny shook her head. "Mind if I ask exactly how we both ended up with massive hangovers?"

"Scotch." He smiled painfully. "You wanted to acquire the taste."

"Oh, yeah. Now I remember. Not one of my greatest decisions." They had pulled the bottle to the table, emptied the refrigerator of what little food he had, and played some crazy drinking game he'd learned in college. So the bedroom acrobatics weren't just a dream, she guessed. As he walked out the door, the yellow sticky note on his backside assured her it was not. She lifted the sheet and surveyed herself again. More sticky notes. Yep, it was real.

When they finished off the scotch, they got into a debate over how much people don't say what they mean in relationships.

How hard it was to tell what they thought. People should just have a sign or sticky note that spelled it out. She remembered him going to the back room and returning with a yellow pad of sticky notes and a pen. He then wrote, "This is one of my favorite parts of you" on it and pasted it to her collarbone.

So that's why he always looked there. Strange.

It became a contest as to which one had more favorites. Clothes came off as they pasted more notes to key areas. At one point he had kissed her so much the sticky notes had transplanted from her breast and neck to his cheek and chin. The friction of the paper between them, sticking to Jenny then Grant when they eventually fell into bed, made her giggle.

"Here you go." Grant pushed the covers aside and sat next to her with two aspirin in his extended hand and a glass of water in the other. When she took it, he tugged a yellow sticky from her hair and kissed her.

She looked at the clock under the lamp and gasped. "I have to go. I probably have all kinds of calls." It was just an excuse but she had nothing else.

"It's only nine in the morning, Jen. I doubt anyone needs a ride home yet. Except maybe you." She smoothed her hair back then draped her hands across raised knees.

"You have a point there." He stared into her eyes. She was sure he expected her to say something more or do something but she hadn't a clue what it would be. A yellow paper clung to her wrist. Plucking it from her skin, she placed it on his mouth. Grant pulled it off and read the words he'd written: "I want to kiss here."

"Stay," he said. When she started to protest, he held a hand up. "Just for breakfast. I'll cook but I promise I won't try to feed it to you."

She sighed. How could she refuse that? "Okay. And maybe I can handle the fork thing."

"Forget the fork. I have a better idea. Let's read all the sticky notes again now that we have a light on and we're semi-sober?" His eyes slid to one pasted at her belly button and he wiggled his brows. Jenny laughed.

*

That evening when she reached in her pocket for her keys to go to her first job, the stack of yellow notes slipped out and floated to the floor. The top one made her laugh again. Despite her best efforts and grouchiest snarls, she recognized she had trouble going through the day without thinking about Grant or wanting to talk to him. Against her better judgment, things definitely were personal. More personal than was safe.

"You're in love with Uncle Grant," the small feminine voice stated from her living room.

Jenny's eyes shot to the small form. *NO! It's been three weeks—I thought it was over. No more ghosts.*

"You are." Shilo smiled. "I knew it. Did you like the wedding? Wasn't Mommy pretty?"

"Yes." *To all your questions, dammit.*

Chapter 31

Jenny surveyed her face in the hall mirror. She massaged her scalp and forehead, feeling for bumps. Perhaps she had fallen last night and didn't remember? Maybe another concussion was causing the apparition. The last time started with a bump on the head. She turned her head to the left, then right, surveying each side with a turned up nose. No bumps. *There has to be. Why else would I still see her?*

"I'm not." She rushed from the apartment to her car, started it up, set the GPS to her first destination, and pulled out of the lot.

"Of course you are," Shilo argued. "Why don't you call him? I bet he'd like that."

"He's working." Jenny looked at the clock on her dash. "Well, at least he might be. It's a little late. Besides, I'm working too. I have to pick up a customer in thirty minutes."

"You can't talk to people when you work?"

"Of course I can, but I don't want to bother him." Jenny listened to her navigation system remind her to turn left in 100 feet.

"Why would that bother him?"

"You ask a lot of questions for a non-existent person."

"I'm not non-ex…whatever that is."

Jenny tried not to scowl. *If a person is dead, do they still exist? Obviously they do. Otherwise, I'd officially be crazy.*

"All right, I'll call him." Jenny dialed his number. On the fourth ring, she reached to hit the "end" button. "See, he's not answering. He must be busy."

"Jen?" *Rats. He answered.* "Are you there?"

"Hi." She had no idea what to say next. "How'd you know it was me?"

"I programmed your number into my phone a few weeks ago." She wondered when that happened. That has to mean something, right? It was before, well, before *everything*.

"Oh." Now she didn't feel so bad about admitting she had programmed him in also.

"Why'd you call? Is everything okay?"

I don't know, some random ghost told me to. She laughed nervously. "Yeah, fine. I just had a few minutes before my first pickup."

"Wow, I guess that means you thought about me. Hey, I have to go into a quick meeting but—"

"I'm sorry I shouldn't have bothered you."

"No, I'm glad you did. Listen, call me when you get done tonight, okay?"

"It'll be too late. You'll be asleep."

"I doubt that. For some reason, I keep seeing little yellow pieces of paper floating around in my head. Just call me. Sorry, but I have to go. Bye." He hung up.

Great conversation.

"He doesn't like phones much. I remember him saying that once." Shilo crossed her arms. "But he's glad you called. I know it."

"You know it. Shilo, why do you keep bothering me?" Jenny pulled the car to the side of the road, and adjusted sideways to confront the child...or whatever she was. It was time to get this over with. Cleanse it out of her system. Out of her mind. Get on with her life. Whatever was causing this needed to stop. But Shilo was gone. Jenny glanced around furtively searching for the dark curls and voice. Nothing.

"He's never going to understand this. Or believe it, for that matter," Jenny muttered.

*

Work became almost overwhelming the following days. New Year's celebrations brought a deluge of new customers, group pickups, and interesting stories to catalogue for future training sessions. She even ended up taking a customer to the hospital after he inserted sparklers in each ear. The spackling of burn marks on his cheeks and earlobes would stir interesting discussion when he returned to work.

Jenny wasn't sure whether to laugh or shake her head at his stupidity. *Didn't you read the warning on the package?* She put on her customer smile and patiently escorted him to the emergency room door. She didn't go further. She couldn't. After depositing him on his front step hours later, she took his keys and promised to deliver his car later. *Some people should just stay home on holidays—for their own safety.*

She had called Grant as he asked, and he met her at her apartment that night, and each night thereafter Grant ended up staying each time and left early to get to work. He had asked her if she minded each night. She shrugged and said, "Up to you."

Apparently that wasn't the answer he hoped for, because the last time she said it he frowned and shook his head. Still, she was too tired to discuss it much and he didn't push. Four days after New Year's, her phone rang around 10 at night. Him.

She answered and tried to sound cheerful as her passenger slept in the back seat.

"I'm not coming by tonight, Jen."

"No problem."

"You're not going to ask why?" He sounded irritated.

"It's none of my business. I assume you're busy."

"Yeah, that's it."

She heard voices calling him to join them.

"Better get back, sounds like you're missed," she said.

He's at a party. She wondered if it was one like she attended before. She hung up before he could say more than "Jen." Why did that piss her off? It was his job to attend those things. An image popped into her head of David and the crowned starlet he'd stepped out with. She also remembered the fact that Grant hadn't said anything about a party or asked her to attend. *Great. I knew it wouldn't last.*

*

Grant stared at the phone. *Did she really hang up on me?* She didn't even ask or wait for an explanation. He wondered if she even cared to know. Truthfully, she had not seemed to want him at her apartment these last few nights. She didn't say so and he wasn't one to jump to conclusions but she seemed disinterested. He wanted to be there and that was good enough. Still, after Emma's fiasco, he wasn't about to wear out his welcome. Give her some room, he told himself. He flipped the phone closed and turned around to the room full of people. *Shit. Speak of the Devil.*

"Grant!" Emma glided toward him with a pasted on smile. He looked around for Hodge, hoping for an exit excuse.

"Emma. You look well." He walked past her.

"Thank you, honey. I am." She slipped an arm through his and stepped in beside him. "Have you missed me?"

He lifted her fingers from his arm and dropped them. "Not really. What are you doing here? Does Hodge know you crashed his party?"

"I came to see you, actually. Don't you think it's about time you got over your mad? I miss you, honey." She drew her lips into a practiced pout and looked around to see who might be watching.

"That's a laugh. The last time I saw you, you had your hands on someone else's ass. I seriously doubt you've thought about me more than a minute, Emma. Missed your meal ticket, maybe, but not me." He trod toward the bar.

"Come on, Grant. You know you can't be mad at me forever. You love me," she called after him.

Grant stopped in his tracks and whirled back. "No, Emma. I don't love you. I never did. I *thought* I did once, but now I realize it was never that. Lust, maybe—or possibly it was just better than nothing. Regardless, I'm seeing someone now and I'm done with you."

Emma glanced nervously to the people standing nearby then laughed hesitantly. "You're just trying to make me jealous, aren't you! Of course, you are. No need, honey. I'm back and I plan to stay."

"Like hell," he muttered. Grant slipped through the throng of people, found Hodge, and asked him why she was here.

Hodge's eyes popped. "I didn't know she was. She must have sweet-talked the guys at the door to let her in. I sure didn't see her." Hodge frowned and peeked around. "Want me to run her off?"

"No, don't worry about it. I'm going anyway. Lauren's got things under control so you don't need me tonight."

"You planning to see Jenny?" Hodge asked.

"Not tonight. She's working." *And she doesn't seem to want to see me any more than I want to see Emma.*

*

Grant went home and slept alone. It was a restless and unsatisfying slumber. When he woke, his mood darkened significantly. He seriously needed a vacation. Until now, he never thought it possible because Hodge needed him. With Lauren back on the scene, personal time would be easier to find. Grant decided he'd broach the subject with Hodge today.

While his coffee brewed, Grant went online and checked email then poked around for travel opportunities. There was something dull and lifeless about traveling alone. Even the thought of it lacked appeal. He closed his laptop just as a rap on the door sounded. He checked the landing outside the door. Jenny with two coffee cups from Starbucks. *Things are looking up.*

She waltzed in, handing him a cup as she passed, and planted herself on one of the kitchen stools that lined the counter. "Okay, so I'll ask," she said. "Why?"

"You mean why didn't I come over last night?"

"Of course. What else?"

"I don't know. Sometimes you get a little cryptic. Last night you said it wasn't your business. For all I know you could have meant just about anything."

"It isn't my business. You don't owe me an explanation and I don't expect you to show up every night."

"Then I guess we're good." Another rap on the door interrupted him. *Now who could be here?* He strode to the door and whisked it open.

"Emma?" Grant gritted his teeth. *Not now.*

"Hey there, sweetie. I was almost ready to pull out my key but I thought I'd knock first."

"Why are you here?" he asked.

Jenny came up behind him and stared at the two. Emma slipped through the door and extended a hand to her.

"Hello. I'm Emma."

"The ex?"

"Um, not exactly ex." Emma shot a coy look at Grant. "I thought we settled that last night, honey."

"Last night," Jenny repeated.

Grant groaned.

"And who might you be?" Emma asked. The saccharin voice sounded like fingernails scratching glass.

He opened his mouth to introduce Jenny but before the words came out, Jenny's hand was up. "I'm Jenny. The driver."

Why did she say that?

"Grant has a driver? Sweetie, you're moving up in the world, aren't you?" Emma stroked his cheek.

The action made Jenny step backward and sidle toward the door. "Well, technically, I work for Lauren." Jenny used her business voice. "Mr. Tucker, I'll be waiting downstairs."

Grant saw cold-as-ice daggers in Jenny's eyes and Emma seemed to enjoy it thoroughly. He knew she wouldn't wait. He imagined the sound of rubber peeling out as soon as she reached her car. There was a part of him that wanted her to speak up and put Emma in her place. A part of him that wanted her to acknowledge what he had thought was between them. He supposed it was more inconsequential to her. The door closed with a clap behind her.

"When did drivers get so pretty?" Emma smiled. "What a glamorous life you have. Still, I see you haven't sold my car yet. Wanted to hang on to a part of me?"

"No. Don't kid yourself." Grant grabbed the cups from the counter and walked to the door. "Emma. Leave." He didn't bother to look at her as he followed Jenny.

Emma. Bad Timing. Bad Karma. And incredibly Bad Woman.

*

As Grant expected, when he reached the lot her car squealed away. He shrugged. Let her steam for a while. Might be interesting to see where this goes. Jenny's never acted like anything mattered to her when it came to him; maybe it was time to challenge her thought process.

They'd never really talked about being together, or a relationship. Shit, he wasn't even sure he wanted that. She certainly had an acidic side to her personality. Although that apparently disappeared once she dropped the front. The sticky-note thing came to mind. Her way of saying what she didn't seem to be able to voice. He had the small squares of paper in his wallet, his favorite on top. Two of them actually, both labeled, "I like these around me." She had stuck one on each of his biceps.

"God dammit, Jenny." He stomped to his car, fumbled his keys into the ignition and headed toward the freeway.

Chapter 32

Grant's car growled to a stop behind hers, blocking any hope of exiting the parking spot. Not that she intended to leave. No, she intended to lock herself in her apartment and curse him for a while, then go to work. After all, why should he be different from David or any other guy she dated? Face it, she was meant to be alone. She was capable of handling things herself. Grant had only complicated things by keeping her up all night, writing notes, and playing drinking games. His showing up every night, staying over, made it difficult to keep up with her bookkeeping. Yes. Grant Tucker was bad for business.

"You didn't wait for my answer," he called when she started to make an escape.

"Answer to what?"

"Your question—the one you asked when you brought this." He handed her a coffee cup. "It's probably ice cold now."

She didn't drink it. He had something to say so she waited him out.

"Hodge had a celebration for another contract signing, a young girl who's going to star in an upcoming television sitcom. I found her so I had to be there." He sipped the coffee once then walked the cup to a nearby dumpster and tossed it. "Jen, if you'd given me any indication that you wanted me to be with you, I would have jumped in the car and been at your door in a heartbeat. You always sound so disinterested. You said more on those damn little sticky notes than I've ever heard come out of your mouth."

"I never expected you to be—"

He held up a hand. "I know. I know. You never expected me to be around all the time. You don't want that. I get it. Strange, too, because I never thought I'd really want to be. Sometimes you're so grouchy and angry I want to pull my hair out. I get it though, because I'm kind of that way myself sometimes. The other night, I had a chance to see you being yourself. No big roadblocks to maneuver around or walls to break down. You were finally open with me."

"I thought things were moving forward. Obviously, I didn't know about Emma."

"There's nothing to know. She showed up at Hodge's last night, uninvited. I spoke to her for about five minutes and left."

"She isn't staying…I mean…she has a key." Jenny walked her cup to the dumpster and joined it with his. She had a key to the apartment that they had shared.

"A key to my apartment which doesn't work because I changed the locks two months after she left."

"But you lived with her. That's serious."

"I thought so at the time. I know better now. It's only serious if both people are on the same wavelength. Emma's only serious about Emma." He brushed a hand down her arm and grasped her fingers. "Let's go up."

"Still, she's beautiful, and you—" *Bought her a car.*

"Not so beautiful if you know her." Grant's cell phone rang. He glanced at the display and sighed. "It's Hodge. I'd better take it."

While he spoke, Jenny opened the apartment and walked in with him trailing behind. He stopped inside the door, closed it, and leaned against the wall, listening.

"I'll be there in an hour," Grant said before hanging up.

"Problems?" Jenny asked.

"Apparently so." The furrows in his brow deepened. "Josh is in the hospital. I have to go."

She gasped. "What happened? Is he okay?"

"Not sure. Hodge just said to meet him at United Methodist.

Stress-related breakdown or fatigue—something." He reached for the door handle. "You want to come?"

"No!" She forced a calmer tone into her voice. "I'm terrible at those things. I get nauseous just walking into a hospital."

"What if I said I wanted you to? Would you do it?" He leveled his gaze straight into her eyes.

Great. Put the guilt trip on me. A stronger woman would say no but I'm not that woman. She opened her mouth to reply but no appropriate excuse came. Clamping her lips back together, she shook her head then converted it to a nod. "I'll get my purse."

"You don't have to if you don't want to."

"Do you want me to or not? Just tell me." She put hands on hips and matched his stare.

Without answering, Grant pulled her right hand from her hip, tightened his fingers around it and pulled her with him.

*

An hour later, they walked up to a waiting room where a very agitated Hodge paced. Lauren listened as the doctor spoke to them.

Jenny's throat constricted. After eight years, this room still looked the same. It disappointed her that even the smell was familiar. Clorox and antiseptic. One for mopping the blood from the floor, the other for mopping the infection from the injured.

She forced herself not to hyperventilate. Breathe in, breathe out. Easy. Concentrate. Breathe In.

"Hello, there." The doctor's eyes took in both of them approaching.

"Oh my God." Jenny exhaled the pent up breath. This was the same doctor. The same waiting room. Oh, God, please not the same circumstances.

Grant cocked his head in confusion. "Jen, are you okay?" She wagged her head furtively.

"No. This is where…that's Dad's doctor…same room. Same smell. No. Not okay. He's not okay." She slumped against him. Her vision clouded and she knew if she didn't sit down, she'd likely keel over. "Have to sit," she mumbled as she melted into a padded bench. *It's okay, honey.* She could hear her Dad as he spoke to her that day in the car. *You're going to be okay. Everything's going to be fine.* But it wasn't.

Grant approached the back of Lauren's chair and listened while the doctor finished his directions. Jenny felt as if she witnessed herself in the room eight years earlier. She had been in the same chair where Lauren now sat. Her mother stood in Grant's place with her arms resting on Jenny's slumped shoulders.

The doctor displayed no similar signs of recognition. Why should he? He'd probably given those announcements to hundreds, if not thousands, of families over the past years. Was it fair to expect him to remember each family? Or each death?

"No! He's not dead," Jenny spouted. Every shocked face turned to her.

"Of course he's not dead, honey," Lauren's soothing voice answered. "He's had an incident with exhaustion that's all. They're keeping him for observation." The tightness around her mouth made it clear there was more, but Lauren wasn't voicing it publicly.

"Our future family doctor was so busy taking care of everyone else, he neglected to do the same for himself."

"Really?" Jenny's mouth dropped. A quick look at each face assured her it was true. She let her shoulders drop and sighed. "Thank God. I thought it was happening again."

"What was happening again?" Hodge asked.

Jenny looked around at all the faces. She couldn't read Grant's eyes. He hazarded a glance at the doctor then moved closer. Had she scared him?

She sucked in a deep breath and held her eyes tightly closed.

God, please make it all go away. She had said this over and over then. Why didn't he listen? It hadn't worked so she just decided if it couldn't be fixed, then it had to be ignored. Forgotten. She had been able to do so for years. She had locked it away since she walked out of the hospital with her mother the day the doctor told them both he couldn't save Dad. The impact to the pole had tossed her Dad so hard against the windshield; it had fractured his skull, severed his spine, punctured both lungs, and crushed his pelvis. The internal bleeding had been too significant. It all came back in a rush. She wanted it to stop. Her closed eyes gave no relief so she blinked them open.

"The accident. My dad's accident eight years ago. He was driving me home from college. We were almost to the house. A rock flew into his windshield and shattered it. He couldn't see." Jenny couldn't stop the words. She'd never said them before, and now, they had to come. She couldn't hold them back. "He slammed on the brakes, but there was this young man…a teenager, I think. He was chasing a soccer ball and laughing. Dad couldn't see him. I screamed. Someone else screamed. Dad swerved and hit a light pole head on. We didn't have airbags back then. His head went straight into the windshield. He put his arm out for me and held me back but he hit it hard because he tried to protect *me*."

Grant couldn't mask the pain her words brought, nor the sympathy that overwhelmed him. She hesitated when he closed his eyes. Still the words had to come and she kept talking.

"There was this little girl that screamed. He didn't even see her because he was trying to miss the boy and the windshield was so broken, it was like looking through a hard rain. His fingers bit into my collarbone right here." She raised her hand and passed it along the spot, feeling the pressure again. "He held tight until he started to slump. There was blood. I couldn't see the left side of his face. Still he smiled at me. 'See, honey,' he said, 'you saved that boy's life.'

If that rock hadn't hit us we never would have been able to stop. We were going too fast. But he had already hit the brakes so he just swerved. Into the pole. Dad said, 'Don't worry; it's going to be okay. Sometimes things happen for a reason. Even bad things. I'm proud of you, sweetie.' He blinked, trying to clear the blood from his eyes as it trickled further onto his face." Jenny's throat cramped again and she swallowed.

Lauren hissed out a painful squeal and clenched her eyes. Then she did something really odd: she nodded as if she knew what came next.

"There was a little girl. Dad never saw her. He died on the way to the hospital and never knew. She was so tiny you couldn't even see her over the hood of the car. I heard her scream but didn't *see* her." The tears stung in the back of Jenny's eyes, then slowly spilled down her cheeks. "I saved the boy but I killed the little girl. I didn't even know her name then and I killed her."

Grant turned away hiding his face from her. Lauren let out a wail and clamped her hand over her mouth.

"Her name was Shilo, Jenny, and you didn't kill her. It was an accident," Hodge murmured.

Chapter 33

Jenny hunched over her computer and typed in the business's monthly budget. It had been five days since she stumbled out of the hospital with tears streaming down her cheeks as she repeatedly mumbled, "I'm so sorry."

Grant drove her home that night, but when they reached her apartment she couldn't bear for him to come up. How could he want to be with her when she'd been the catalyst that changed his life? Her mistake had catapulted him into a career that was not of his choice. It also ripped Hodge and Lauren apart, and plummeted Josh into a world of anxiety, stress, and self-mutilation. *How can I face them again? It wouldn't be right.*

She wondered what their life would have been like if not for her mistake. If she hadn't screamed, they may have still missed Josh, and Shilo would be fine. *She would have been a teenager talking about boys and school dances.*

"And that would have been just gross," Shilo's voice said. Jenny shot her eyes to the figure over her shoulder. "I hate boys and I would never, ever, ever dance with one. What are you doing, Ms. Jenny?"

"Shilo, I'm so sorry. I didn't mean to hurt you. I didn't *mean to kill you*. I'm so sorry."

"You didn't. It was an accident. Your dad was right. Sometimes things happen for a reason. Like me. And you. And Josh."

"But Dad didn't know about you. I should have seen—"

"Yes, he did. Why do you think I'm here with you?"

Jenny shook her head. "Because I'm going crazy with guilt, I guess. Or you're haunting me because I screamed and killed you."

Shilo slammed a hand against the table. "NO! *You didn't kill me. You SAVED Josh.* And I'm here to save you."

"I thought you were here for Josh." Jenny reminded her of their earlier conversation.

"I just said that because I knew you wouldn't listen. You blocked it all out. That's what your dad said."

"My dad said?"

"Yeah. He couldn't come back. He'd already done what he was 'spose to. He asked me to help you and he said you'd never listen 'cause you're kind of stubborn, but that you had to know how important you are. He said you deserved to be happy and that you didn't want to 'cause of me. You thought you didn't 'serve it."

The ashen-faced little girl with big brown eyes smiled at her. "You deserve it, Miss Jenny. That's why I'm here. Why I was here the whole time and…why I'm leaving now. Your dad said to tell you that just because you haven't been inside the big guy's door for a while, it doesn't mean he hasn't been in yours."

"My dad? You're telling me he's here too?"

"Not him, silly. *THAT BIG GUY*" She pointed upward. "Bye, Miss Jenny. Be happy."

Jenny swore she heard her father's voice saying the words along with Shilo. Then her image vanished. She basically evaporated into the curtains.

She swallowed the lump in her throat, buried her head, and frantically typed on the keyboard, entering invoices, calculating billings, and posting her new service orders.

Deserved to be happy.

What made her deserve to be happy when they were gone? Her scream had completely rearranged the future of two families and broken them to shatters. She thought of Grant. What future would he have had if it hadn't happened? He certainly wouldn't be in entertainment. She felt pretty confident of that.

She glanced out the window at the sun beaming in. As much as it hadn't been his choice, maybe it was a good fit. He stabilized them. He had a way of doing that, even for her. She imagined it was rather a caustic way at times but even that seemed to have good intentions. The abrasiveness had diminished over time.

Know how important you are.

How can I be more important than someone else? Isn't every life important? She struggled to remember Shilo's explanation.

Her purse vibrated and Grant's muffled ringtone said, "Jenny someone wants you."

She frowned and tapped a pencil to the stack of bills in front of her.

"I wish," she said.

Jenny, someone wants you. It repeated. She padded over and pulled the phone from her purse. She swiped a finger across and started to say her name.

"Jenny, someone wants you." The voice was louder now. She stared at her iPhone.

"Jenny, I want you."

She pivoted her eyes to the door and brought a hand up to her mouth. They were here. Grant's dark, smoldering eyes watched her. *You deserve to be happy,* Shilo had said. Elation bubbled through her like a warm bath. In his hand he lightly held a leash that only pretended to contain the dog that sat next to him happily drooling on her carpet. Jenny smiled. Okay, maybe she'd try this happiness thing.

"I love you, Grant Tucker."

In the mood for more Crimson Romance? Check out *Identity Crisis* by Eliza Daly at *CrimsonRomance.com*.